the rogue

Also by Maisey Yates

Secrets from a Happy Marriage
Confessions from the Quilting Circle
The Lost and Found Girl
Cruel Summer

Four Corners Ranch

Merry Christmas Cowboy
Cowboy Wild
The Rough Rider
The Holiday Heartbreaker
The Troublemaker
The Rival
Hero for the Holidays
The Outsider

Gold Valley

Smooth-Talking Cowboy
Untamed Cowboy
Good Time Cowboy
A Tall, Dark Cowboy Christmas
Unbroken Cowboy
Cowboy to the Core
Lone Wolf Cowboy
Cowboy Christmas Redemption
The Bad Boy of Redemption Ranch
The Hero of Hope Springs
The Last Christmas Cowboy
The Heartbreaker of Echo Pass
Rodeo Christmas at Evergreen Ranch
The True Cowboy of Sunset Ridge

For more books by Maisey Yates, visit maiseyyates.com.

MAISEY YATES

the rogue

CANARY STREET PRESS

If you purchased this book without a cover you should be aware that this book is stolen property. It was reported as "unsold and destroyed" to the publisher, and neither the author nor the publisher has received any payment for this "stripped book."

**CANARY
STREET
PRESS**™

Recycling programs for this product may not exist in your area.

ISBN-13: 978-1-335-77710-2

The Rogue

Copyright © 2025 by Maisey Yates

All rights reserved. No part of this book may be used or reproduced in any manner whatsoever without written permission.

Without limiting the author's and publisher's exclusive rights, any unauthorized use of this publication to train generative artificial intelligence (AI) technologies is expressly prohibited.

This is a work of fiction. Names, characters, places and incidents are either the product of the author's imagination or are used fictitiously. Any resemblance to actual persons, living or dead, businesses, companies, events or locales is entirely coincidental.

For questions and comments about the quality of this book, please contact us at CustomerService@Harlequin.com.

TM is a trademark of Harlequin Enterprises ULC.

Canary Street Press
22 Adelaide St. West, 41st Floor
Toronto, Ontario M5H 4E3, Canada
CanaryStPress.com

Printed in U.S.A.

To Flo, forever

*the
rogue*

CHAPTER ONE

Ruby Matthews had her life together. She had a perfect little house, with a perfect little yard. She had a very perfect little dog. She had the perfect engagement ring and the perfect fiancé—deployed at the moment—and a perfect wedding dress in her closet waiting for her very perfect day.

It was important to Rue that she had those things, because her life growing up had been very, very far from perfect. Things being the way they were now felt right, after the chaos of her upbringing.

Everything had a place. A perfect, neat place where it belonged.

All of her yarn organized by weight and fiber in little baskets in her extra bedroom.

Her dresses belonged in rainbow-colored order in her closet.

Her beloved grandmother's ashes belonged beneath a cherry tree at King's Crest, the place she loved most in the world.

Asher belonged by her side as her husband, and their wedding was in one month, which meant it was almost time for that to happen.

And Justice? He belonged right up at the front of the church when she and Asher had their wedding.

Because he was her best friend in the whole wide world, and he was her man of honor. It was his place.

Oh, Justice.

It was impossible to oversell the impact of Justice King. When he walked into a room, he created a ripple. You couldn't *not* notice. He was tall, halfway over six foot, with broad shoulders and sandy brown hair. His eyes were a deep green that seemed almost otherworldy. His jaw was square, his nose straight, his lips . . .

She had heard a woman say once that his lips were made for sin.

Rue wasn't sure what that meant but it had stuck with her.

He was her best friend. The greatest guy she knew.

Except he was late for his suit fitting because he was a careening, disastrous mess who washed his face only when she reminded him to. Or when he was going out to pick up women, which he did a lot.

It could be argued that Justice's place was actually in the dog pound, because the man was nothing but a hound. But she was way too fond of him to argue that point.

She was getting anxious because she was had been waiting with the seamstress in her front room for ten minutes, and Justice hadn't answered his text and he was eight whole minutes late. The seamstress had been early.

Rue herself was always early, and Justice was always late.

It made her want to . . .

But just then his truck pulled into the driveway and

her heart lifted. She was so, so glad to see him. Because time was wasting and she hated wasted time.

He parked his truck and walked through her front door without knocking. Which made her feel a strange note of wistfulness, because when she moved in with Asher, Justice wouldn't be able to just do that. She and Asher would be being newlyweds and having . . . sex and intense conversations about meal planning. At least that was her understanding of newly married life based on TV and books. She would not be basing her marriage off her parents.

No matter what, the shift would change Justice's position in her life.

She frowned.

"You're late," she said.

"Sorry, Rue," he said, his voice sounding scratchy and unrepentant. "I'll do better next time."

He always said that. Rue could only assume that his version of *best* worked for her on some level or she wouldn't have made him such an integral part of her existence.

"When, at the next tux fitting or my next wedding?" she asked.

He grinned. "Yep."

"The only way I'll be having two weddings is if the first one is ruined because the man of honor is late." She gave him the evil eye and Sue Quackenbush, the seamstress, gave him a swift once-over.

"Come on over here," she said.

She began to measure him without preamble, and Rue watched the proceedings closely. Justice gave her a smile and a wink as Sue measured down his inseam.

"Careful," he said.

"I know what I'm doing," she responded, brusquely.

Rue liked it when a woman wasn't flustered by Justice. It was far too easy for him to get a reaction out of women. They shouldn't reward his bad behavior.

"Where were you?" Rue asked, because suddenly she was suspicious.

"In bed."

She couldn't help herself; she let out an exasperated sigh. "You're a cowboy, Justice. How do you end up sleeping past noon?"

"Easy. I party till the cows come home. Then I feed the cows. Then I go to bed."

"Lord." She scrubbed her hand over her forehead.

"Okay," said Sue. "Go in the next room and put these on." She pulled some pants, a vest, a shirt and a jacket off her rolling clothes rack. "They'll be close. Then I'll put some pins in and make the alterations."

Justice went into her bedroom without checking with her first. It was clean, thankfully. She knew that.

He emerged a few minutes later and she was stunned speechless. Motionless. Thoughtless.

She knew Justice better than she knew anyone. She knew him after a hard day's work. She knew him as a third-grade boy who wouldn't read and who'd had to take lessons from her, a girl a whole grade younger than him. She knew him as a protector, a terrible poker player, a first-rate playboy.

But she'd never known him in a tux.

Good. Lord.

He was too powerful. She was going to have to warn her female family members, and Asher's, who came from out of town, to be safe and vigilant where he was concerned because . . .

In a tux he was *lethal*.

All the broad, muscular lines of his body were so sharp in that suit. The black bow tie made him look like Cowboy James Bond.

She'd seen him cleaned up, but this was another level.

Justice, the man she'd known since childhood, had actually rendered her speechless.

"Well . . . well, that's fantastic," she said.

"Yes," Sue agreed. "Just a few alterations to make."

She was speedy with her pins, and far too quickly, Justice was back and changing out of the tux. "You're going to make a great decoration at the wedding," Rue said.

She was only half kidding. Having him on stage looking like that was a boon. She could save on flowers. Who needed them when you had all that cowboy to look at?

"Thanks, Rue, I always wanted to settle down and live a quiet life as something more aesthetic than useful. I'd be a great paperweight."

In spite of herself, Sue, who was really quite stoic, blushed. Justice was a whole thing and he couldn't be stopped.

"I'll have the altered suit back by the end of the week," Sue said.

"Great," Rue responded. "I'll talk to you then."

Sue hung everything on her rolling rack and collected her supplies, before leaving Justice and Rue alone in the house.

"I bet I could pull her if I wanted to," he said.

"She has been married for thirty years and has nine children."

"Your point?"

"Lord above, Justice, not everyone is an idiot over . . . that sort of thing." She gestured wildly at him.

"If they aren't then they aren't doing it right."

She cleared her throat. "So where were you really?"

"In bed. Really. I had a late night."

Oh. That was code for hooking up. She knew Justice well.

Good for him, really.

It was fine that her sex life was sporadic.

She wasn't jealous.

It was a hazard of an eight-year engagement to a man who'd been deployed for the majority of that time.

She wasn't *that* sexual anyway. She liked sex. She liked being close to Asher. But it wasn't a huge factor in her life. What she liked best was the stability. The promise that he would be there for her always.

The certainty she felt with him.

He was her high school sweetheart. Her one and only. Their wedding was finally on the horizon and that was *real*.

So, Justice could wham-bam-thank-you-ma'am whoever he wanted to. That was empty. She had *love*. So there.

So very there.

"Well, at least you showed up without the scent of the work day clinging to you." If she smelled too deeply there might be a hint of perfume, though.

She wouldn't smell deeply.

"You coming for dinner tonight?" he asked.

She spent most nights with the King family. After her grandmother's death last year she'd felt so alone. Her grandma had been the most constant figure in her life. She might not have raised her, but going to her house every day after she'd done school at the little one-room schoolhouse at Four Corners Ranch had been her salvation.

Her parents' house had always been a mess of angry words and beer bottles. Rue hated the disorganization. Her own room had always been spotless.

Her grandmother's house had been a haven of sunlight and cookies. She and Justice had both spent days there, often. Her death had been tough for him too, not that he'd actually said that. Justice wasn't a big one for emotional sincerity.

Though, after the funeral he'd seen her crying behind the church and he'd taken her in his arms, hard and tight.

He'd smelled like the earth, the sun and Justice. So familiar, and so necessary in that moment when the church had been full of all the family she didn't know that well, while they said goodbye to the one person she had.

She cried into his jacket and left tear stains behind.

It had helped her hold it together later so she hadn't had to cry on Asher.

But ever since then she'd eaten dinner at the main house at King's Crest more often than not. King's Crest was Justice's family ranch, part of the broader ranching collective of Four Corners Ranch, the largest ranching spread in the state of Oregon.

Sullivan's Point was home to produce, baked goods

and a farm store. McCloud's Landing was an equine therapy center. Garrett's Watch was a cattle ranch, and King's had been too up until recently. They still did their cattle, but they were expanding. They had a new wedding venue they were almost finished with. It was going to be gorgeous but she couldn't wait for it to get done to be married there.

Also, as much as she loved King's Crest, she really did think she needed a church wedding. It felt more grounded and traditional. But the reception would be at King's. They'd offered her the barn and outdoor area they used for town hall meetings—the big all-ranch gatherings they had once a month to discuss their business and make new proposals, dance, eat and have a good time.

Asher had been a little bit *meh* about it, but the truth was, he was always a little *meh* about the ranch.

He didn't *get* it, that was the thing. How could he?

Four Corners had always been a family. Even if, much like her own, it was dysfunctional in some ways. The school had been small, and they'd all known each other—even if she and Justice had been closer to each other than to anyone else.

Justice was popular, he always had been. He played kickball, baseball and backyard football with the rowdier kids. She had taught some of the other kids who preferred to sit to crochet, then eventually knit and the ones who were interested would sit with her in relative silence while sports occurred.

They'd had different kinds of home lives. She'd never really talked about her situation with anyone but Justice.

The dirt, the trees, the view of the mountains, that would always be a profound part of her. Asher seemed to find it inconvenient that she liked to spend time there.

But it was fine. Asher would get it eventually, she was sure. Because no, she wasn't going to keep eating dinner six nights a week at King's when they were married, but they would definitely go over sometimes. That was just how it was.

Justice and his family were part of her life.

"Yes," she said. "I'd love to come to dinner. I might bring some bouquet pictures too. Maybe Penny and Bix can give some input."

"You think Bix is going to tell you what flowers to get?"

Bix was Justice's brother Daughtry's fiancée. She was unorthodox to say the least. Rue had an interesting time with her. Not that Penny was much better. A headstrong, feral woman who had been taken in by the Kings when she was a teenager, after her dad had died.

"Maybe I'll hold back unless Fia's there." His sister-in-law. There was no point showing flowers to his sister, Arizona, either.

It was sometimes a little sad not to have a passel of close female friends, though she did like the women of King's Crest. But Justice was the one whose opinion would always matter most. He would always be the one who mattered most.

"Probably a good plan."

"I only have a month, Justice. Thirty days. And then Asher and I are finally going to be married and . . ."

"And what flowers you carried won't really matter."

She looked up at him, shocked by his uncharacteristic show of . . . sentimentality. It was deeply unlike him. "That's really sweet, Justice."

"Is it? You didn't ask me why the flowers won't matter."

"Oh. Dear. Why won't they matter?"

"Because men don't give a shit about flowers. All he'll care about is what you're wearing, or not, under the wedding dress."

She scoffed and tried to hold back the color she could feel bleeding into her cheeks. He was outrageous sometimes and it was embarrassing, even though she should be used to it. "That isn't true."

"It is," he said. "Trust me, I'm a man."

"But you aren't a man in love," she said.

"What difference would that make? I'm still never going to care more about a bouquet than a bra."

"But the whole thing matters when you're in love. All of it. It's not about sex. It's about caring, and saying vows and . . ."

"The sex should matter," he said.

"But it isn't the point."

He squinted. "It's not?"

"No. Your thoughts on that are why you're stuck in bar-hookup Groundhog Day, where you wake up at the same time every morning with a different woman in your bed, doomed to repeat it again the next day."

"First of all, is that supposed to sound bad?"

"Yes!"

"Second, I don't wake up in the morning with anyone but me. I don't spend the night with women I don't know. It's dangerous. You could get robbed. I practice safe sex."

He smiled then, and she couldn't be annoyed at him. Because that was how he was.

"Okay, get out of my house," she said, pushing at his shoulder. "I have to go take inventory at the yarn store."

Her grandmother's yarn store was forty minutes away, in Mapleton, and it had been part of her inheritance. It was an established shop with a full staff, but Rue worked there full-time and she loved it. She was a serious yarn addict. Her stash was the only thing in her house that was overflowing.

It was organized, though.

By fiber, weight and color.

"Okay then, see you at dinner."

He left then, and got in his truck. As she watched him drive away, she couldn't help but sigh in a contented sort of way.

Everything was perfect.

Everything was in its rightful place.

CHAPTER TWO

JUSTICE STACKED ROCKS until his muscles ached. Until the tyranny of the night before released its hold on his head, and his muscles. The only way to survive partying this hard was to work harder.

The older he got, the more that was true.

At thirty-three he was hardly an old man, but the hard living was definitely beginning to catch up with him. So he was doing the best he could to outrun it any which way he could. Because the alternative was to grow the fuck up.

He wasn't planning on doing that anytime soon.

He wondered, not for the first time, what his life would be like when he was less tethered to Rue. Sometimes she felt like the only thing holding him to basic human decency.

She was the only and best part of his valor.

It wasn't like she was moving away or doing anything drastic. Rue never did anything drastic. She was a constant. The eternal port in the storm that he had grown up in. His best friend in the entire world. His better half, some might say.

She deserved the world.

He was happy as hell that she had found a man that made her happy. That she was moving on and having the kind of normal life that they hadn't been able to imagine when they were kids.

Watching her win at this made him feel . . . He was proud of her. She deserved this. She deserved everything and more.

"You're up early."

He turned and saw his brother Denver standing there, staring at him. His tone was dry. Because it was 4:30 p.m., he was not up early. He had gotten up early to go to Rue's. But this was a normal time for him to be up and about.

"Fuck you," he said.

"Good morning," his brother returned.

"I've already run errands today. Don't be so high and mighty."

"Oh yeah? What were you up to?"

"I had to go to a tux fitting. The wedding is in just couple of weeks." There was no need to specify which wedding. It was the only wedding that mattered.

"Oh, that's right. The wedding. I can't believe it."

"Yeah. Me neither.

"Do you ever feel weird about that?" Denver asked. "Like everybody getting married and moving on. Even Penny."

They both shook their heads. *Even* Penny—who their family had taken in back when she was a little sprite—was off and married.

Landry was, Daughtry was getting hitched soon.

Honestly, he felt much the same about them that he did about Rue. It was good for them. It was good if you could run from the shit in your past and get better.

"Yeah, I guess it's a little bit strange. But . . . I don't want to change anything. I'm happy."

"Are you?" Denver asked.

"Yeah. I mean, I got laid last night."

"Thank you for sharing, Justice," Denver said dryly. "I really value knowing about your sex life."

"I like to keep an open line of communication, bro. It's good for the soul."

"You're *bragging*."

Justice shrugged. "You could get laid if you felt like it."

"Some of us work. I mean, we really work, we don't stroll into the barn at our leisure and stand around propping up various ranching implements."

"Your thoughts on my life aside," Justice said, "I've done what I set out to do. I never wanted to fuck anybody up the way that Dad did us. The way that he did Mom. And here I am. I'm a decent brother, I like to think. I do help you on the ranch, whatever you say, and I have a lifelong friend. And I have managed to maintain that friendship since I was eight years old. Given our upbringing, I feel like that is winning. Great for other people if they want something that looks a little bit more traditional. I don't."

"Can't say that I do either," said Denver.

"Yeah. I mean, that's kind of a big hell no."

"And that's fine," said Denver.

He couldn't remember the last time he ever thought his big brother questioned much of anything, but he could see that he was.

"What's got your panties in a twist?" Justice asked.

"We're the last two," Denver said.

"The last to what?"

"Everyone else on this whole fucking ranch is gone and gotten themselves married. The Garretts, the McClouds and the Sullivans. *All married.*"

"Honestly, you say that and all I hear is that everybody went and stepped in a bear trap. Then I hear you musing about whether or not *we* should want to step in the same bear trap."

Denver laughed. "I dunno. I guess my concern more is that there is something wrong with us."

"Who cares if there is? We haven't dragged anybody into our shit. That, as far as I can see, is the best and only part of virtue when you're fucked up."

"Good point."

"Go out and get laid, Denver," Justice said. "That will deal with all of your emotional turmoil. You'll remember that there are ways to connect with people that don't require you upending your entire life."

"Yeah. I know."

In all seriousness, his brother was a good dude. But he was hard. And harder to know. They were all like that, he supposed. They had a bit of a reputation around town for being . . . unsociable. Daughtry had made it his mission to improve the King family name in town, after their dad had done a good job of running it through the mud. The rest of them . . . Their younger sister, Arizona, had always been known to be prickly and mean. Landry was legendary if only for the explosion that had occurred between him and Fia Sullivan when they were in high school. Denver was well-known for being a hard-ass of epic proportions.

And Justice? Well. He was known for having fun.

He was a good time, not a long time, and everyone knew it.

He couldn't say that it had earned him any respect around town, but it had certainly allowed the townspeople to see that the Kings could be harmless. Or if not harmless, something a little closer to fun than deathly serious assholes. Or scumbags.

So there was that.

Of course, Officer Daughtry had gone and married a reformed criminal, Landry and Fia had gotten together—but only after they had revealed they'd secretly had a child together back when they were teenagers, who they were now raising together—and Arizona had reunited with the love of her life, which had sorted her personality quirks right out. The Kings were on the straight and narrow, except for Daughtry. Who had been kicked off of it a little bit. But honestly, it looked good on him. Happiness looked good on all of his brothers.

He had been happy for a long time, personally. Because he had figured out the secret to that. He had a full life. A good family. Good friend. And he had manageable expectations for himself. And that was the best a man could do in his situation, he figured.

The alternative was marinating in trauma and other bullshit and he wasn't interested in that, thanks. Thinking too much didn't lead anywhere good.

"You coming out to dinner tonight?"

"Yeah, I figured."

"Let's head that way."

He hopped in his brother's truck and let him drive him across the property. King's Crest was, in his opinion, the jewel of Four Corners Ranch. He knew that the other families would fight for that distinction. But Justice had never shied away from a good fistfight. So, it didn't worry him any. His brothers' trucks were sitting in front of the farmhouse when they arrived. The stately old place had been in the family for generations.

Just like the ranch itself.

A collective run by the McClouds, the Kings, the Garretts and the Sullivans since the 1880s. It was the largest ranching operation in the state of Oregon. They weren't factory. They worked the land by hand; they had over a hundred employees. The employees often lived on the ranch, worked on the ranch. Their kids went to school on the ranch. They were an ecosystem in and of themselves. And it was only growing. The Sullivans had made a store on the property where they could sell their items directly. And the Kings were in the process of working at diversifying their cattle operation.

They were building a venue so that people could have conferences, weddings, birthday parties. Guest cabins for people to stay in. Justice was happy to go along for the ride. His favorite thing that they had started up was headed by his sister-in-law Bix, who had an affinity for brewing, and had started a beer label for the place. They had all gotten together and come up with their own distinct variety of beer, and it was about to go into stores, which was definitely a boon.

Bix had been a moonshiner prior to her marriage to Daughtry, and she was the cutest, scrappiest little thing. He really did think his brother had won the lottery with that one.

Bix and Daughtry were about in the farmhouse when

they arrived, and so were Arizona and her husband, Micah.

"Hey kids," Justice said when he came in.

"Well," Arizona said. "As I live and breathe. Justice King. Without a hangover."

"Oh, I had one. I just worked it out."

"Good for you," she said. "Is Rue coming?"

"I expect so. Unless she has wedding stuff."

Asher wasn't back in town yet, so she was still spending most nights out at King's Crest. But that was normal. Asher hadn't been a Four Corners Ranch kid. Meaning he hadn't gone to school on the property, even though he was from the area. He had been bussed to school an hour away in Mapleton, and so she hadn't met him until she had started working at her grandmother's store in town. She had fallen for him pretty quickly. At least, that was how Justice had felt. She was cautious and sweet, was Rue. And she had never been big into the dating scene. He couldn't blame her.

Her parents had been a hot mess and a half. Certainly not the kind to give you aspirations of great romance.

So she'd been extremely choosy when it came to dates and all of that. He had actually been a little bit disturbed when she'd gotten serious about Asher. When they'd started . . . apparently sleeping together.

It wasn't like she had gone and announced it to Justice. There was just a point where it was clear that was happening. Justice couldn't say he'd taken kindly to that. To his perfect Rue becoming a sexual being. She was like a sister to him, and it had felt like another thing he wanted to protect her from.

He just hadn't wanted her to get hurt.

But she hadn't gotten hurt. Asher and Rue had stayed together. It was definitely hard on her when Asher was gone. But one thing he admired so much about Rue was that she was levelheaded even when she was falling in love. He'd always heard that women got a bit loopy over that kind of thing. Hell, he'd seen men do it too. Love, he knew, was one of the single most dangerous things on earth. It gave one person an extraordinary amount of power over another, and it could create a hell of a lot of damage.

The way that Rue had managed to get into a relationship, and stay in that relationship, while maintaining her home, her career and their friendship, had actually shown him something. But then, Rue had always been a window into some foreign, fascinating thing. She had always been different. Different than what they had been raised in. Different than what they had been surrounded by. A source of peace.

He had never been able to quiet himself long enough to learn anything in school. But when Rue taught him, he was able to sit and listen. She broke it down for him in such a way that she made it all feel possible. He wouldn't even know how to read if it wasn't for her. Forget algebra. So, if anybody could do love and marriage and make it all work, keep their sanity and all of that, he really wasn't surprised that it was Ruby Matthews.

His phone vibrated, and he looked down. Right on time he had a text from Rue saying that she would be there fairly directly. He smiled. He didn't respond. She knew he saw it.

She wouldn't expect for him to respond directly either. It just wasn't how they did things.

They began to get dinner on the table—barbecue and all the trimmings, which was a staple of the King family diet. They did beef. And they did it well. And anything the Kings did well, they did hard. From work to sex.

He liked that about them. They were definitely a better iteration of the family name than their father had been. And to that he could raise a glass.

Rue appeared a bit later with a craft bag hanging off of her arm, and a folder under her other.

"Hey," he said, moving to the door and taking everything from her, unburdening her immediately.

"Hi," she said, smiling.

"Tell me," Arizona said, sticking her head out of the kitchen, a mischievous grin on her face. "Are you really going to get my brother to wear a tux?"

"Yes," said Rue. "Because I'm getting married in a church like a civilized person, and he has to dress like a civilized person."

"The trouble is," Micah said, "I've never had the impression that he was a civilized person."

"I'm not," said Justice.

Denver chose that moment to join the conversation. "Oh, he sure as hell isn't. But he will move heaven and earth to make sure that Rue has the wedding that she wants. He's not civilized. He's a damned good friend."

"That's the truth," said Rue.

Rue, for her part, gave him a level of loyalty that he knew few people ever saw. He often wasn't quite sure what he had done to merit it. Yeah, he'd been there for her. He was protective of her. He cared for her. But in comparison, he was an absolute disaster area. Walking caution tape. And she was . . . perfect.

"I will show up and do whatever I'm told to do," he said. "This is her wedding, and the bride gets whatever she wants."

"You're a good man, Justice King," Arizona said.

"Oh I'm positively great when I'm on loan. But I wouldn't be any good long-term."

Rue laughed. "I don't know. We're pretty long-term."

"You know what I mean."

"Yeah," she said, wrinkling her nose.

That hurt a little bit, but it was fair. Rue was realistic about him. There was nothing wrong with that. She knew him. She knew him well.

They served up dinner, and sat around the table. And he watched as Rue smiled and interacted with his siblings. Family, maybe. That was maybe what he offered. Because for all that they had been broken and damaged during their upbringing, the Kings had done a good job of rallying around each other, and holding each other tight. They had been through hell, in some regards. Their father had been a pretty high-level narcissist who had done a lot of damage in the community. And had twisted up his kids all kinds of ways. It was what had given Justice a healthy distrust for love. Because he had watched their father manipulate how much they had loved him. How much they had wanted to please him. That was when Justice had exited people-pleasing stage left. It had been clear to him that there was nothing but danger in that. And that was when he decided the life of a hellion was the one for him.

It was safer. For all involved.

"He looks great in his tux," Rue said.

That knocked him out of his reverie a bit. She thought he looked great?

"Do I?" he asked, wanting to press more on that.

"You know you do," she said. "You know you *always* look good."

"It's a tragedy," Arizona said, shaking her head. "No matter how many times I warned the female populace about him, his powers are too strong."

He rolled his eyes. "Listen. We all have to play to our strengths." The truth was, he knew that he was shaped the kind of way women liked.

He was good-looking, he supposed.

But more than that—and the real point of pride as far as he was concerned—he was fucking *fantastic* in bed.

Part of being raised by a sociopath was making a decision about whether or not you were ever going to use people the way he did.

A man whore—and Justice was a man whore, no doubt—could become a user if he didn't decide that he wouldn't be.

Which was why he went out of his way to be the best lay possible. If a woman picked him to be her evening's entertainment, then he made sure he gave her a hell of a good time. He wasn't a selfish lover. He made sure his lovers had orgasms until they were shaking. Maybe it was a kink. But hell, he knew his limits emotionally, which meant he physically made sure to be the best anyone ever had.

He made it his mission to rock worlds. It was his version of being a better man.

He might not be able to offer forever, but he compensated for what he couldn't offer with world shattering pleasure.

They finished dinner, and he walked Rue out to her truck. "I didn't get a chance to show you all the stuff in the folders. I'm trying to choose flowers."

"Oh. Did you want to come back to my place for a bit?"

"No," she said. "It's okay. I . . . Asher ended up getting delayed back at the base. So he isn't going to be here for a couple more days. Would you help out?"

"Whatever you need."

"Well, I need help choosing some things for the bouquet. Not the flowers—I had to have those grown over a year ago, but she thought that it was a good idea for me to hold off on ribbons and things until closer to the time, so now I have an array of things to look at. Just fine details. And then, I need to do my final dress fitting with Sue. I was kind of hoping you would come."

"You want me at your dress fitting?"

"The final one. To make sure everything's good to go. In case I lost weight or gained it, or whatever. Obviously most of this was done a year ago."

"Obviously," he said.

There was nothing obvious about that to him. But then, that was Rue. Always prepared. And he couldn't imagine that she actually needed his input on anything. But, she did like to double-check a box, and so he knew it was important to her to make sure that everything was thoroughly managed.

"What time do you need to meet?"

"I need to go to the florist at nine."

He grimaced.

"Is that okay?" she asked.

"Yeah," he said. "I just won't go out tonight."

Because the truth was, he would do anything for Rue. She was on the path to her perfect life, and he wasn't going to let anything mess that up.

CHAPTER THREE

SHE DIDN'T KNOW why she was so nervous. She really had every decision about the wedding made.

She'd made the decision to get married in February, on Valentine's Day. It was a tightrope walk. Between touching a theme but also trying to not look like a whole craft store.

She had taken that very seriously.

The problem was, she was a little bit cheesy. Her parents hadn't liked the holidays, and she did. Every single one of them. Christmas was an explosion of joy in her house. Halloween was haunted. Thanksgiving was turkey-ful and Valentine's Day was red lights, red flowers and hearts.

So this was going to be pushing the line on taste, but she felt like she had it. Like she was tightrope walking it like a champ. But now she was worried she was going to see things together and think it looked like an event rental store had emptied its contents into an elementary school classroom party.

So she had to be sure.

It was who she was as a person. But she was still nervous that Justice wasn't going to get to her house on time, and consequently they would not be able to get to Mapleton on time. Which was why she had told him that she needed to leave at nine, when she actually needed to leave at nine thirty. He rolled in at 8:59 on the dot. She scrambled out of the house and climbed into his passenger seat. "You're early," she said.

"I wasn't going to be late. You have to get to an appointment."

"You were late yesterday," she accused.

"I know. I'm sorry. This is your wedding. I need to be more on top of it."

"Don't be this nice. It freaks me out."

"Am I not nice generally?"

He headed down the highway, and Rue pulled out her folder, leafing through some of her pictures. "You're nice," she said. "Consistently. Fantastically. You are also a rake. A rogue. And I like that about you. I *expect* it about you. I actually told you to be there a whole half hour earlier than I needed you to be."

"Treacherous," he said, but he didn't seem mad.

He was never mad at her.

She was never mad at him either, regardless of what a hard time she sometimes gave him.

The truth was, she admired Justice. Not in a way that made her want to emulate him. But the way he lived his life was just strangely commendable to her.

Her parents had been chaotic, but they had *hurt* people with it. They had hurt her with it. They had gone around using sex as a weapon, acting unhinged in their attraction for each other. Justice didn't do that. He was promiscuous, putting it mildly, but he always seemed to treat everybody that he encountered with respect. Especially the women that he slept with. He never played games with them. He never hurt them. He was scrupulous in his misbehavior, and it was a revelation to her that such a thing could occur. She had only ever seen this kind of behavior as a sort of walking DUI. A potential hazard to all and everyone around them. Until him.

"I'm going to throw you a bachelorette party," he said suddenly.

"Oh, I don't need anything like that."

"Don't look scandalized, Rue. We'll have a party at King's Crest the night before the wedding. It'll be great."

"Asher will be back in town."

"I know. But are you really going to spend the night before your wedding with the guy? You're going to spend the rest of your life with him."

"A fair point," she said. "But I don't know. Doesn't it seem . . . ?"

"Doesn't seem traditional to fuck your groom the night *before* your wedding night."

"Justice," she said, sounding scandalized. She could see that he loved it.

Rue felt a strange pang in her stomach. She didn't care for it. She did not . . . They did not . . . It wasn't like that. And hearing Justice call it all wrong like that made her feel tetchy.

"I'm just saying. You have the rest of your life with the guy. You oughtta spend your last night of freedom getting silly with your best friend."

It warmed her, she decided, that Justice cared like that. Which had to be the pang. And he was right. It was *traditional* to spend the night away from the groom. There was definitely something about that which appealed to her.

"Okay," she said. "I will submit to your bachelorette party. But no strippers."

"Oh damn," he said. "I was really looking forward to it."

He looked both innocent and devilish at the same time. A Justice King special.

"I don't even know what to make of that," she said.

"I'm messing with you. You know I would never. It's not you. Your wedding is about you. Not me."

It did feel so extraordinarily lucky to have a friend like him. When they arrived at the florist, he looked vaguely overwhelmed by the intensity of the blooms around them. But he sat quietly and attentively the entire meeting and it reminded her a whole lot of watching him in school. Restless energy pouring through him while he tried to sit and listen. Absently, she touched the top of his hand. He went still.

"It's nice that you're involving the groom," the florist said.

They both jumped, and Rue put her hand back in her lap.

"Oh," she said. "He's not the groom. He's my best man. My man of honor. He's my . . . He's my best friend."

"Oh," the woman said, looking surprised. "I'm sorry. I assumed."

Well, Rue supposed she couldn't blame her. It was probably weird for a bride to walk into the shop with a man she was not related to—and who was absolutely gorgeous—and have him not be the groom.

She didn't touch him again, though.

She had known him forever.

So she had a lot of intuition when it came to his feelings. Though, he would claim he didn't have any. But it was a lie. When Justice was unsettled, a little bit of physical touch always seemed to quiet him. It wasn't like they were *hugely* touchy with each other. That would be weird. But this—her casually touching his hand—was a habit that went back to their school days.

He wasn't really that much help with the flowers, but he reinforced her decisions. All of her ribbon choices, all of her little charm choices for the ends of the ribbon. And then the wrap for his boutonniere.

She didn't have any bridesmaids. It was just Justice. He was the one constant in her life. She wouldn't have any family at her wedding. It would be Asher's family, and the Four Corners crowd. She felt . . . sad about that. Maybe sadder than she should.

"Do we have time to grab a bite before we head back for your fitting?"

"Yeah," she said. "It's pretty early for lunch."

"That's what brunch is for, Ruby," he said, grinning.

"You're very practical."

"Don't say that, it will ruin my rep."

The way he was with her would ruin his rep. If anyone know he was so damned sweet they would question everything they knew about legendary seducer Justice King. She had to admit, she liked that.

She had this part of him.

Only she had it.

They went over to a small cafe and Justice ordered astronomically sweet-looking pancakes, and encouraged her to get even sweeter looking French toast, which she did.

She wondered if this would change when she got married. Or, rather, probably not so much when she got married but at the end of Asher's contract with the military.

Right now, part of why she and Justice spent so much time together was that Asher was usually out of state, or even out of the country. They had definitely talked about her following him, but they had done their whole relationship like this. Spending time together when he was on leave, her coming out to visit when he was stationed somewhere, it was difficult, but they had managed. And there had always been an understanding that they would marry and he would take a job with his dad at his pipe-fitting business. And during that time he would use his military benefits to go to school. He wanted to be an engineer. It was all coming a little bit later, but that was because of how he had chosen to balance things.

They had a plan. A good one.

But yeah, she would be eating breakfast with him most mornings. Dinner at night. So it would change the amount of time she and Justice spent together. But that was a good thing.

That was the point of getting married. You were making a new life. Making a family. With the person that you loved, and she did love Asher. Their relationship had always been so easy. He made her feel good about herself. He was so much like her. Organized and certain. Neat as a pin. They had fun planning their future together. He was going to give her that continued stability. And for a control freak like her it was literally the best-case scenario.

He was a man whose ideals matched up perfectly with her own. She really couldn't have asked for anything better.

But there was definitely a small hint of sadness. For the thing she would be leaving behind. For the fact that she and Justice wouldn't be able to be just like they had always been. It was hard for her to let go of anything. Justice had always provided a certain amount of stability, security and emotional support. Asher had always been totally comfortable with the relationship, and she knew that was weird. She wasn't just going to find that with any guy. In fact, a couple of guys she had made vague attempts at dating prior to Asher had all stopped very quickly in part because they had been completely weirded out by Justice's continued presence.

And she hadn't wanted anything remotely resembling jealousy in her vicinity.

That was too much like her parents. Accusations of cheating, and then real cheating, and she just couldn't abide it.

Infidelity was an absolute *no* for her. But jealousy? That was even worse. Well. Not worse, maybe, but she just was never going to get herself tangled into something like that. She wasn't going to cheat. And she couldn't handle being with a man who was going to be insecure about that. It was just a hard no.

They drank way too much coffee, and were buzzing on that and sugar by the time they got back into his truck and headed toward the house for her dress fitting. She knew a moment of extreme nervousness.

Justice was going to see her wedding dress.

She didn't know what kind of reaction she wanted from him. Just that she needed it to be a big one. She had been very certain about what she wanted, and even though the woman at the bridal shop had told her that she would end up buying something completely different than what she had in mind, Rue had known that wasn't true. She had known exactly what she was going to get. A strapless gown with a belt at the waist that had a small detail, and an A-line skirt. Not a ball gown, but not clingy either. She knew she wanted heavy satin, and not much adornment. She had gone and gotten exactly that. The dress was entirely white except for the sash around the waist, which was a lovely taupe color that went with her crimson flowers. And the sage green, crushed velvet ribbon she had chosen today complemented it all beautifully. Subtle pops of color, nothing too wild.

A little Valentine flavor without being the full-on Cupid.

She was utterly pleased with herself. But, because she had been so certain of what she was buying she hadn't brought Justice in with her. Otherwise she might have. But she had just known. She had a vision of herself that was so clear it had transcended any uncertainty.

So yeah, really nobody but the seamstress had seen the dress, and she really wanted him to like it.

She realized that the look on his face when she came out in the dress was incredibly important to her.

It was too late for her to get a new dress, so if she didn't get a reaction out of it, then that was just going to be terrible. Of course, Justice and Asher were very different men. She didn't want Justice to react the way that Asher was going to anyway. Besides, Justice would probably want to marry a woman in a minidress that had a plunging neckline. *Obvious* was his stock-in-trade.

He would never get married, though. It made her kind of sad. If a little bit meanly . . . pleased at the same time. But she didn't even want to articulate that to herself. It was just . . . she knew that she wasn't going to see him as much anymore after she got married. If he got married . . . Well, of all the issues she had had early on balancing the feelings of the men she was dating with her relationship with him, and then finally finding someone who was okay with it, but who still demanded a heavy amount of her attention . . . She didn't want to share Justice with another woman.

Which wasn't really a problem. He didn't *date*. He hooked up, and he never brought those women around. She usually felt like the only woman in his life and she appreciated that.

They rolled up to the house and she grabbed her French toast leftovers container—Justice didn't have any leftovers—and they both went inside.

"Boots off, cowboy," she said as she took her own shoes off right by the door.

He shot her an indulgent look, and took his boots off.

She looked from him, to her neat, orderly house, to her wedding ring, and back to Justice. The one who'd known her most of her life. The one who had been through absolutely everything with her.

"Look at us," she whispered. "We're grown-ups."

Sometimes it amazed her. That they'd made it this far. That she had her house, and he was still standing. And that they still had each other. Because no one else in her life had lasted longer than Justice King.

"We are indeed," he said.

He walked over to her couch and sat heavily on it, the male sound he made when he connected with the cushion hitting her strangely.

"Okay," she said. "I'm going to go put the dress on, because Sue is going to be here soon. If you laugh at me, I will kill you."

"I'm not going to laugh at you."

"Remember my prom dress?" she asked.

"Yeah," he said.

They had a dance in the barn at Four Corners that year, coordinated by their teacher, and poor Rue had done her very best to cobble something together with parents who just didn't help at all, and a grandmother who had been deeply conservative.

Justice had called her *Prairie Dawn*. It had been fair enough. But it had still hurt her feelings. He'd spent the whole night apologizing to her, but she'd been wounded in spite of the apologies.

"I'm *not* going to laugh," he said again.

"If you do," she said, "I will kill you."

"You won't," he said. "Because you'll get blood on your dress, *and* on your carpet. So I think we both know I'm safe."

"I could strangle you."

He laughed. "You wouldn't. That's a messy way to

kill someone too. Takes a long time. Takes real determination. It's not like in the movies."

She squinted. "Do you doubt that I have the determination?"

"I would throw you off like a little flea, Rue. You could try, but you would not succeed."

"Let's not test the theory."

She went into her bedroom, and pulled the gorgeous dress out of her closet. Every time she saw it her heart expanded. She took her clothes off and folded them neatly, and slipped into the little half corset that she had to hold everything in place, before stepping into the gown. She did a contortionist act to get it zipped up. But she had lived alone long enough that she was very good at that.

She took her veil out of the box and looked at herself critically in the mirror as she put her hair up in a high bun and pinned it in quickly.

She had to put heels on; otherwise the dress wouldn't fall right. She got into the closet and put on her gorgeous sandals. They sparkled all over. Even though they wouldn't show, she loved them. They were flashier than anything else at the wedding. Nobody would see them. But *she* knew. And she liked them.

She took a deep breath and opened up the bedroom door. She had a direct view of Justice sitting on the couch as she came out.

She didn't know what she had expected from him. But his face was like a mask. Completely immovable, and fixed. She had never seen him look so grave. He just looked at her, and he didn't say anything.

She moved closer, and stood there, and still he didn't move, one hand on his left knee, the other on his right, his jaw squared up tight, his teeth clenched. His blue eyes glittered as he looked at her, the only movement that she could discern at all.

"What?" she asked.

"I . . ."

She turned slowly. "Do you like it?"

He stood up from the couch, and moved to her, pulling her hard up against him, the hug so unexpected it took her breath away. All she could hear was her own heart beating in her head, and then his as her face was pressed to his hard chest.

He released her quickly, the whole thing lasting maybe one second.

"Oh," he said. "You're just really fucking beautiful. And I am . . . I am damned proud of you, Rue. Look at you. We're grown-ups. But you're *really* one. You made it."

It was so sincere, and so deep that she just didn't know what to do with it.

"Thank you," she said. "I wanted it really bad."

He reached up and brushed a strand of hair out of her eyes, and her stomach swooped. He smiled, and she felt like everything was going to be okay. Everything.

He linked his arm with hers and turned to the side. "I should be giving you away, you know?"

She looked up and caught their reflection in the mirror just behind her dining table. Her in a wedding dress, and him in a black T-shirt and a black cowboy hat right beside her. She just stared for a second. And then it was like someone had slapped her and she had to look away. She took a step back from him. "You could," she said. "You . . . you could."

"It's okay. Nobody needs to give you away, Rue. Besides. You been banging that guy for eight years."

"Stop," she said. And she laughed, the tension in her chest dissipating. Thank God.

"You have to stop, because it's ridiculous."

"Newsflash, Ruby. I am ridiculous."

"It's part of your charm," she said.

Sue arrived about ten minutes later, and made final adjustments to the dress, which she completed right there because they were so small.

And then it was time for Justice to go back to work on the ranch. And she felt relieved after a fashion. Which was an odd sensation, but there had been something heavy about the whole day. She wasn't in the mood to unpack it. It was just the impending change of it all. But she was fixed in her decision, and she was happy about it.

And the truth was, she and Justice would weather the change in their relationship. They had weathered everything else.

Now the only thing she really had to worry about was surviving her bachelorette party.

CHAPTER FOUR

ARIZONA AND FIA had gone entirely overboard with their help for the bachelorette party, and Justice adored them for it.

He opened up a bag that was filled with absolutely garbage party favors. They were humiliating. They were embarrassing. They were tasteless as hell. And he loved them. "You are brilliant," he said, reaching into the bag and taking out a necklace that was made up entirely of small, miniature naked men.

Arizona grinned. Like a shark. "We want her to be dressed up for the party."

"She's going to be *horrified*," he said.

He had lied a little bit when he'd said that the party was going to be tailored to her needs. The truth was, he had done her a kindness by deciding to have it at King's. Keeping it all in the family. Because it was going to be raucous, and he was going to pull her out of her comfort zone. Because that was what best men did on the eve of their friend's wedding. It was just what happened. It was what *needed* to happen.

"I can't believe she's getting married," Fia said, looking a little bit wistful.

"Why do you say that?" Justice asked.

"It just feels very final," Fia said, shrugging.

"Final in what sense?" he pressed.

"I . . ." She exchanged a glance with Arizona.

"What?"

It was Arizona who finally relented. "We thought *you* would marry her. I mean, eventually. Maybe in a decade. But . . . I just thought it would be you."

"You thought I was going to *marry her*?" Something akin to horror stole through him. The idea of Rue being stuck with him . . . "Have you *met* me? Absolutely not. Absolutely not."

"You care about each other. Clearly. You have since you were kids. We've all watched it," Arizona said.

"Yeah. We *care* about each other. That's not the same thing as wanting to get married."

"It's not like I don't think men and women can be platonic friends," Arizona said.

"I don't," said Fia.

"That's a little bit regressive, Fia," said Arizona.

"In my experience sex is regressive, Arizona."

"*Gross*. Because you have sex with my brother."

"All the time," said Fia.

The women regarded each other, and Justice now wanted an escape button, his admiration for them dimming slightly.

"Here's the thing, I don't care what you say." He directed that at Fia. "Men and women can be friends. Rue is my best friend. In the whole world. And it has never even almost been anything else."

Yeah, when he had seen her in her wedding dress earlier he had been knocked on his ass. She was beautiful. He wasn't blind. He was familiar enough with women and how they were shaped that even though she dressed much more conservatively than any woman he would ever consider taking to bed, he was aware that she was hot. The wedding dress had been . . . a shock. Because it was like a reality check he couldn't ignore. She was getting married. Life was changing. He could do without that, frankly. But it was balanced by the fact that he was happy for her. Thrilled for her.

"It's weird to react this way," he said to both of them. "If I had a male friend getting married you wouldn't be moaning about the fact that he hadn't married me instead."

"Well, it depends," Arizona said.

"On what?"

"If I thought you'd be good together romantically."

"Oh *please*," he said. "You're liars."

"Liars with good taste in party favors, though," Arizona said.

"The value I place on that is waning, little sister."

He groused through all the setup. But was cheered mildly by the obscene balloons. And the even more obscene candy hearts that were going in different bowls stationed around the living room.

"You're annoying," he said to both of them. "But this really is fantastic."

His siblings and Fia, plus significant others, arrived shortly after that. They had decided to make it an extended-family affair.

The alcohol was flowing freely, and Bix had brought some of her special, higher proof alcohol, which he imagined Daughtry in no way approved of. But hey, if Daughtry didn't approve, then it was a good party.

When Daughtry walked in, in uniform, they all groaned. "Whoop whoop," Bix shouted. "*Five-O Five-O.*"

"The police are here," Arizona wailed.

"Maybe it's just the stripper," Justice said, reaching into his pocket and taking out his wallet.

"Adorable," Daughtry said, his expression suggesting he did not, in fact, find it adorable.

Then they all took their places and waited for Rue. His pocket buzzed.

"She'll be here in five minutes."

And right on the dot, she was.

She opened up the door, wearing a long coat, which she discarded and revealed a cute floral dress beneath that was definitely not weather appropriate.

She looked so much like the girl he'd always known. But also the woman she'd become.

His family all hooted and shouted and it did the work to knock him out of his sudden fog.

She looked shocked to see such a full house.

"Oh my," she said.

And Justice walked across the living room, holding a sash aloft that said Bride. "Welcome," he said. "Guest of honor."

"Thank you, man of honor," she said. "I didn't expect such a big turnout."

"I've a feeling there's going to be a few things you didn't expect tonight."

And that was when he grabbed the necklace of naked men and bestowed it upon her. She frowned and looked down, and then her face turned bright red. "You can't be serious."

"It's a bachelorette party," Arizona shouted. "So let the fun begin."

And it did. There was food. Cake. And even though Rue barely drank, she tasted some of Bix's brew and got surprisingly into the spirit of it all.

They paired off for games, and he and Rue were on the same team. There was balloon shaving and myriad other nonsense, which she would've said he hated, but it was all just traditional and delightful and hilarious, and he felt happy that he could give it to her.

Because she looked filled with joy, and that was all he had wanted. Wanted for her to love this. Wanted for her to have the best wedding. The best lead-up to the wedding. The best life. It mattered so damned much.

They were trying to play pin-the-veil-on-the-bride, with a big life-size tracing of a person on the wall, but Daughtry was a dick, and he had moved the poster so that it was sitting weirdly high when it was Rue's turn. She was spinning around, and trying to find it. Justice stood up and, without thinking, grabbed her around the waist and hefted her toward the wall. She shrieked and kicked, and his hand made contact with her bare thigh. He felt like he'd been kicked, but he lifted her up to the poster on the wall anyway and let her pin it before setting her down slowly. Which put his palms on a lot more of her leg than he had counted on. She lifted her blindfold up, and wrinkled her nose. "That was cheating."

"Look how good you did," he said, pointing to the veil, which was actually on the wall above the poster.

"Cheaters don't prosper," Rue said, smacking him on the shoulder, and if she had any feelings about his hands being all over her legs, she certainly wasn't acting like she did. Which was good. That didn't need to become a problem.

He had to question why the hell *he* was having a reaction to touching her legs? They touched each other casually pretty much all the time. *No*, he didn't touch her bare thigh as a general rule, but he'd had sex just a few days ago. It wasn't like he was hard up or anything. And she was *Rue*, for God's sake. Her legs were a fixture in his life, as was the rest of her, and there was no reason for anything to feel illicit or anything like that. *For God's sake.*

He had let Bix's moonshine get to his head. It pissed him off, because he had felt like his sister and sister-in-law were being so out-of-pocket earlier. He didn't like that he was feeling weird over physical contact with her body now.

So he decided the best thing to do would be to throw another drink on it, and keep the party rolling.

And they did. Loudly.

"I can't stay up all night," she said softly when they were all sitting around in the living room listening to Denver tell raucous stories.

"Yeah. I guess you need your beauty sleep."

"I guess."

"I'll walk you out."

It was freezing outside. Not even her coat could possibly be keeping her warm with that little dress beneath it. And his palm still burned.

She was getting married tomorrow.

"I remember when you first came to school," he said. He hadn't intended to take a little walk down memory lane, but hell. It was preferable to focusing on the way his hands felt.

"You do?"

"Yeah. I do. I heard that we had some new ranch hands. Though, we had those all the time. But that it was a family. And they had a kid. I was really disappointed that you were a girl."

She laughed. "Wow. I didn't know that. Our friendship is built on lies."

"Sorry," he said.

"When did you get over your disappointment?"

"About the time you pulled me aside because you noticed that I was struggling with my reading. You managed to do it in a way that didn't make me feel like an idiot. In a way that didn't make me feel embarrassed. For the first time, when you sat there and put your finger on the page I felt like I could actually focus on it. There was something about the way that you explained it that held my attention. I'll never forget that. After that, I figured maybe we ought to be friends."

"Well, I was disappointed that you were a boy. I wanted to get to know some girls my age. But I had a hard time with it. There were the Sullivans, but they had each other. And that bond seemed really strong. It was difficult to get around that. I don't know. It was like a magnet pushed me toward you. And at some point I quit caring that you were a boy. At some point, I was just happy to have a friend."

"I still remember you crying because your parents were fighting and . . ."

"When was that?"

He laughed. "When wasn't it? I don't know. It was easier, right? For us to band together. To kind of cling to each other rather than deal with our families. Because Lord knows they were just a mess."

"They were. But it never seemed bad here. Before we were here we were in Sacramento. And my dad had worked, but only sometimes. Tension was really high, and we lived in a tiny apartment. We moved here and there were other kids. We moved here and at least the basic necessities felt handled."

"I never asked you this, and that seems kind of stupid. Did you move here because your grandma was already here?"

"Yeah," she said. "I guess my mom grew up in the area. And my grandma never left. But it isn't like we talked a whole lot about that. There weren't open lines of communication. I mean, you know I don't talk to them now."

"Yeah. Well. I don't talk to mine either."

They looked at each other. It was a terrible thing to have in common. Parents that were just so terrible they might as well be dead to you because not speaking to them at all was the only way you could manage your damned life. And yet, it had always been the bad things they had in common. The good things . . . they were different. But it was why they worked.

"What do you need to make tomorrow the best day possible?" he said.

She looked up at him, the adoration on her face just about knocking him for six.

"You're going to be there. I'm marrying Asher. Everything is going to be perfect. That's all I need." She wrapped her arms around his neck.

He wrapped his arms around her waist, letting her linger on a hug. The familiar weight of her, combined with the scent of her shampoo, was one of the most comforting things he could even think of.

"Thank you for tonight. Thank you for being such an important part of my life."

"Thanks for teaching me how to read," he said.

She let go of him. "Anytime."

After Rue drove away, he went into the house. The bridal veils were still pinned to the wall, and there was still lewd paraphernalia strewn all about. The dishes had been collected and he could hear chatter and glass clattering against itself in the other room. He walked into the kitchen, where Daughtry, Bix, Landry, Fia, Arizona, Micah and Denver all were working at putting everything away.

"Thank you," he said.

"Of course," came the response, along with varying degrees of dismissive noises.

"Could y'all come to the church early with me tomorrow to help set up?"

"Rue is important to all of us," Arizona said. "Of course we'll be there."

And the underlying thing of all that was that he was important to them too. And it mattered to him.

He thought about that as he headed back to his own cabin on the property. He and Denver might never get married and have kids. They might never be normal in the way the rest of them were. But the King family had built something better than what they'd had before. They had made something real out of all the messed-up nonsense that had come before. And that was something.

He was going to hang on to that.

CHAPTER FIVE

The knot in Rue's stomach refused to go away. It was with her from the time she woke up on the day of her wedding, all the way on the drive to the church, and it persisted.

Which was weird because everything was in its place. There was nothing to be nervous about. It had ended up that she hadn't actually seen Asher, and that was causing her a little bit of anxiety. But his flight had been delayed, and then she had her bachelorette party, and there was a point where it really was bad luck to see each other, and as much as she didn't believe in that, it was the tradition of all of it. Justice had been right about that.

But it had been a couple of months since she'd last been with him, and yeah, it just felt . . . funny to be marrying him after that much distance. But that was just the way of it with the military.

It was excitement, really. She remembered reading one time that excitement and anxiety were actually the same physical sensation in the body and it was up to your brain to interpret what you were actually experiencing. So then she decided on excitement. Because it was her wedding day after all. She dressed and did her makeup, her hair a simple style that she could manage on her own. She enjoyed the silence and the solitude. It was, she supposed, one of the perks of not having a big wedding party. Her man of honor was off helping set up. And he didn't have to text her for her to know that.

Not that he ever texted.

She heard a knock on the door and she opened it. It was Justice, looking incredible in his tux. They stood there and looked at each other, her in her dress, him in the tux.

"You're beautiful," he said finally.

"You're not so bad yourself, cowboy."

It just felt an especially grown-up thing to do, getting married. Especially right now that she was looking at her childhood best friend. The one who had been there for her through so much. Everything. No one understood her the way that Justice did. He was unique in that regard.

"How is everything looking?"

"We're good to go," he said. "Guests haven't started arriving yet, but the sanctuary's looking perfect, we've got all the flowers set out. I know the reception venue is handling all of that. So . . . you have absolutely nothing left to worry about."

He stepped into the room and closed the door behind him. She was suddenly aware of how small the space was.

"Are you okay?"

"Yeah. Why wouldn't I be?"

"When Arizona got married she was a little bit . . . I don't know. *Sad* really isn't the word. I think we've all accepted the limitations of our parents. It's been a long time. We're grown. We get it. But I think there are moments like this where you just feel real conscious of what all is and isn't right. It is not right that your mom isn't here with you helping you get ready. It's not right that your grandma's gone. It's not right that your dad isn't here to give you away. I guess even more so that your mom and dad aren't the kind of parents that should be here. Because if they were here they would just be making the wedding worse."

"That is the truth," she said. "I really am okay." She meant it. The people that mattered would be here. And she couldn't complain about that.

"I have something for you."

"You do?"

"Yeah. Because when you get married you need something old, something new, something borrowed, something blue, right?"

"Oh my goodness. Where did you even learn that, Justice King?"

"It's cowboy wisdom. Everybody knows it. I figure you got quite a few new things. But you don't have family here. I have something for you. You can borrow it. Because that's an important bit. You have to be borrowing it. So I need it back in like thirty years. Okay?"

He reached into his pocket and he took out a necklace. It had a blue sapphire in the center, and the middle was clearly aged.

"What is this?"

"The King family is one messed-up legacy after another. But it all started with my great-great-great-great-great grandfather Elias King, and his wife, Sadie. They came out West for a chance at a better life. I don't know that they had one. But what I do know is that we're still here. Trying. This belonged to her. She brought it with her from Missouri. And I believe it came over on the crossing from England some fifty years before."

Her jaw dropped. "You can't give me a family heirloom."

"I'm loaning it to you. Because it took my family on this journey. The journey to a better life. And all I know is I'm living a better one than my parents did. It's a reminder. To keep being on the journey."

Her hands were shaking so much that she almost didn't even want to pick it up. Didn't want him to see.

"I'll put it on you," he said.

He lifted the necklace and undid the clasp, then lifted it, leaning in. Her breath caught, her heart thundering hard. His eyes never left hers as he brought the chain around her neck and slowly clasped it, letting the gem fall between her breasts. She felt them suddenly. She was just very aware she had them. Heavy, sensitive. His eyes drifted down to the jewel, and it made her feel unbearably . . . aware. Of her skin. Of her fingertips. Of the way he smelled.

She didn't know what to do. She felt frozen. Lost. Found. All at once. Maybe it was because of the enormity of it all. The wedding. The intensity. Because dammit all, the man had given her this necklace to wear. He had fulfilled all these traditions; he had shown up for her. In a way she hadn't expected. In a way she hadn't thought she might need. That was all.

Suddenly, she found her breath, and took a step back. "Thank you."

There was another knock on the door and she stiffened. "Oh. I better . . ." She opened it, and froze. Because there was Asher. His sandy brown hair a mess, wearing a white T-shirt and blue jeans, and not a tux. He looked like he hadn't slept.

"You're not supposed to see my wedding dress," she said. Because for some reason it was the first thing she thought of, even though she had a lot of follow-up questions. But it had just come out of her mouth. She hadn't been able to stop it.

"I . . . I need to talk to you."

"Okay," she said.

"Without him here."

Justice turned, and there was something in his expression that she couldn't name. Justice was probably four or five inches taller than Asher, and somehow right then it was more apparent than usual.

And then Justice was just Justice again, an easy smile on his face.

"Howdy," said Justice.

"I just need a minute," Asher said.

Normally Justice and Asher got along great, but there was tension in Justice now. The way he looked at her was so sharp she felt it cutting into her.

"Justice," she said. "I need to talk to my fiancé."

Because it was silly that he was standing there acting like a bouncer when her almost-husband was there.

"All right," he said.

He turned and walked outside and shut the door behind him.

"What's going on? Why aren't you ready?"

"I'm really sorry," he said, looking wooden and stiff. "I have really fucked this up."

She didn't know what she'd been expecting to hear. But it hadn't been *that*.

"What happened?"

Maybe his suit wasn't here? Had he forgotten to pick it up? No. She had picked it up. So there weren't any problems with that. She had made sure that it would all be fine. That it would be perfect.

"Everything's okay," she said.

"No, Rue. It's not. It's not okay. I . . . You know I got delayed, and the military called me back and had me stay that extra couple weeks."

"Yes. I do know that . . . It's why I haven't seen you."

"I didn't anticipate it. And . . ." He scrubbed his hands over his face. "Dammit. Rue, I slept with someone else."

"What?" The word was hollow. The ground was hollow. She was hollow.

She couldn't think. Couldn't speak more beyond that one, devastated word.

She couldn't reconcile those words coming out of that man's mouth. That man who knew her so well. Her fears, her hopes, her plans. Who was part of those plans, had made them with her.

And he knew . . . he knew how much fidelity meant to her. How much sex meant to her.

He knew he was the only man she'd ever slept with.

"She . . . We were on deployment together last year, and we kind of got to know each other, and I . . . I love you. *I love you*. I was super clear on that. But one thing led to another, and things just got really out of hand. I'd never experienced anything like that before. I had never experienced being attracted to somebody like that. It was just the one time. I thought we had, you know, four months until the wedding and I could let it go. But then I got delayed, and she and I were at the same base and . . . it happened again. It happened . . . and I don't think I can go through with this. I thought that I could forget that it happened when it was a year before the wedding—"

"What?" There was a buzzing sound in her ears. She couldn't breathe. "You had sex with somebody else?"

"Yes."

"And you weren't going to tell me? You were going to marry me when you . . . You know how I feel about that. You know how I feel about infidelity."

"I was on deployment," he said. "It's . . . I hadn't had sex for so long and she was there and it blindsided me. I felt like I was just a lot weaker than usual, and that it wouldn't ever be a problem again but—"

"That's *my* decision," she almost choked on the words. "Not yours. You were going to marry me and not tell me and the only thing that made you confess is that you did it again. Because this time it was close enough that it bothers you?"

"Yeah," he said, looking lost. Looking like a stranger.

"I don't understand this. I don't get what I'm hearing right now."

"It's just it was . . . I can't marry you knowing that I'm . . . this attracted to somebody else."

"You're attracted to her. But you don't love her?"

"That's the worst part, Rue. I love *you*. I just . . . I lose my head when she's around. And I thought that I was going to get on top of that and I thought that I was going to—"

"You threw everything away to *fuck*? What does that even . . . ? How is that more important than eight years? Than love? I don't understand. I don't understand how you threw away everything that *we* are—high school sweethearts and and . . . all because of sex."

"I didn't mean to."

She sputtered, her disbelief coming in halting gasps. "You didn't mean to. You didn't mean to. I'd . . . I don't even know what to say. There are people coming here. My . . . my friends . . . We paid for all of this. We've been planning this for so long."

Those things didn't really matter. Not in comparison to the devastation of the whole rest of her life. The way everything she'd hoped for and planned was destroyed. But it was the easiest thing to hang onto right now.

"I know," he said. "And I thought that I could come and put my tuxedo on and just not tell you. Because there is a very big part of me that still wants to do this. I want the life that we planned. I want . . ."

"You . . . you have a plan for everything. You never do anything without thinking . . . You never . . ."

"I *know*," he said, his voice desperate. Lost. She wanted to comfort him, that was the messed up thing. "And I did this without thinking. I . . . I'm so sorry." To her horror tears filled his eyes. "I never wanted to hurt you. I . . . They . . . It wasn't supposed to be this way. And it wasn't you. It was me. I . . ."

"You are damned right it was you. I did everything that I could've done. I was here. I was faithful to you.

I have never even been almost tempted to cheat on you."

The necklace sat heavy on her now. She touched it, and ignored the sensation in her fingertips.

"I worked and I planned this wedding. I invested everything into our future. And just . . . How dare you?"

His shoulders shook, his distress, his regret so evident that it only stoked the fires of her rage. Why couldn't he be an asshole? Why couldn't he accuse her of being unfaithful while he was away? *Blame* her. Why did he have to stand there and somehow be so damned decent in the middle of admitting that he was a cheating scumbag? In the middle of breaking her heart, breaking her life, ruining her wedding. It wasn't fair.

"Am I not good in bed?" she asked.

"Rue, you're . . . you're great, you're beautiful . . ."

"You're not attracted to me." Her voice sounded so small. She hated it.

"I *am*. It's just there was chemistry with her and I didn't . . ."

"Tell me that something is wrong with me," she said, pleading now. "*Please*. Because if not then this just feels random and unfair. Give me something that I can fix. Come on. Because some of this has to be my fault."

"It's not your fault," he said. "It's my fault. I messed up. I wrecked everything."

"*No*. I can't accept it," she said.

Because she had a plan, and she had met the perfect man, and she had trusted him. With all of her. And so if she could find a good man that she trusted and he could do this, and it had nothing to do with anything she had done, this . . . This unraveling, this betrayal that had nothing to do with her performance, meant she wasn't going to be able to move on. She was never going to be able to . . . She just couldn't accept it. She couldn't.

"It wasn't you," he said. "I didn't want to hurt you. I didn't want to lose this. But I also can't lie to you. I told myself that I could. That I could keep it from you and that I could still have everything. But I can't do that to you, Rue. Because I know about your family. Because I get why you hate infidelity so much. I do. You're right. What I was planning on doing was shit. But this isn't better. And if I could go back and change it . . ." He put his hands over his face. "I would."

He was lying.

She knew him well enough to see that he was lying.

He wouldn't change it.

He felt bad, but he wanted to walk away. He felt bad, but he wanted the sex he'd had with whoever this woman was more than he wanted *their* life. And he couldn't even be honest about it. With himself or with her. What the hell was that about?

"Are you going to be with her now?"

"I don't know. I don't know. I . . . I'm really sorry."

"What is *sorry* supposed to mean to me? I planned for this. Everything was perfect. I had a bachelorette party." She started to hyperventilate. "We were supposed to go to that gorgeous lodge for a week for our honeymoon and now . . . now it's all nothing. It's nothing. So what good does sorry do me?"

"It doesn't fix anything. I get that. I'm not even

asking you to forgive me. I just want you to know. That I regret . . . hurting you."

"What good does that do me? You tell me. All these people are showing up. I'm wearing the dress. What good does that do me? What does your sorry mean? It's . . . it's bullshit," she said. "Can't you at least accuse me of cheating on you with Justice?"

"You didn't," he said, looking wide-eyed and shocked. Trusting.

"No," she said. "I didn't. But can't you be unreasonable and unhinged, and nothing like the man that I've spent the last eight years with, instead of being . . . *you*? I want you to turn into a monster," she said, her voice breaking. "Because it was a monstrous thing to cheat on me, Asher. It was. But you're standing there and you're still you. I wish you could make me hate you."

"I'm so sorry."

What a bland sentence.

I'm so sorry.

It didn't fix anything. It didn't change the moment, or alter her feelings.

She'd thought once that if her parents ever had a moment of self-awareness and apologized to her she'd be healed in some fashion.

But that was a lie.

She realized that now. Apologies were empty when you were still losing everything you wanted. It was empty when the sorry fixed nothing and left you without an enemy to rage against.

"Bullshit." She closed her eyes and a tear slid down her cheek. She wiped it away. "This is bullshit."

"I know. I know, babe . . ."

She wasn't letting him have this. She wasn't letting him get off the hook because he was hanging his head and being ashamed. She couldn't. She wouldn't.

"I'm not your *babe*. I cannot believe that I spent eight years waiting for you. Waiting for *this*. All so you can have a collapse now? Why couldn't you have fucked somebody else *eight years ago*? You didn't deserve this *time*. You didn't deserve my love. You didn't deserve my virginity. My trust. You're just like my parents and you don't even have the decency to be . . . ugly and awful in the middle of all of it the way that they are." His eyes were shining, the pain and regret there so real. It just made it all worse.

"Rue, what can I do . . . ?"

"Nothing. Take your key, and go to my house, and get all of your things out of it. I know there isn't much. But I want you to take all of it. I don't want it. I don't want it, I don't want you. I don't want to see you."

"Rue . . ."

"No. I don't care. I just don't ever want to see you again."

He nodded, and opened up the door, walking away, and it took less than a minute for Justice to be right there. He looked at her, and her bright eyes, at the fury radiating off of her. And suddenly, when she looked into those blue eyes, it was murder she saw there.

"Justice . . ." she said, reaching out and grabbing hold of his arm.

"Where the fuck is he headed?"

"Justice," she said again.

"Did he fucking break your heart?"

"He . . . he called off the wedding."

"What the fuck?"

"He had sex with somebody else," she said, the words stinging her throat.

"What the fuck?"

Justice wasn't yelling. His voice was low. Even. Dangerous.

"Yeah. He . . . Apparently there was a woman that he met on deployment and it happened a few months ago, and he just wasn't going to tell me."

"Wait here."

CHAPTER SIX

JUSTICE COULD ONLY see red. He was beyond rational thought. He was beyond understanding. He was beyond everything but his desire to destroy the man who had hurt his Rue. Who had taken her perfect day and turned it into a nightmare.

He was going to bend that man into the shape of a pretzel. And then . . .

"Asher."

Asher was halfway to the front door of the church, and he stopped and turned.

"Listen," he said, putting his hands up.

Justice growled. He crossed the space and without giving him a chance to say another word, punched him in the mouth.

Asher went down. It wasn't like he was a weak guy. He was in the military. But he was a damned sight smaller than Justice, and Justice had a feeling that even though he had never been enlisted, he could take this guy.

"Justice," he said, breathing hard, and not making a move to hit Justice back, which made him feel like he couldn't hit him again, even though he wanted to.

"You get the hell outta here," said Justice. "Or I will kill you. Do you understand me? I don't mean it as a metaphor. I will kill you. They won't be able to find your body. It'll be the mulch I feed to the cows."

The cows would not eat a human being; the cows were vegetarians. It didn't matter. Because Justice had a feeling that the cows would know that he deserved to be eaten.

"I'm sorry," Asher said.

All the goodwill Justice had ever felt toward Asher was gone. Justice had tolerated him–liked him even–because he made Rue happy. Now he'd made her cry. So that was it.

"Like that means anything. It's an *insult*. Get out of here. She should never have to look at you again. She shouldn't have to deal with you, she shouldn't have to see you. Nothing. Do you understand me?"

"I get it . . ."

"I can't believe that I thought you were all right. I never thought you were good enough for her, because nobody could be. But she loved you. She really did. Do you have any idea how much that meant?"

Rue had risked herself to love him. She had given herself to him. She had . . .

She had broken down all those walls for him, and this was what he had done to her? The doors to the sanctuary opened, and his siblings appeared.

They looked at him, and then they looked back at Asher.

"I'm going," said Asher, putting his hands up in surrender.

And then he walked out of the church. A whimper instead of obeying. Probably for the best, since Justice didn't especially want to get arrested today. But he was willing to. He was absolutely willing to.

"What happened?" Daughtry asked.

"He cheated on Rue. He called the wedding off. I would've killed them. But I thought maybe you didn't want to arrest your own brother."

"I might've looked the other way," Daughtry said.

Because that was how much they all loved Rue.

"I have to go to Rue."

"Yeah. Hey. We'll explain this to the guests. She doesn't need to do it."

"Damn straight," said Justice.

He trusted that to his siblings. He didn't trust Rue to anyone but him.

He went straight back into the dressing room, where she was sitting on the floor, her knees held up to her chest. "What am I going to do?"

She looked lost and miserable. His favorite little go-getter totally devastated by this. This woman who was never without a plan. There she was all curled up like a kid again. Like when her parents had hurt her.

"Aw, Rue," he said, getting down on the floor beside her. He put his arm around her, and held her up against him. "First of all. You're going to be fine."

"Am I?" she asked, her voice watery.

"Yes. You are. Because you have been through way worse than this. And there is no ineffectual, weak-willed man who deserves to take a damn thing from you."

"But he did," she said, wiping tears away. "Eight years of my life. I invested eight years of my life in him."

"That isn't all you did," he said. "You kept the yarn shop going, and you made your grandmother's house a home. You lived your own life. It wasn't all about him. Ever. You're one of the most levelheaded people I've ever known, and you were levelheaded when it came to him too. I always admired it. Because so many people completely lose it when they get into a relationship. Like they forget how to function. Forget how to think. But you never did. You never gave all of yourself to him. You're still here."

They sat in silence for a long time. "I should give you your necklace back," she said.

"No," he said. "Don't do that." His stomach was tight. "You keep it. Because it was about you making a better life. You're still going to do that. You don't need him to do that. You only need yourself."

She looked up at him, her face tear streaked. It killed him. "But that's lonely. I was so tired of being alone. You asked me earlier how I felt about my parents not being here, and the truth is I felt okay. Because I was making a family. With him. Finally. Now I'm not going to have that. I don't have a family. And I . . ."

"You have me," he said. "You have the Kings. I know it's not what you mean. I know it's not what you wanted. But you have us."

"Thank you," she said, her voice thin.

He pulled her in tighter, and she rested her hand flat on his chest. He covered it with his own, and sat with her like that. Him in the tux, her in the bridal gown.

"What did you do?" she asked finally.

"I punched him in the face."

She jerked away. "You didn't."

"I did. He's going to go back home to that other woman with a fat lip and a sizable bruise. I'm not sorry about it."

"You can't just punch people, you know. It's assault and stuff."

He shrugged. "It turns out I did, though. So what's anyone going to do about it?"

She sighed. The way that she did when he was feral, accepting that she couldn't change him. In context with everything, at least that felt normal.

"I'll never forgive him," he said. "For ruining your special day."

She leaned back against the wall. "I thought that I'd been through enough. Honestly."

"Me too."

"I want to leave," she said.

"I'll take you home."

"I don't want to go home. Because he's there. He's at my house clearing out all of his stuff. I told him that I didn't want to see him again. So he needs to get it all now, because whatever else is there . . . I was going to throw it away."

"Then you're coming home with me. You can stay the night."

"Thank you. What about the guests?"

"Daughtry is taking care of it. We're going to go up the back, and you don't have to see anybody. I've got you, Rue."

Because what was the point of being a disreputable best friend if you didn't use your skills sneaking out the back when your good-girl best friend was in need? There was no point.

He'd wanted to be good for her today. But the thing about him and Rue was that they complemented each other. So if right now she needed him to be bad, that was what he would do.

WHEN RUE WOKE up, she couldn't figure out where she was. The ceiling was unfamiliar, and the bedsheets were scratchy. It wasn't her house, with her gloriously high-thread-count sheets. It certainly wasn't the cute B&B that she had intended to go to with Asher for their wedding night.

Asher.

She sat bolt upright. *The wedding.* The wedding hadn't happened. The wedding had been called off. For a solid thirty seconds she sat there in the bed she hadn't identified yet, wondering if that had been a dream. Wondering if today was actually the wedding day. Willing it to be.

But slowly, she was able to focus on the rest of the room. Slowly, she was coming to terms with what day it actually was. And . . .

She was at Justice's house. In his spare room.

Sleeping on a little twin bed, the dubious sheets a testament to his bachelorhood.

She groaned, and put her head in her hands. She had cried last night until her eyes were sandpaper. Yeah. Now she remembered everything. Justice had taken her home, Arizona had brought over some clothes, she had changed and then she had gone into the bedroom and curled up in this bed. She had slept fitfully at first, and then like she had been rendered unconscious. Which was why she was so disoriented now. She looked at the basic digital clock on the nightstand. It was ten thirty in the morning. She couldn't remember the last time she had slept in that late.

And she still felt exhausted. All the way down to her bones.

She grabbed her phone. It had . . . exploded. Everyone who had known her well enough to be invited to the wedding—clients from the yarn store, distant cousins, other local shop owners—had texted her to find out if she was okay. She really couldn't deal with it. Not right now.

She always answered her texts. She judged Justice and his eternal red bubble that sat on his text window. The man had 150 unread texts. What kind of monster had that many unread texts? But today, she realized she was going to be that monster.

There was one text that she saw that she felt too curious to ignore. Or maybe *curiosity* was the wrong word. It was just grim. But . . .

She touched Asher's name and opened it up.

> Everything is cleared from the house. I wish that we could talk. I love you. And the idea that I'm not going to see you again kills me. But I understand. I do.

All she could do was stare at it. If he loved her, how had he been able to have sex with somebody else? Or even more importantly, how could that have felt so important in the moment? How could it have felt so essential? If she was really the perfect woman for him then why had it been so much more important for him to have an orgasm than to spend his life with her?

She rolled out of bed, and looked at herself in the mirror. She was an absolute nightmare. Her hair was a rat's nest, her eyes were swollen nearly shut. Her misery was bleeding out of her pores.

Asher didn't deserve for her to feel this level of heartbreak. But she had loved him, or she wouldn't have been intending to marry him in the first place. She ground her back teeth together and opened up the bedroom door. She heard footsteps, and then she made her way into the kitchen, where she saw Justice, shirtless and wearing low-slung jeans and no shoes, taking the carafe off the coffeemaker and holding it beneath the spigot.

"Good morning," he said.

"Nothing is good," she said.

"Okay. How awful is today?"

He turned around, and she was struck by how gorgeous he looked. Because she looked hideous. It suddenly felt all the more notable that he never did. Whether he was hung over or coming off of punching her ex-fiancé in the face, Justice King was a glorious sight. His shoulders were broad, his chest well-muscled; the golden hair sprinkled over those muscles looked . . . textured. It made her fingertips itch a little bit, and she couldn't really say why. He looked a bit sleepy eyed, and that was completely different to the swollen pig eyes she was currently sporting. That heavy, hooded blue gaze looked more like a woman had just rolled over in bed to the sight of him staring at her.

Justice was a lethal weapon.

His rage yesterday on her behalf had been . . . It had been the nicest, most amazing thing anyone had ever done for her. She really did think he might've happily risked prison. It touched her in a way that it maybe shouldn't.

"This is a really sucky day," she said, stomping deliberately over to the dining table and plunking down hard. The living area and the dining room and the kitchen of his place were actually pretty nice. Partly because she had helped him put everything together. His bedroom was decent too, owing to the fact that he had told her what he really wanted was a decent place to bring women back to. She had helped him with his dark wood furniture, and his very plush bedding. He clearly had not transferred the lesson over to his guest room. But then, she supposed women didn't sleep in his guest room.

"I know, Rue." He started brewing the coffee, and then he opened up his fridge. "Yogurt?"

"Yes," she sniffed. He got out plain yogurt, granola, sliced strawberries and honey, and proceeded to make a bowl that looked a lot like what she often had for breakfast.

"Do you just have all this on hand?"

"I went to the store after you went to sleep," he said.

Which meant he had driven back to Mapleton. He was just so . . . He was so good to her.

"Thank you."

"You really need somebody right now."

"Yeah. I do. I . . . I don't even know what to say. I don't know what to make of any of this."

"It sucks. But, I'll take you back home today, and you can figure it out."

"I guess I have to. Nobody's going to do it for me."

"I'll give an assist," he said.

She ate, and drank some coffee, and was disappointed to discover it didn't actually make her feel more human. But then she got into Justice's truck, and they drove a few minutes to her house.

"It occurs to me that my car is in Mapleton," she said.

"No. We took care of that too. Bix drove it back."

"Where did she get a key?"

"I find it best not to ask questions where Bix is concerned. Because either she hot-wired it or she lifted your key off you at some point. Either way, she managed to get it back."

"Well . . . tell her thank you," she said.

"Believe me. I already did."

"This is the most humiliating thing that's ever happened. I got left at the altar, and everybody knows. I have like a hundred texts from people asking if I'm okay. And . . . no. I'm not okay. I don't know how I could ever be expected to be okay. It's . . . it's awful. My life is . . . nothing that I thought it was twenty-four hours ago. I was getting ready to get married yesterday morning. And now . . . the inside of my mouth tastes like a musty old carpet, and I have no idea what I'm doing."

"A toothbrush might help with your mouth. As for the rest . . . I don't really know what I'm doing either."

They pulled up to the house, and she saw her car parked in the driveway. That at least felt sane.

They walked up to the front of the house, and she noticed a yellow paper on the door. And then, she noticed that there were padlocks on the doorknob.

"What is this?"

"The hell?" Justice grabbed the paper and tore it off the door. "It's a notice of foreclosure. And property seizure."

"What?"

"Yeah. It says . . . it says that because of the failure to pay on a loan taken out by David and Mary Matthews, as cosigned by Nina Hallstrom, the property is being seized by this company."

"What?"

"Did you know that this had been put up as collateral?"

"No, I had no idea. But we never . . . I guess we never transferred the paperwork. I've just been paying the payments."

"I don't know that it would've mattered. I doubt you would've been able to transfer ownership because it was tied up as collateral for this. I don't think your grandmother would've been able to . . . Did she ask you not to go and change anything?"

"Yes. She mentioned that the terms that she had were so good and nothing was ever going to be able to be that good so . . ."

"Because of this. And she probably didn't want to tell you because . . . she had loaned money to your parents. She cosigned for them."

"What was she thinking?" She was still in shock, not able to fully process the implications of any of this.

Because how was this possible? How was it possible that all of these things in her life were unraveling all at the same time? "I can't get in to get my things..."

"Well, fuck that."

Justice butted his shoulder up to the door and elbowed it hard as he jerked the handle. She could hear the lock break as the door pushed open.

"Justice!"

"What. Don't you want into your own house to get your own things?"

"Well, yes," she said.

"Then don't wait for the locked door to open up on its own."

How was it possible that she was reduced to breaking into her own house? She had never done a shady thing in her entire life and here she was sneaking out of churches and sneaking into her home. Here she was, dealing with the fallout of a broken wedding, and her, with her eternally answered text messages, now permanently broken apart by this canceled wedding, completely frozen and unable to respond. This wasn't fair. It wasn't the life she had invested in. That was for sure.

"Pack a bag."

"I..."

"Some suitcases, even. We'll go back to my place."

"I can stay at the yarn store..."

"No," he said. "You're not staying at the yarn store. I'm going to pack your bed up and put it in the back of my truck. In fact, we'll pack up as much as we can, and we'll take it to my house."

"What then?" she asked.

"We're going to have to try to get ahold of the

bank," he said. "Sort all this out. See what we need to do. But the point is, you're not going to be without shelter. You're going to come and live with me."

"Justice, I'd—"

"Ruby Matthews, you listen to me. If it wasn't for you I wouldn't have passed high school. It wasn't for you, I probably wouldn't have even made it out of elementary school. You taught me to read. You paid attention to me. You listened to me. You took care of me. You were the one that was always there. You've always been there. And I will be damned if I don't show up for you."

Her breathing was shallow, her heart thundering. She was pretty sure she was in shock, because it was really the only way to explain why she hadn't completely lost it at this point. But one thing that felt very important right then was that she tell him this. She put her hand on his forearm. "Justice, you've always been there for me. It's not uneven. This . . . this has been above and beyond."

"No, it's not. There's no such thing."

He was truly the most important person in her life. Her touchstone. Especially now. He was everything. And right then, she really felt it. Because her attempt at expanding herself hadn't done a damn thing.

Working on autopilot, she gathered her clothes. Gathered her favorite kitchen gadgets. Left her living room furniture. Justice had efficiently lifted her bed and her other bedroom furniture out of the space and put them in his truck. She folded up her very lovely sheets.

"Am I really going to lose this house?"

"I don't know. I hope not. I hope that we can figure something out. But until then, I'm just going to make sure that you're as comfortable as possible."

"This is surreal," she said.

"Yeah. I know. I'm sorry."

When he said *sorry* it *meant* something. Unlike when Asher had said it.

He hadn't even done anything wrong. He had done all the things right. As a friend, he was unparalleled. It was very obvious to her in that moment, though, exactly where her support system was. And where it wasn't.

Because somehow her parents, their issues and all their unresolved baggage had just come home to roost. In spite of the fact that she hadn't spoken to them for all this time.

So all she did was pack up her life. Her neatly ordered life. The one that had been perfect two days ago.

She realized she was still wearing that necklace.

She reached beneath the sweatshirt she had on and touched it. Was this what it felt like? Leaving everything behind and moving to a new home? Did it feel more like an end than a beginning? Back then when you hadn't been able to look up pictures of the place you were going, hadn't been able to get all kinds of information at your fingertips? Or had his ancestor been excited. Had she chosen it? Or was she just being dragged around by the whims of men? Because that was a whole lot of what Rue felt like.

When Justice reappeared she released her hold on the necklace and tried to look . . . together. Because she had been dissolved in his presence for a while now, and that really wasn't their dynamic. She was usually put together. But she just didn't feel put together right now.

She didn't feel like herself. It was the most disorienting, insane situation she had ever been in.

Feeling dazed, she walked outside.

"What do you think she's like?"

Justice was just closing the bed of his truck. "Excuse me?"

"The woman. The one that Asher slept with. She was deployed with him. That means she was in the military. What do you suppose a woman like that is . . . ? What is she offering him that I'm not? What . . . ? If he loved me then why did sex make him forget that? Why did it seem so important?"

"I don't understand the question, Rue."

"Well, I don't understand any of it. I don't understand how he lost his sense of us."

"Sex makes you crazy sometimes. And I'm not excusing him. Not at all. It's just . . . you know."

"I don't," she said. "I'm completely dumbfounded. I had sex with him for eight years. And only him. I mean, he's the only man I've ever had sex with."

Justice's face went rigid. But she kept talking.

"Nothing about the sex we had was enough to make me lose my mind. Not ever. I was always firmly contained within myself. So what is that? How was he able to be so different with somebody else? Is that where I failed him? Because he said it wasn't, but it sounds like it was different, it sounds like . . ."

"I don't know," he said. "As far as what the hell he was thinking, I don't. But I do know that men are really good at making up stories that allow them to get laid when they feel like it. So who knows, Rue, maybe she was a siren. Maybe she didn't have a gag reflex."

"What does that mean?"

Justice looked . . . pained. "Maybe she didn't . . . Maybe she didn't gag when she . . ."

"What?"

Justice's face was now a mask of regret. "When she gave him a blowjob."

Rue frowned. "I never gagged when I gave him one."

Justice winced, opened his mouth, then closed it. Then opened it again. "I . . . have follow-up questions. But I'm not going to ask them. Listen, whatever the story, it doesn't really matter. Because it isn't about you. And I don't even know that it's about her. It's about him. He made the decision. End of story. Because yeah. The desire to get off can be all-consuming. But it doesn't make you forget the person that you love. At least I'm pretty sure. I've never been in love. I've never cheated on anybody. Because I've never set myself up to be in that kind of situation."

"Neither have I. I loved him. I never even let myself consider getting close enough to somebody else to do that. I don't understand how he could do it to me."

The words were broken; she felt broken. She felt ignorant and small and naive. She had never even imagined that he might cheat on her, and she had grown up in the kind of environment where people acted like that. Where they lost their minds over sex. Where satisfaction and jealousy and all of those kinds of things made her parents act unhinged. And they were clearly still unhinged.

"Are you okay to drive?"

"Yeah," she said.

She wasn't sure that it was true. But she got behind the wheel of her car all the same and followed Justice back to King's Crest. When they got there, he got out of his truck as she exited her car. "I told everybody."

"You did?"

"Yeah. I told them not to make you tell the story. So that should just be handled."

"Thank you," she said.

"You're going to make it through this. We'll figure it out."

"I had the next three weeks off," she said. "For the honeymoon. All my shifts are covered."

They had planned on spending their wedding night at a B&B in Copper Ridge, then they were supposed to be spending two weeks fixing her house up. Making it theirs. And then they planned to go to the most beautiful resort she'd ever seen, with a spa and mountain views. A suite with a fireplace and a private hot tub.

It had been her perfect getaway. Nothing like she'd ever had as a child.

And nothing she would have now either, so great.

"Good. Take the time off. Let's figure out the house thing. Let's figure out all the things."

"You don't have to help me. I have the time. I just . . . Thank you for giving me the space. Because if I had to worry about where I was going to sleep on top of everything else I really don't know how I was going to . . ."

Her entire life had imploded. That realization hit her in a wave. Her entire life had just caved in on her.

"Well, in honor of the fact that you don't have anything going for a little bit, I say we go out and have some fun this week."

"What?"

"Hey," he said. "You're not living like you right now. Maybe you should live like me."

CHAPTER SEVEN

THE VERY FIRST thing Rue had to deal with was figuring out what the heck to do about her house. Of course, the notices had gone up on a Sunday so she couldn't call anyone about it, which left her with the Mondayest Monday ever.

The beginning of what would have been the first week of her married life. The kind of day Rue usually saw as a fresh start began by just feeling stale and awful and generally horrendous.

Justice hadn't gone out last night, which she knew was weird for him, and even still she half expected to run into a half-dressed woman somewhere in the house. She knew that Justice wasn't one for restraint, but he was being saintly. He was always good to her. He was always nice. But this sort of sainted-savior thing with nothing that she could even begin to reciprocate was starting to get to her, and then added to that, when she woke up there were no half-naked women; she just didn't even know how to orient herself.

Everything was already weird.

When Justice came into the house while she was making coffee, having clearly been out, she couldn't hold it in. "Oh. Did you have sex somewhere else?"

"Excuse me?" He looked scandalized. He looked

like he might have clutched his pearls if he was wearing some.

"Don't look at me like that," she said. "It was a perfectly reasonable thing to ask."

"It was the fuck not. I prefer to dance around things in double entendre, Rue. I prefer to show up looking laconic and disheveled, and laugh and make asides that could be interpreted in multiple ways. I am a gentleman. I do not kiss and tell."

"No, you just bang and insinuate."

"As God intended."

"Well, I'm asking," she said.

And she actually didn't know why she was. Why she was preoccupied with that. She had just been thinking about the fact that he was being overly saintly and solicitous and she didn't want him to feel like he had to do that. Because she wanted things to be normal, and this would be normal, except it also felt . . .

Maybe she was just feeling insecure. And she was projecting it onto Justice. There was the little issue of feeling possessive of him.

It *did* happen sometimes.

In fairness, he sometimes behaved the same with her. They could both be a little bit territorial. It was just that they were so close. It was just that they were best friends. And right now she needed him. So much.

He was here. Asher wasn't here, because she didn't want him to be. She never wanted to see his ferrety face ever again. That should have been her first clue that something was amiss. He was a little ferrety. Justice had said that, in fact. Very early. But, given the fact that Justice had never been in a relationship, she didn't think that his opinion had mattered.

Perhaps she should have listened to what she had thought of at the time was a rather shallow evaluation of someone. Nonetheless, the idea of Justice going out and being with someone else right now when she was alone upset her, and while she knew that was not fair, especially because she was contradicting her own internal musings, it was still how she felt.

"I was up feeding cows, if you must know."

"Now I don't know if you would tell me."

"I would tell you. I'm not embarrassed."

"You've been taking care of me. And I feel like this is probably cramping your style."

"I'm not Asher," he said, doing what Justice did with her, always cutting straight down to the heart of it. Often before she even could. "I don't consider you an inconvenience or a barrier to my sex life. I'm taking care of you and staying with you because I want to. Okay?"

"Well, it doesn't have to . . . I mean, I don't want to run into a woman here . . ."

"I don't bring women back here."

"You . . . you don't?"

"No."

"But it's so nice. I mean, the room I was staying in needed some work, but your room is very nice. And now that we have my bed in the guest room . . ."

"I don't bring women here," he said. "I don't know why that's hard to believe."

"Because it just looks like the kind of place that you bring women to."

"I don't. Do you know why? If I brought women here then they would want to spend the night. Worse, I would feel obligated to let them. It's not neutral territory. If I go to their place, they can throw me out, or I can see myself out."

"You don't . . . you don't spend the night with people?"

"No," he said, looking at her like she was crazy.

"I don't know that," she said, spreading her hands. "Why would I know that?"

"I'm not really sure why you know it now," he said.

"Because I feel . . . I feel naive. Which isn't fair. I was in a relationship for eight years. Half the time he was gone, and he and I had . . . Our connection was so based on this vision that we had for the future. Our theoretical future. It was so . . . cerebral, I guess? That doesn't even feel like the right word. It was companionable. We wanted all the same things. I really, really valued that. There was something calling about him. There was something . . . comforting. And now I'm starting to think that was a shelter, and I shouldn't have been hiding in it. Because he wanted something else." She stood there, feeling wounded. Baffled. "He was out fighting a war. You would think that he would want something stable waiting at home. You would think that sex under gunfire wouldn't take precedence."

Justice let out a long breath and stuffed his hands in his pockets. "I hate to break it to you. But I think sex under gunfire makes a lot of sense. Trauma bond and all of that. Intensity."

He looked at her then. Really looked at her. His

blue eyes felt hot, burning into her, and she didn't care for that. Because it was a little bit too much. She also didn't want to peel back the layer to get beneath the top of what he had just said. It was all a little too close to the bone.

Trauma bond.

Yeah, that felt . . .

Well, like something the two of them might share.

"But you don't even spend the night with people," she said.

"Because *I* don't want intensity," he said. "I want to have fun. I don't want to be navigating weird morning-afters, and I don't want to know anything beyond the girl's name, okay?"

She rolled her eyes. "There has to be a middle ground."

"I am not a man of middle grounds, Rue, so I can't help you there. I do assume you need a little bit of help with the bank today."

She bristled. "I don't need help with the bank."

She wanted help with the bank. But she was a grown woman, and she could drive into Mapleton and speak to someone herself. It was a small-town bank, and she imagined that she would get further with them going right up to the counter and explaining the situation.

She didn't need Justice for that.

She kind of *wanted* him, though. Which was a bit annoying.

"I don't care if you need me or not. I'm going."

"Well . . . surely you have things to do."

"Surely I do not have things to do that are more important than helping you through this current crisis."

She felt discomfort gnawing at her. It was adjacent to the feeling she had when Justice had first walked in and she had felt vaguely jealous, but it wasn't exactly the same. This was more like fear.

Everything was being weighted toward her. Everything was about her.

That just didn't happen in her life. To her parents, she was an inconvenience. She had never been all that important. And it really . . . it really made her feel so . . . edgy when he did things like this. When he was just so good and present and pouring all this stuff into her, it made her feel like she had to reciprocate. Like she had to make herself important.

Maybe she could organize his sock drawer.

"Okay. I really would like for you to go with me. But I just feel like this can't be all about me. I'm not used to this. To being the one who needs help. To being the one who is a mess. I'm not used to it because . . ."

Because she couldn't afford it. She had never been able to. Her parents would never have taken care of her, and she desperately didn't want to be a burden to her grandmother. Her grandmother had been wonderful, and she had never made Rue feel like a burden, but Rue was so aware of her own presence. Of the space she took up. Because . . . she had to be. She'd become painfully aware of what it meant to take care of herself from the time she was little, so when anybody else stepped in to do it, she was really aware of it. Of the labor.

Their teacher had always paid extra attention to her, and Rue had felt like she had to be an exemplary student to make up for it. To make the investment worth it.

And with Justice . . . She had helped him with his homework. She had taught him to read. She had soothed his hangovers. She was used to giving *him* things. And he had been so relentlessly giving to her in the run-up to the wedding, and now this.

"Like what's going on with you?" The words came out lamely, and just kind of landed between them with a thud.

"Are you serious right now?"

"I'm serious. Sometimes, Justice, I feel like you know everything about me. Everything about my life, and I don't know anything about yours."

He never slept over with women, apparently. She hadn't known that. Not that they made a habit of talking about sex—but they were friends and they did share things. Sex wasn't a totally taboo topic for them.

"That's not true," he said. "It's just that it's a lot less work to see down to—" she made a scoffing noise "—the bottom of a kiddie pool than it is to see the bottom of the ocean."

"Oh please," she said. "You're just so committed to this whole shallow thing that you do. It isn't honest. I know you. I've known you for all these years and you're the most caring . . . You're the most caring, sweet man—"

"Hang on a second. I am not sweet."

"You *are*."

He looked genuinely appalled. "Have you ever left this ranch? Have you ever talked to . . . a single other person about me? I am a destroyer of worlds. I have never been one to shy away from a bar fight. There have been marriages in this county that were hanging on by a thread and I cut that thread. Gave the missus a good time, and an escape route. I am not sweet."

"You're very sweet to me," she said, ignoring all of his bluster, because what was even the point in engaging with it?

"You're my friend. And you're the only person on this damned earth who bears that title. So stop applying good intent to me, when you have no idea. Because you don't know who I am when I'm away from you."

"Aha," she said, pointing her finger at him. "That is my point."

"Because it's bullshit you don't want to see," he said. "You don't want this. You want the Justice that you know. Trust me."

"You said that I should live like you. So how can I do that if I don't actually know who you are?"

"I didn't mean . . . I did not mean that you should actually literally pattern any part of your life after mine. Let's go to the bank."

He turned and started to stomp out of the house. "Are you going in that?"

He looked down at his black shirt, blue jeans and cowboy boots. "What's wrong with this?"

"Nothing. For wrangling cattle."

"I was unaware that the bank had a dress code."

"I'd like to go in *not* looking like we're a pair of dissolute reprobates."

"Well, that's what I am."

She rolled her eyes and walked past him out to the truck. "See," he said, moving past her and getting in the driver's side, hanging out the halfway-open door. "I'm not sweet. And I'm not going to do what you tell me."

He closed the door, and she growled, then stepped over to the passenger side and opened the door up. She got in and buckled ferociously. One thing she would say about Justice was that he was a safe space. Because in the past fifteen minutes she had cycled through jealousy, insecurity and deep, unending irritation. All with the same person. All with an underlying sense of security.

Yes, for a moment she had felt worried. For a moment she had felt insecure. But she didn't have to feel that way with him.

"The real problem is the banker is still going to flirt with you," she said as they drove down the long dirt driveway that would take them out to the main road.

"I know," he said.

"You're so confident."

He lifted a shoulder. "In certain things. I have no reason not to be."

That made her want to howl. Because she had so many reasons to *not* be confident right now. Apparently hanging out with Justice for the better part of her life hadn't done anything to make her absorb any of that confidence.

"I'm going to need some of that," she said.

"Some of what?"

"Your confidence. Because you are . . . You're you. You know?"

"Yeah. I am me."

"I don't know how you have all that confidence. I've

never had it, I have always just wanted to be secure. And now I don't even have that. I need . . . I need swagger."

He laughed. A good flaw, really.

"Swagger. Is that what you think I have?"

"Yes."

"Rue, swagger is for men who need to put on a show. I'm good."

She slapped her hand on her thigh. "There it is again. Full confidence. No brakes. It's insane, really."

"Listen. I never put myself into situations where I can't be confident. I know that when it comes to ranching I can get the job done. Ditto taking a woman to bed."

Those words made her face feel hot. She gritted her teeth and didn't overthink it. "Great. I had the one lover, who I thought was fine enough with my skills in bed. And now I don't have that. Not even a little bit. I don't know how to get back . . ."

She didn't have a house. She wasn't getting married.

"I am so tired of myself," she said.

"There may not be a quick fix for it," he said. "But this is the first stop."

"I need music. But not sad music."

"You sure?" he asked.

"Yes. I'm sure. I don't want sad music."

"I could play you your favorite emo band."

"Don't," she said, but she smiled.

Which was how she found herself rocking out in Justice's truck to music from the early 2000s. That carried them all the way to Mapleton and saved her from being completely maudlin. And she marveled again at Justice's ability to carry her through multiple moods in one extended moment.

The bank was in an old brick building on Mapleton's main street, and Justice pulled up to the curb, while Rue worked at psyching herself up.

"You know what's wrong with all of this," she said as she got out of the truck.

"What's that?" he asked.

"It's that none of this is moving at a slow enough pace for me to make a binder or laminate anything."

"Well. We could laminate Asher's dick."

It was such an unexpected thing to hear on a public street, and she couldn't help herself. She laughed. She didn't just laugh; she began to laugh hysterically. Because she was hysterical. Because everything that had happened in the last couple of days was outrageous. And here she was just marinating in all of it. Unable to escape. She would be dealing with the issue with the house even if she and Asher had gotten married, and if she stood back for a second she could realize that. That the issue with the house was separate. That it was something she and Asher would be dealing with together instead of her and Justice. But it felt entwined. It certainly compounded the issue. It was just . . . horrendous. And she was wounded, angry, and the idea of laminating her ex-fiancé's penis was really the most ridiculous and hilarious thing she had ever thought of.

"You okay there?"

"I'm fine," she wheezed. "I mean, I'm not fine. Nothing is fine. Everything is terrible. But that was hilarious. Like genuinely the funniest thing you could've said."

"I'm here all week."

She wiped the tears out of her eyes. "Now I have to go do serious banking."

"Well, at least you'll do it with a little bit more of a bounce in your step."

"You're ridiculous."

"I know."

They walked in together, and Rue approached the banker's desk cautiously. "I have to speak to someone about a home loan."

"An established loan?"

"Yes. It's a little bit complicated, though. It was my grandmother's, and she died, and there's an account for it, and the money just comes out."

"Do you have the loan number?"

"Yes."

She gave all the information to the woman sitting at the desk.

The woman frowned. "We don't own this loan any longer. It was transferred to another mortgage company two months ago."

"What?"

"This kind of thing happens all the time."

"You don't have to . . . ask to sell somebody's mortgage?"

"No," the woman said.

"I don't . . . That's the most ridiculous thing I've ever heard."

"I agree," said Justice. "That doesn't sound right."

"I'm sorry," the woman said. "It is."

"I . . ."

"You would have gotten a notice in the mail."

She always saw her mail. She always got notices. How had she not gotten this? She didn't understand. Somehow, she had made a serious mistake. One that was making this whole thing more complicated.

The woman rubbed her temples, and then gave Rue an apologetic look. "I'm sorry. I'll give you the info that I have."

The woman started printing papers off, and then she handed them to Rue.

"This isn't a local bank."

"No," the woman said. "It's a big mortgage company. They buy a lot of loans in bulk. Hopefully they still have your loan."

"You're kidding me, right? Someone *else* can have my loan already?"

"It does happen," the woman said.

Rue gripped the papers, and tried not to be rude. She knew that it wasn't like the woman had caused the situation. It wasn't her fault. It wasn't like she had done it to Rue personally.

They walked out onto the street, and Rue dialed the number for the loan company immediately. "Hi—"

It was a recorded message. She pressed a zero and stood there tapping her feet while Justice looked at her.

"I'm on hold," she said. A jaunty song started playing in her ear and it made her angrier.

Someone on the other end picked up. And Rue began to explain the situation.

"We don't have your name in the paperwork."

She let out a short breath, knowing that her explanations weren't the best, and having to repeat it like this made it pretty clear to her she should have questioned this before her grandmother passed, but it hadn't seemed important. Now it did. Essential, even. "There was a reason . . . But in my grandmother's will I am the beneficiary. It's just that she didn't have me switch the loan over—"

"It was being held as collateral. The bank has seized it because of the defaults on the loan. There's an auction set for it at the end of February."

"How is this moving so quickly?"

"It wasn't really all that quickly. The loan was in default for a couple of years."

"My grandmother didn't tell me any of this."

"I am sorry," the woman said. "I don't know what your grandmother did or didn't tell you. But the house is being sold to cover the debt. It's a cash auction."

"I can't even get a mortgage to get my house back?"

"No," the woman said.

"But I . . ." And just suddenly, tears started to fall down Rue's cheeks. Extremely angry tears. Because she was just so fed up. With all of this. She had no control, no choices. And none of it was her fault. "But I'm not the one that made this decision."

"Your grandmother left you something that had some baggage," the woman said, her voice apologetic but firm. "These things happen with inheritance. Sometimes they get seized because of unpaid property taxes. It's a land mine." She genuinely did sound sorry, and Rue knew that she didn't have to stay on the phone with her.

It was an ironic thing to say, though.

Her grandmother had left her something with baggage.

Rue already knew that. It was her own mother.

Wherever all that baggage had come from, Rue had loved her grandmother. And she had always been kind to Rue, but she knew people weren't formed from nothing and nowhere, and her mother was no exception. And now, her mother had become the gift that kept on giving.

"Thank you," Rue said. "I . . . I'll figure it out."

Rue turned to Justice. "They're going to auction the house off. I'm going to have to go move the rest of my stuff."

"I'm sorry," he said.

"I just . . . This is so unfair. I didn't do anything. I wasn't the responsible one. So why are they doing this to me? Why . . . What is this happening to me? It doesn't seem fair."

"It doesn't. You're right."

"There's supposed to be a reward for good behavior. There's supposed to be . . . a point to this."

"I don't know. Some people say that virtue is its own reward."

"Well, fuck this rewards program," she said, kicking a stone on the sidewalk. "I hate it. It hasn't given me anything that I want."

She put her hands over her face.

"Rue, it's possible that we could pool the money from the ranch . . ."

"No," she said. "You can't do that. I won't let you. That is taking this whole friendship thing a bridge too far. It's not like I'm going to be homeless. I'll be able to get something together. I will be able to buy another house. I can do it in Mapleton. I can probably find a rental. That's what I'll do. I'll find a rental near the yarn store..."

"You're going to move to Mapleton?"

"It makes sense."

Except it hurt. Because she worked in Mapleton, but Justice was her life. Still. She had to make the drive in one direction or another.

That didn't help. Nothing helped. Everything just felt terrible and disruptive and like the absolute worst thing that could've happened. But she was going to try not to dissolve out there on the streets.

"Do you want to go into the yarn store for a minute?" he asked.

She shook her head. "No. I can't face anyone yet. I can't... I can't."

"Yeah. I get it."

"Can we just go back...?" She almost said *home*. When she said that, she meant King's Crest. She hadn't forgotten that she wasn't staying at her grandmother's. Not anymore.

"We can go back," he said. "Hey, if you want to box up your things that's fine and I get it. But..."

"No. I'll do it."

"Well. I'll stand guard and make sure those lackeys from the repossession company don't try anything."

"Thanks. I wasn't worried about that. And now I am."

"Hell. You should always worry," he said.

"You never worry."

"Because I have you to do it for me. If you stopped, though, I might get myself into trouble."

That was like a little pinhole of sunshine coming through the darkness. It was silly, maybe. But it was a reminder. Of how they balanced each other. Of how she mattered.

"Okay," she said. "We'll move my stuff out."

"You can store it in one of the old outbuildings."

"I'll start looking for a place at the end of February."

"Fine with me. You can stay longer than that."

"I need a binder."

"Then let's go get you a binder," he said.

"I think that's the only thing that could make me feel better."

She bought four binders, three of them with flowers and one of them with a squirrel, and she was pretty happy with that. As far as her happiness scale could go.

"What are they all for?" he asked.

"I don't know yet. It never hurts to have backup binders."

He chuckled. "If you say so."

"Maybe I'll make a binder for you. Oh! I'll help you organize things."

"My house is organized," he said.

She couldn't deny that for a bachelor pad it was pretty neat. And that was especially impressive now that she had the knowledge he didn't bring women back there. So it wasn't really for anyone but him.

It was something they'd never discussed before so she had assumed that there was a level of cleanliness that was performative.

"You are fairly organized."

"I can't have you coming to my house if it looks like a total mess. You would lose all respect for me. *And* you wouldn't visit."

"What?"

It sounded almost as if he was saying it was for her. And that was difficult for her to wrap her head around. More than difficult. It was impossible.

"I fear your judgment," he said.

"I don't judge you," she said.

"You generally don't," he replied. "But I like to be on good behavior so that it never gets to a place where you might."

"My mind is blown by this."

"Glad that I can still surprise you."

"Well, if you need help with anything . . ."

"Do you hear yourself right now?"

"You keep asking me that."

"Because I'm not sure you do. I don't need you to do anything for me."

She huffed. Then she thought about the binders. "Maybe I can use a binder to figure out how to be more like you."

"Well, first of all," he said, "I wouldn't use a binder."

"I need a binder. If there's going to be chaos it has to be controlled."

"What exactly are you talking about here?"

"I don't want to go out. Not yet. Like, I don't want to barhop, and whatever else, because mostly right now I cannot stand the idea of having everybody look at me and think that I'm the poor jilted bride."

"In fairness," he said. "That may last a while."

"Yeah, I know," she said.

"What's your plan then? Hole up at King's Crest?"

"Is that bad? I have the next few weeks off. I don't have to go into public."

"No," he said. "You don't. But that might build it up and do something that's difficult to get past."

"You're an expert on that?"

His expression was neutral. "I know a thing or two about it."

"Okay. So I just need to come up with some things."

"Alternatively, you could let it unfold naturally."

"No. I want a plan."

"Lord."

"I *will* have an adventure," Rue said. "What are all the things that I haven't done because I've been just too cautious?"

His blue gaze landed on her, his expression bland. "I could not rightly say."

"I barely have any experience on horses. I haven't been on one since I was a kid. It looks like fun. And you . . . The way you ride it makes it look like an adventure. I want that."

"I can definitely take you on a ride."

"And . . . oh, I want to do a polar plunge."

"You've got to be kidding me."

"No. I'm not. It's like a completely insane thing to do, and I have always thought so. I hate getting cold, and I don't really like just jumping in the water."

"Why is this turning into doing things you hate? Talk about piling on the martyrdom."

"It's just . . . my life is different. I didn't choose it. I want some things to feel totally different because of some things I chose at least. I want it to feel significant. Maybe I'll hate everything. I probably shouldn't get a tattoo right now."

"No," he said, shaking his head. "Big no on the tattoo."

"But there are things that are not permanent, that are not going to actually injure me that . . . I have this time off. I have this time away and . . . and this was supposed to be special. This was supposed to be my first married vacation. My first . . ." Her throat went tight. Because she hadn't wanted to think about this part. "I'm thirty-two. I was supposed to be getting married and starting my family. The family that I wanted to have. The family I wish that I had all my life, but didn't because . . . I just didn't. This was supposed to be a special, beautiful, idyllic holiday. Maybe the only one before we had kids."

She could sense Justice's discomfort. "Anyway. I don't want to dwell on that. But if my life isn't headed in that direction, I just want something different. Zip lining. I want to go zip lining."

"Maybe when the wind isn't trying to eat your face off."

She really didn't like being cold. Regrettably, most of these ideas she had involved the outdoors. "I can wait for it to warm up."

"A *polar plunge*." He shook his head. "You're on your own. I don't do that shit. I don't do masochism for the sake of it."

"It's not masochistic. It's supposed to be good for you." If anything could provide mental clarity at this point, she needed it. If a baptism in ice would do it, she was all for it.

"A lot of things are supposed to be good for you. And I don't do them because they aren't fun."

"That's my problem. I've done all the sane things, the good things. And for what?"

He rubbed his chin, the sound of his whiskers scratchy. It made her heart trip over itself, just for a beat. "I mean that's the real problem. It didn't get you what you wanted. So you're mad about it. Which means maybe it isn't right for you. So yeah. I agree. You do need to do something different."

"Then I will. That's my plan. My rebellion."

He looked at her sideways. "That's a little scary."

"I have watched you do whatever the hell you wanted to for a lot of years, Justice King. So I expect you to support me."

"You have my support. But if I have to save your ass . . ."

"Isn't that what friends are for?"

He sighed, long-suffering. "You got me there."

CHAPTER EIGHT

IT WASN'T A question of *if* the binder would hit; it was a question of *when*. He knew better than to underestimate Rue when she was in the midst of making a plan. She was unstoppable.

Relentless in her organization. She was a one-woman wrecking ball. If a wrecking ball put labels on things with a label maker, rather than knocking them over.

He was supportive of her. There was no need for her to be as careful as she was. But he . . . Well, he admired it too. So it felt weird that she was so intent on disrupting this thing that he . . . that he valued so much. Not that riding a horse and jumping into cold water was wild. In fact, it was kind of funny that this was what she had come up with. It wasn't like she had asked him to take her to the rodeo so she could snort a line of coke off the rump of the bucking bull. He might have had to stage an intervention at that point.

But it was . . . it was something to do with the dynamic of everything being just a little bit distracted. It felt like the air was electric. And he didn't especially like it. He hadn't even made a joke when he had said that he could take her for a ride. Normally he wouldn't have passed up the double entendre. Well, maybe that wasn't true. Maybe with her he would've gallantly passed it up. Because she was . . . her.

"You all right?"

"Fine," he said.

His older brother was staring at him. They were working on some of the last-minute touches on the new barn venue before the season started in summer. They had reservations and everything. It was getting real. All the changes.

"Totally fine," he said to Denver.

The barn door opened, and Bix and Daughtry came walking through. It wasn't entirely unusual to see Daughtry at the ranch in the middle of the day, but it was a little unusual.

"Landry isn't here?"

"No," Justice said.

That was when the door opened again and Arizona came in. "Landry isn't even here? He texted . . ."

Landry and Fia came in through the back door then. Fia had a wide grin on her face, her eyes sparkling. Landry looked . . . Well, he had never seen his brother look like that.

"What's going on?" Denver asked.

"We've been sitting on this. But we went down to the doctor today, and we saw . . ." Landry couldn't even contain his glee. The grin on his face almost stopped him from speaking clearly. "We're having a baby."

"Wow . . . congratulations," said Daughtry.

"Congratulations," Arizona said, leaning in and pulling him in for a hug. "My little bun in the oven is going to have a cousin."

"Yeah," said Landry, his voice hoarse.

Fia put her hand on his back and rubbed him gently. "I'm just so happy."

"Yeah. Damn," said Denver, clearing his throat. "Good for you two."

Justice knew that this was an especially loaded and weighty thing for them. Landry and Fia had a daughter, but they'd had given her up for adoption when she was born. It had driven a wedge between them for years, and they'd kept it a secret. Then when Lila's parents had died, Landry had been contacted by the adoption agency asking if he wanted to take her in. It had brought Landry and Fia back together, and they'd made a little family. But now . . . now they would get to experience this together. Not in secret.

"What's Lila think?" Denver asked.

He had thought his brother couldn't look any prouder. But he did.

"Oh, she's thrilled. She's already trying to strong-arm us into letting her name him or her. So, if we end up with a kid named Ragnar the Destroyer, you'll know what happened."

Justice's chest felt strange. It was so . . . It kind of blew his mind to see his brother in this position. It had been a few months of watching Landry come into fatherhood. Watching him learn to parent Lila. Then watching him learn to be in a relationship with Fia. Then they'd gotten married. After all those years. All those years of circling each other. Of no one knowing where their bad blood came from. He was like a new man. For one acidic, awful moment, he envied his brother so much he thought he might not be able to keep it off his face. And then the moment passed. Landry was Landry.

The truth was, even when your father was an awful bastard, he wasn't an awful bastard to each of his kids in the same way.

Hell, the McCloud family had a great and obvious example of that. Seamus McCloud had been horrible to all his children in their own special way.

He never laid a finger on Brody. He had manipulated him instead. He'd tried to kill Gus. Gus carried permanent physical scars from that. As for the other boys, they had endured varying degrees of abuse. But it looked different for everyone.

Justice knew the things his dad had put him through had done some particular, specific damage. He didn't waste time worrying about it. He didn't waste time worrying about whether or not he ought to fix it. It was what it was.

He thought back to the conversation he'd had with Rue earlier in the day. The idea that he didn't have women over because he didn't want to deal with it. It was true. But fractionally. He didn't like sharing his space.

Rue was an interesting exception to that rule. She felt like home. She was *her*. Also, she was organized and she wouldn't go moving things without talking to him. He just liked his space. He liked control. Maybe that was the real problem. Right now nothing about life felt predictable. It didn't feel in control.

Rue wanted to get wild and Landry was settling down. It was all just a little bit too off-brand for him. He didn't care for it. It was his sister who peppered Fia with questions, while Bix stood back, eyeing everybody with suspiciously glittery eyes. His brothers didn't ask lots of questions, but their happiness for Landry and Fia was evident.

Daughtry looked at Bix. "What do you think?"

She wrinkled her nose. "I dunno, Sheriff. Not sure I'm ready for you to put a baby in me. Maybe we can just keep practicing."

He laughed. "I'm good with that."

Bix had been such an easy addition to the family because she was as feral as the rest of them. And he wondered if she was uncomfortable in a similar way to him. All this . . . functional family shit.

It made him kind of want to run for the hills, and embrace his brother at the same time. That was the problem. Moments like these made him feel like he was being split in two. It was why he preferred control. Preferred for things to keep bumping along like usual, not . . . get all upended like this.

It was Fia who approached him, and then she stood up on her tiptoes and ruffled his hair. "Justice," she said. "Are you good?"

"I'm good. I just don't know what to do with pregnant women."

There. That was true anyway.

"You don't have to do anything with me. I'm not your responsibility. You do have to be a fun uncle, though."

"I'm already a fun uncle."

Granted, Lila and Arizona's stepson were teenagers, and he found that a damn sight easier to deal with. Babies . . . He didn't the hell know about that. Thinking about how vulnerable little kids were . . . it made his stomach hurt. They were born into this world with no choice of who parented them, and there was no . . .

test to take or anything like that. People made you, gave birth to you, didn't ask you if you wanted to be born, then did whatever the fuck they wanted with you. Didn't seem fair to him.

"I'm happy for you," he continued. "You guys are going to be great. You're already great. But now you get to do sleepless nights and diaper changing together."

"It will be great," said Landry. "Because we didn't get to do it the first time. And now . . . we do."

He hugged his brother and his sister-in-law and sent them on their way, went back to work and was a little bit annoyed that the binder wasn't the only unexpected thing he should've been looking out for.

He didn't really get why everything was changing like this. Of course, it had been bound to change no matter what. Rue had been about to marry somebody else.

He'd been certain it wouldn't change their relationship, though.

He'd been so happy for her, he wondered if he hadn't fully thought all that through. Well, that didn't sound like him at all.

He huffed. Finished out his work for the day and headed on back to his place. And that was where the binder reared its head. Rue was sitting on the floor in front of his coffee table, her eyes overbright.

"I have a plan," she said.

She lifted the first binder, one with flowers. "This one is all about my plan for what I'm going to do with the new phase of my life. Rental options, purchase options, potential locations. Things like that. And this one is about me personally." This binder was the one with the squirrel on it. He didn't know what to make of that. "New hobbies, new activities and new things I'm going to try. Because I have to become a different Rue than I was before, because the old Rue can't come to the phone right now. Do you know why, Justice?"

"I don't."

"Because she's dead."

"That . . . is a little dramatic," he said.

"No," she said. "It's Taylor Swift. But even if it wasn't, it's a metaphor. The only way that I'm going to find a way to not be sad about all this is to let go. I have to make a new life so that I can personally begin to recover from all of this. You have to fill the void, Justice."

"This sounds a lot like unhealthy coping mechanisms to me. And I should know, because I am the king of them."

"You are a King."

"That you are saying things like that with glee makes me think you are either drunk or a little deranged right now."

"I'm not drunk," she said.

"Well, thank God for that."

"But I will be. That is part of my plan. My multistep plan to make the old Rue into the new Rue. And it will involve a night of debauchery."

"What . . . what kind?"

"I'm going to see where the night leads me. I'm going to let Jack Daniel's lead."

"Oh, please don't do that."

"I'm spontaneous now," she said, holding up the squirrel binder that contained all of her plans, likely color coded and itemized. *"Spontaneous."*

"You're heartbroken," he said.

He didn't know why he said it. Maybe as a reminder to her. Maybe as a reminder to him.

"You know, that's the thing," she said. "I'm not. I . . . I don't think that I am."

"You must be. Because this is out of the ordinary."

She clutched the binder to her chest and looked up at him, a sort of desperation in her eyes. "Justice. I am more upset about the life that I'm not going to have than I am about losing Asher. And I don't know if it's because I'm in shock, because the reality of the whole thing hasn't set in yet. Because he was on deployment a lot and we spent a lot of our relationship apart. I'm used to not having him as part of the day-to-day."

She chewed her lip and looked up at him. "It makes sense that I might not miss him until it's been longer than this. But I don't know. Am I upset about losing him? Or am I mad because I was humiliated? Because he basically left me at the altar. Because he thinks another woman is sexier than I am. Am I offended by that? Is it more to do with the fact that I don't get to have the fantasy wedding that I wanted?"

"Are you going to let me answer any of these questions?"

She kept talking like he hadn't spoken. "I have to keep waiting to have kids. To have the family that I want and the life that I want. That's just not a good reason to be with somebody. And I honestly don't know the answer to the question. Because I feel like heartbreak should feel a lot less like rage. A lot less like thwarted plans. And that's what this feels like to me. I'm angry.

Because I didn't get what I wanted. But when I think of all the things that I'm mad about missing, he isn't one of them." She closed her eyes. "I mean not specifically."

That made him feel oddly triumphant. And he wasn't sure what to do with that. Or why the feeling existed.

"Rue," he said. "Listen, it makes sense. It makes sense that you can't love the guy like you did before you found out who he really was. What he prioritized. Maybe that's all it is. I'm not saying that I want you to be heartbroken. I don't. But you make it sound like you were ready to marry a man you didn't even love."

"What if I was? Do I even know what love is? Why would I know that? I mean, for me it has always been about security. How could it not be? My parents didn't give each other any security. They made things worse. They lied to each other, they manipulated each other. Our house wasn't a sanctuary. It was a war zone."

"I am very familiar," he said.

"I know you are. So maybe I just decided that love was the opposite of those things. I feel like I need to undo all the ideas that I ever had about what my life should look like. Everything that I did to be the opposite of my parents."

"This sounds . . ." But he sighed, because what else could he do. He was just going to have to be her . . . her emotional support pack mule. Taking her and all of her baggage up Mount Debauchery. Because he knew how to carry it. Because he knew how to handle the treacherous road. Because he could keep her from doing anything truly stupid. Of that he was certain.

"All right," he said slowly. "Just let me know when you want to start."

"Oh good," she said, opening up the binder. "I want to ride tomorrow."

"That's fine, what did you have in mind?"

"Well, I asked around the ranch to find out what the best trail ride was, and—"

"You didn't ask me?"

"No, because I wanted to present you with my finished plan. I didn't want to involve you in the *making* of the plan." She smiled. It was so cute he . . . couldn't look away for a second. "I wanted to surprise you."

"I'll tell you what, Rue. Let's try this for spontaneity. I'm going to choose the route that we ride. Okay?"

She lifted her nose, and looked down toward him suspiciously. "I don't know how I feel about that."

"Luckily, I didn't ask you." He took his cowboy hat off his head and plunked it down on Rue's head. She looked up, and the hat lowered over her eyebrows. Then she frowned. "This is sweaty."

"I was working hard."

"I was too," she said. "I did make you dinner."

"You did not. We can go to the farmhouse."

"No. I did," she said.

"That was sweet, kid. Thank you."

He went into the kitchen to find a lasagna, and who the hell is mad to find a lasagna? Not him. So he sat across from her at the table eating lasagna and garlic bread and tried not to think about how his life felt like the same life that had been a couple of days ago but in a different font. The same elements, somehow completely rearranged to make something entirely different.

"Got some good news today," he said, dragging his garlic bread through the remaining sauce on his plate.

"Oh yeah?"

"Landry and Fia are having a baby."

Rue looked up at him, her eyes glassy, and he wondered if it had actually been insensitive to tell her that. She clearly wanted a baby. But then she smiled. "I am so happy for them. After . . . after everything."

"Yeah. I know. It's good. They deserve it."

"That's . . . It's really wonderful." She patted her eyes.

"I think it's going to take a lot for Daughtry to talk Bix into having kids."

"Well, I guess everybody handles the hard stuff they've been through in different ways."

"That's the truth."

Like Rue trying to plan her way into being wild. And Justice just . . . cutting ties with caring about much of anything. He held on to his family, and he held on to Bix. That was about it. You couldn't control other people. There was just too damned much she couldn't control.

And when you loved too many people you were open to manipulation.

So Justice kept things free and easy, and he was happy that way. Minimal ties, minimal everything. Just the way he liked it.

Now, the ties he had were intense, but he knew how to manage them. And that was what it all came down to. Control. He knew Rue. He knew what she was going to do. And he was going to choose the damned trail they were going on. He would take her up Cracker Jack Mountain; there was snow up there. The pine trees would look exceptional. It would be a good long ride, and she would get a good view. It was a mountain out on the property so they could just ride down a trail to get on that one, rather than loading the horses up into a trailer and driving somewhere.

Yeah. That's what he would do.

He would pack them a lunch. He would get Fia to do it. Well. She was pregnant. So maybe one of her sisters would do it. But if the food came from the Sullivan sisters it would be great.

"Let's head out about ten tomorrow."

She looked at him, faux innocence sparkling in her eyes. "Super early morning, Justice."

"Hush up, varmint. You can't be mean to your guide."

"My guide?"

"To sin, Ruby. Your guide to sin. Well. And trailheads. I'll meet you out at the main barn."

"You're saying that like we don't live together right now."

Well, hell. So he was.

"All right. But I guess I will keep seeing you all evening, and I'll see you tomorrow at coffee time."

She laughed. "Must be a trial."

"When there's lasagna, of course it's not. So I guess I did lie to you. You do have to do something to pay me back. You need to keep making me lasagna."

She rolled her eyes. "Only because I am not doing anything else all day."

"I thought the binders were work."

"Oh, they were," she said. "So was listening to Taylor Swift and singing at the top of my lungs while I cried."

He didn't say anything. But he was glad he had to work today.

"All right. I'll clean the kitchen. You scamper off and finish up any last-minute details you need to put in your notebook. But remember, I'm your guide. So I reserve the right to upend your plans at any moment and substitute them with better plans."

"I didn't agree to that."

He looked at her and lifted a brow. "I didn't ask."

The air seemed to get heavy between them then. It was like when he touched her thigh at the bachelorette party. Which officially felt like it had been ten years ago, instead of just a few days earlier. Another life, another Rue.

And he tried not to sit in the discomfort of the change of it all.

"Right. Well, I'm going to go have a shower."

"Good," he said, the word coming out more clipped than he had intended it to.

He spent the rest of the evening getting their picnic planned, figuring out which horses to take, exactly what trail. Looking at all the weather conditions. He would have to bring blankets. One for them to sit on, with a tarp underneath it, and a blanket for her to wrap in so she wouldn't get cold.

When he was going to sleep, he had the vague idea that it had been a lot like what planning a date must be like.

But it wasn't one. Because Justice King had never been on a date, and he sure as hell wasn't going on one with his best friend.

CHAPTER NINE

Rue met Justice at the barn, as bundled up as she thought she could be while still managing to maneuver herself onto a horse.

"You look a bit . . ."

She frowned. "What?"

"Like a blueberry."

She was indeed in blue snow gear that made her look a bit spherical.

"That's rude."

"It is a little bit rude, I admit it. But also it's funny. And true."

"Okay," she said. "I think I can get myself up on the horse."

"Let's see it," he said, crossing his arms and regarding her far too closely.

She'd had . . . a weird day yesterday. But she felt a lot more balanced now that she had gotten her plans down. She had been grateful for the space to cry and be ridiculous. But that had set her off on this spiral of an idea that she hadn't actually been in love with Asher. Maybe Justice was right. Maybe it was just that seeing him like that had knocked her so decisively out of love she was never going to be able to access the feelings she might've had once upon a time.

Maybe.

But she was a little bit worried that what it amounted to was that she had a huge blind spot. She had convinced herself that falling in love with an idea was the same as loving a person.

It unnerved her. She considered herself to be pretty self-aware. It was the antidote to her parents and all of their drama. Because what they did, they did blindly. Wildly. Without taking into account the feelings or needs of others. And so she had tried to never be like that. But . . . that she could have gotten that close to marrying somebody without really being sure what love meant was astonishing.

She wasn't going to marinate in it right now, though. Because she wasn't marrying the guy. And she had time to put things back together. To put them in perspective. That, she supposed, was the gift. The gift of all of this. It was like being given a second chance. So here she was, about to get on the horse.

"I got a picnic basket from the Sullivans," he said, hefting himself easily up onto his mount. A gorgeous paint with a persnickety personality. Her own was a black, docile steed, and she was grateful for that, because she didn't have the experience for persnickety.

"Well, that is cheering," she said, managing to get herself hoisted up onto the horse. It had been several years since she had done this.

But it felt like a step in a new direction. She could do this. She could go riding sometimes. Maybe she would lease some ranchland. Or board a horse with the Kings. Of course, she didn't really need to do that because they had a surplus of horses. But maybe she would start riding sometimes. She would get outside in nature. She would do more than just sit and knit in front of murder mysteries on TV for a hobby. But she did like that. She was trying to imagine different lives. That was the whole goal right now.

That last one scared her a little bit. She had been lying to Justice when she said it had to be led by Jack Daniel's. She hadn't told him the truth. What she wanted to do was go out and find some guy to show her exactly what crazy, betrayal-making sex was all about. She had been with one man. And that man had been part of stunting the growth of her sexuality. Part of, because she couldn't blame him entirely. She had to own up to that herself.

It had been one of the things she just hadn't thought that much about. But she had not wanted to say that to Justice, because he would get all weird. Because he . . .

Her brain sort of tripped over itself and she stopped thinking about it. Because she was with Justice. Not that he could read her mind, but she didn't need any weirdness. And he would get so overprotective. He would just . . . He would lose it.

He had been snarly enough when Asher had come into her life.

Hadn't trusted him, hadn't been happy when she had moved in with him.

It was funny, because she truly considered them the kind of friends where their relationship transcended the fact that he was a man and she was a woman. But they did not talk about their sex lives, and when they did, it immediately got uncomfortable. At least for her.

She didn't think much of anything made Justice uncomfortable. Nice for him.

But that was when she became especially aware that her best friend was a man. An attractive man. And that was where the thought process stopped. Which was okay with her.

"So where are we going?" she asked, desperate to get to a part of thinking that didn't involve Asher. She needed to move on.

"You'll see. Just follow my lead."

She didn't have a choice, because he wasn't giving her real directions. Fine.

She had always thought Four Corners Ranch was the most beautiful place in the world. And being out here like this on the back of a horse with the heavy gray clouds looming over them, fat with the promise of snow, and the crisp bite in the air promising the same, she felt it renewed her in her bones. And she knew a moment of relief. She was looking for a new direction, but there were parts of herself she didn't want to lose. Not ever. The part of her that loved this place. The part of her that got solace from spending time with Justice.

For some reason she was thrown back into the memory of when they had first come here when she was a child. She had been so afraid at first. Of everything. The wide-open spaces, the horses. It was just so different than the dry, arid landscape she was used to, different than the big apartment complex with the fenced-in pool that had graffiti spray-painted onto the cement beside it.

Trying to sleep at night had been so difficult. Because usually the sound of traffic and sirens joined the sound of her parents fighting and helped minimize it. And at Four Corners everything was so quiet. Crickets and coyotes were the only noise.

She simply hadn't known what she thought of it in the beginning. But she'd also accepted it, because she was a child who was used to being dragged around at the whims of her parents. It was her reality.

And gradually it had become her salvation. The best thing that had ever happened to her.

It had given her a sense of family she hadn't had before. Trauma bonding.

She frowned as her horse meandered behind Justice's. He had said that about Asher and the woman he hooked up with on deployment. It sounded like it would be a decent enough description for what they had.

She looked at his back, tall and straight, his shoulders broad. That familiar cowboy hat fixed on his head. Justice was inextricably linked to the land. He was part of it. As sure as the mountains, as sure as the pine trees that rose up to meet the sky. The dirt that was on his boots at the end of the day was also in his blood. She liked that about him. Always had. He had taught her that you could plant your own tree rather than relying on the concept of a family tree to provide connection.

There was a lot of blood, sweat and regret poured into the ground here. So many dysfunctional families, and yet the children had all stayed to make something better. Because the roots were their own, and there was something deep there that Rue found touching. Comforting. Something that resonated. She would be all right. Because whatever changes she made, her roots were here. And that wouldn't change. She just needed to mix it up a little bit. She had meant for this to be an entirely new sort of endeavor, but the funny thing was, it had actually reminded her a fair amount about the past. Before Asher. Before life had fully formed her. And maybe it was a good reminder simply because when she had moved here as a child she had changed. She was still fundamentally herself, but it had brought her new, wonderful things.

Maybe this all would too.

Or maybe the fresh air had just infected her with unrealistic optimism that would ultimately leave her feeling singed. But she would take the good mood as it came.

The trail began to wind upward, the hard ground suddenly frosted, and up ahead, covered in snow.

"Oh," she said.

"That's why I chose this. I figured you might like a winter wonderland."

"That was a good guess."

It touched her, how thoughtful he was about things like this. About her.

Justice was her safe space. A fundamental truth that also hadn't changed as time went on.

She was grateful. So very grateful.

"This reminds me of sneaking out," she said. "Running over to King's Crest through the fields in the evening so that I could get some peace and quiet."

"What a bummer you had to come to our place to get that," he said.

"You were all there," she said. "And that gave me what I was looking for. You took care of me. I just remember the way that we carved out a place of our own."

And as the years had gone on, they had carved out some different spaces. When they were kids and they had taken refuge it was always in the old barn. They would bring snacks, and sit on a blanket. Turn the lantern on and talk. Avoid their parents. Avoid anything that felt difficult.

Then Justice had carved out a space at the bar. In one-night stands and casual hookups.

She could remember the first time she realized he was doing that.

Having sex.

She had caught him sneaking back from one of the ranchhand cabins and had figured out he was sleeping with an older girl whose dad worked on the ranch.

She hadn't said anything to him. She'd felt scalded by it, though. And weirdly jealous. She'd been fifteen; he'd been sixteen.

She hadn't wanted to have sex. Not with him or anyone. But it had been threatening to her that there was another woman who knew something about him that she didn't.

She had ultimately decided to let that escapade be his and his alone. At a certain point, she'd just had to not think about it. Or rather, she put wallpaper over it. It was so apparent that the wall was there, but she wasn't able to see the texture of it, not able to see the details. It was covered over, made palatable. And that was how she had handled it all the way up until now. That was his space. Just like the yarn store was hers. Like her grandmother's home had become another space. His wildness a thing of fierce beauty that she admired from afar, but didn't question too deeply, or examine too closely.

Of course, she had been poking at it these last few days. But maybe that was part of trying to figure out why she had ended up here. Why she had ended up thwarted in spite of trying so damned hard. Being so careful. So responsible. But what had it gotten her?

"What made you decide to . . . I don't know, to be you?"

"What?"

"I'm curious. Because I remember what made me decide to be careful. My mom told me one time that she got pregnant with me by accident. Right after she met my dad. They had thought they were doing the right thing by getting married, but everything had been a disaster since then. But they were stuck together because of me. The accidental pregnancy caused all of their unhappiness."

"What? That's some bullshit," said Justice. "They made their choices. You didn't. Babies don't choose to be born."

"I know. I'm not going to pretend that didn't create some serious issues." She huffed. "But honestly, my biggest takeaway from that was you needed to be careful because there were some things you couldn't take back. There were some decisions that could change the course of your life. It's why I waited so long to be in a relationship. I wanted to be sure that if I did start dating somebody, that if I was, you know, physically intimate with somebody, I could either handle the consequences on my own or they were someone I could stand to deal with. I just remember deciding to be careful. And I was wondering when you decided not to be."

"I'm careful, Rue. Don't ever look at what I do and who I am and think it comes from a lack of care."

Her stomach twisted. "That came out different than I meant it. I didn't mean to imply that you were careless. But it feels like you're able to move through life with the degree of lightness that I just don't have. You do things because they feel good. And I don't know how you ended up getting there."

"I find it easier to get through life if I just don't think that deeply. But the beginning of that comes from caring a hell of a lot that I didn't fuck somebody else's life up the way that my dad fucked up all of ours. The beginning of it starts with caring a hell of a lot. I don't want to be the cause of somebody else's pain and suffering. I treat everybody with dignity. I treat them all how any person would want to be treated. Whether it's a woman I'm taking to bed or a person I'm buying a beer from. I don't treat people like they're disposable. But I also don't get deeply involved in them. And there is a way to do that. My life is my life. I like to control it. I like the set pieces to be fixed. Everything is permanent, everything is where I want it. And that means I can go out, have a good time and come back and nothing's changed. I decided a long time ago that if I made it clear who I was and what I was about that I could have a pretty full life. I have King's Crest, I have my siblings, I have you. I can go out, hook up, come back, you're all here."

"You're not selfish," she said.

"I don't know. It could be argued that—"

"No," she said. "Anybody looking at you and itemizing what you do on a daily basis might be tempted to stereotype you as careless. I was just close to saying that myself when I absolutely didn't mean it. They would be tempted to think so. But I think you're actually just a whole different breed."

"I didn't decide to keep myself safe," he said. "I decided I had to figure out how to keep others safe. I'm not like my old man. I know that. I have never been quite that much of a narcissist. But I got a good look early on at how you can manipulate other people and what it does to them. I never wanted that. If anything, I set out to prove that you can have a good time, a pretty damned full life without fucking up other people. Work hard, be respectful where you need to be, be disrespectful in a fun way when you're naked, and don't stir shit up."

"Destroyer of worlds, are you?"

"I just don't want to be characterized as sweet."

"Why? God forbid somebody see you?"

"I don't need anybody to see me."

"Oh Justice."

That was the most ridiculous lie he'd ever told. That he didn't do things to protect himself. But all things considered, she thought she might let him have the lie. Because why dig too deep into it today? Her life had been upended; she didn't need to go rearranging his.

It was okay to let the subject drop, she decided.

The scenery was stunning, and as they wound up the mountain the snow got thicker. White and heavy on the dark green trees, blanketing everything in silence. There was no sound other than the horses' hooves on the ground, the swish and flick of their tales. And every so often a bird would call to another, and fly from tree to tree, disrupting the snow and stillness as they went.

Rue and Justice didn't speak. One of the most incredible things about having a friend like him. Sometimes you didn't need words. You could just be together and get something out of that. Comfort.

She tried to think if she had ever found Asher comfortable in a similar way. Talking, planning, those things had made her feel bonded to him, but silence had never felt this easy. It was strange, because they had so much in common. She and Justice didn't on paper. Not that it was a comparable relationship. Not really.

She felt so much calmer now. More centered, and thank God. The last few days had felt so manic. Just an endless slog of discomfort. She wanted to fix it when there simply were no quick fixes.

She kept hitting highs and lows. When she'd been googling simple, adventurous things she could do yesterday during her binder building, she'd felt high. Dizzy and amped-up. Skydiving was a no, though she saw there were a lot of women who went through divorces and went skydiving, and she loved that for them. Just not for her.

Mountain climbing was also a no—but that was when she'd decided on trail riding.

Bungee jumping—no.

Running—another one people often took up when life turned against them.

Big no.

That was when she'd somehow ended up reading about cold-water plunges, which had taken her to the phenomena of polar plunges—usually done in groups for charity, where people leaped boldly into freezing water. It seemed daring, but not dangerous—in the right environment. And so she'd added it to the list.

In her mind, it had felt like she could maybe make some sort of peace with discomfort. Maybe.

Eventually she was going to have to leave King's Crest and actually see people. Eventually she was going to have to figure out what to do about her self-confidence, which had been shot full of holes.

But this was an okay place to start.

When they arrived at the clearing at the peak, she maneuvered her horse around and looked out at the view below. Stunned by the glory of it. Justice dismounted and began to get into the pack that was resting on his horse's haunches. He pulled out blankets, and she realized for the first time that he had a big picnic basket.

"Well, that's just perfect," she said.

He chuckled. "Yeah. I tried to come prepared. The snow is a little deeper than I was thinking, but I do have a tarp to keep you dry."

He set everything out, right there in the snow, with the pine trees towering around them, and the view of the ranch stretching out below. Green fields dotted with cows standing in stark contrast to the snow they'd found at this elevation.

It was so peaceful. So quiet. A new version of their barn from back in the day.

It was a brief feeling, more of an impression than wholly thought out words, but for a moment she felt like she'd never be as happy as when they'd been kids in that barn. It was over quickly, and it left her startled.

They hadn't been happy. They'd been kids surviving the best they knew how.

And yet for one moment she'd missed it. The simplicity of it.

The two of them against the world.

This almost felt the same. Almost.

"This is lovely," she said, the words becoming all the more intense as he began unloading the picnic basket and revealing the contents. Cheese and mushroom tart and puff pastry chicken galette. Not to mention cinnamon rolls that had been put in a thermal container to keep them warm.

It was just so . . . so thoughtful in a way she couldn't imagine anyone else ever being.

Her stomach went hollow, because it wasn't them against the world right now. It was them, living in their very messy lives. Well, her life was messy. His was what he'd made it, nothing more, nothing less.

She swallowed hard.

"Thank you. This is making up for the reception dinner I didn't get to have."

She opted to grab a cinnamon roll while it was still sticky and hot. Dessert first. Another thing that new Rue did, she decided.

"You're welcome," he said.

He surprised her by taking out a bottle of wine next.

"You don't even like wine," she said.

"But I knew that you would like it," he responded.

He filled her glass halfway, and she noticed he didn't take any.

"Are you the designated navigator?"

"Someone has to be, Ruby. You're a loose cannon."

They sat for a long while, eating, making light conversation. She asked him about the building happening at King's Crest, and he told her how they had weddings lined up for the whole summer.

She wasn't sure how she'd feel about seeing other people's weddings.

Right now it seemed like it might be okay.

She lay back on the blanket and looked up at the gray sky. Feeling warm out there in the middle of the snow, and oddly cocooned.

It had always been like this with him.

She sat up when he moved, and he took a step away from the blanket and stood on the edge of the mountainside, looking down at the view below. There was something about seeing him like that that made her heart cramp painfully. And she became aware of how often lately her heart did things when she looked at Justice.

He turned his head to the side, and her eyes came to rest on his square, hard-cut jaw, the curve of his lips. His blue eyes. He had been so damned handsome in his tuxedo, but out here, with that black cowboy hat on his head, his jacket on, beat-up jeans that molded to his thighs, he was . . . him.

Not the man who went out to the bar and charmed women, but the man *she* knew.

The one that thought everything through, even his debauchery. The one who had to decide to keep things shallow, because deep in his core he wasn't that kind of man. He was loyal. He was true. In ways that people who didn't really know him would never fully understand. Then he turned to face her and it was like getting hit in the head with a rock.

He was so handsome. She knew that. She knew he was handsome. She would have to be a fool not to recognize that. But it hit her then different.

Because he was the kind of handsome that knew how to make women lose their minds. That knew how to make them set aside their better judgment, trade it right away for a night in his bed, in his arms. She understood them. Right then, she understood. She wanted to make that feeling go away. Wanted to make that revelation disappear. She didn't want to look down at his hands and notice that they were big and rough and strong. And then remember the times when he held her. Like on the night of the bachelorette party when he had picked her up off the ground and those rough hands had made contact with her thigh. She'd dismissed it then. She just hadn't let herself linger on it. But for some reason now she was lingering.

His lips quirked upward into a smile, and she saw her friend again. But she couldn't quite get that other image out of her mind. Or the memory of his hands on her skin to fade.

"You ready to go?"

"Sure," she said, feeling a little bit dizzy.

"Did it live up to your expectations?"

She had to swim through a murky sea of her own thoughts to try to figure out what he even meant by that. "Riding horses," she said.

"Yes."

"Yeah. I . . . I love this." Finally, she got her head back on track. "I really did. I loved everything about it. I loved spending time with you. And I loved getting out on the ranch. It reminded me of better times."

"Good," he said, the corner of his mouth tipping up into a smile. "I'm glad to hear that."

It was like everything slowed down. Like she was back in the barn all those years ago, and here too.

And with that feeling came a pull toward him she wanted badly to ignore.

She nodded, feeling a little bit like she couldn't breathe. She helped him pack up the things, and they got on the horses and rode back down the hill.

She couldn't go there. She had to put everything back in its own little box. Where it had always been. Because every time something like this had bubbled to the surface she had been really good at putting it away. She wasn't jealous of that girl who had slept with him when they were in high school. She was just annoyed that she knew him in a way that Rue didn't.

She wasn't envious of pieces of his lifestyle because she wanted to live it with him; it was just a fascinating window into a life she didn't have.

That was all. That was all, *that was all*.

Her life was already in pieces.

She couldn't afford to shake its very foundation.

Rebellion was one thing. But she refused to destroy the most important thing in her life.

CHAPTER TEN

"You're being kidnapped."

Rue opened her bedroom door when she heard the female voice on the other side.

It was Fia, with Arizona and Bix, all looking determined.

"Why . . . why?"

"Because," Fia said, "we know you're sad, and you have every right to be because screw that guy. But we thought you needed a girls' night and since King's Crest is your safe space we thought we would do it here."

"Here?"

"Not here, here, we're going to Bix's because Daughtry is working."

"Come on!" Bix said cheerfully, grabbing Rue by the arm.

"I'm not dressed!" She had stripped down to her sweats after the trail ride and had taken a nap.

"You're just fine for our version of girls' night," Arizona said.

"I've never had one," Bix said, looking large eyed. "Please come."

It was, she told herself, sympathy for Bix that propelled her on, and not the sheer force of will of the women involved.

She was piled into Arizona's truck and they took the two-minute drive across a field to Bix and Daughtry's house. It was small and charming, with a neatly kept front yard that had endless planter pots—empty now due to the cold weather.

There were red lights strung up on every exterior surface, giving the whole place a glow. "I never really had any holidays growing up," Bix said, explaining as they went in and found it to be an even more explosive Valentine theme in there than it had been outside. "I might go a little overboard with everything."

"This is impressive," Rue said, trying not to feel sad over her empty house and how she would usually have put all her decorations out by now.

"Thank you. Now that I'm not living in a van, or with criminals, I can actually enjoy putting out cute things!"

It was only after she'd taken in all the glittering decor that she realized there were also plates of food. On every surface. Cheese, crackers, meat. Chips. Dips. Fancy things, Super Bowl–style things . . . it was a lot.

"In case you need to eat your feelings," Arizona said solemnly.

Fia produced a couple bottles of wine and held them out. "And in case you need to drink them, though only you and Bix can have it since Arizona and are gestating humans."

"She can have it," Bix said. "I'm not a big drinker."

A funny sentence coming from a former moonshiner who was now the resident brewer at King's Crest. But Rue had accepted long ago that Bix was a funny one.

It was part of her charm.

"I'll go easy on it," she said. "Though I appreciate the thought. I'm trying not to slide entirely into a depression. Though, Justice is doing a good job of helping me stay busy."

"I heard he took you on a ride today."

Of course they had collaborated with Justice on this kidnap. "Yes," she said. "I haven't actually done a lot of riding ever really. I did it a few times when I was a kid because I was learning to be a country girl. But it wasn't something that I got all that into. Mostly I spent my free time either running around with Justice or being at my grandma's."

She was a little bit older than Arizona and Fia, and Bix hadn't grown up here, so she wouldn't have been surprised if even the ones she had shared the ranch with in childhood didn't know a whole lot about how she had spent her time.

"Well, you were one of my brothers' friends," Arizona said. "Obviously you had cooties like they did, even though you were a girl."

"I would've been proud to share cooties with Justice," she said.

She clapped her hand over her mouth to suppress a squeak when she realized how that sounded.

Arizona laughed. "Well. That's unexpected."

"And not what I meant," said Rue.

"Yes, I know. You are platonically involved with my brother."

Rue felt twitchy having that introduced into the conversation because her feelings were so on edge it was like she had a teeter-totter inside of her. It had been making her feel strange things, think strange things. The same sorts of thoughts that burst into her mind and bloomed like a flower before she could grasp on to them and see what they were actually trying to grow into.

Earlier today it had been . . . a little bit treacherous.

"I'm sorry that asshole cheated on you," Arizona said. "I don't know anything about that, but I did end up bitter and twisted for years because the man that I fell in love with when I was a teenager left me." She didn't know Arizona all that well, but she did know there was more to the story than that.

She had been in a life-changing car accident shortly afterward that had left her scarred and with a permanent limp. But for years Arizona had been mean and standoffish to anybody who tried to get close to her, including Rue. Not that she had ever seriously tried to make friends with her, but she was Justice's sister, so she had spent time trying to get to know her, and for a long time that had been an impossible thing.

"I really don't want that," she said.

"Micah Stone broke my heart," Arizona said. "He didn't mean to. It wasn't a bad thing that he chose not to get involved with a seventeen-year-old girl who had way too many feelings for him. But it felt like it to me. I really let it poison a whole lot of good years of my life. I'm with him now because it was meant to be. The only thing I regret is that I wasted those years that I had by myself. Because they were valuable on their own. Because I'm valuable on my own. It took a little bit of untangling for me to realize that. Our dad really did a number on all of us, so I can't even really blame

Micah for how I handled that. But I know your parents aren't exactly a walk in the park so . . ."

"I appreciate it," Rue said, sitting down on the couch and picking up one of the jalapeno poppers. "I do. I don't want to be bitter, and I don't want to be stuck. I'm . . . I'm so happy for both of you," she said, gesturing to Fia and Arizona. "But I'm thirty-two. And I really did think that I was going to be able to start my own family. I was with him for eight years. I thought this was it. I thought this was the beginning of my life. And now I have to figure out what else it looks like." Not even getting into the fact that she now had a massive dent in her ego.

"That's its own kind of painful," Arizona said, frowning. "I wasn't exactly worried about my biological clock when I was seventeen."

"I'm getting worried about mine," she said.

"It'll be okay," Fia said, moving to her and rubbing her back. "We're almost the same age."

"I know," she said. "It's more that I'm worried if I have to meet another guy and it takes me eight years to trust him enough to marry him then . . . You know."

"Maybe Justice could be your sperm donor."

Bix offered that cheerfully from her corner of the sofa, and Rue felt like she had been shot between the legs with an arrow. "What?"

"He is a fine genetic specimen," Bix said. "I hear you can just use a turkey baster to . . ."

"Bix!" Arizona and Fia shouted.

"Also, you could do it the old-fashioned way," Bix said. "The King men are good in bed."

"Should I see myself out?" Arizona asked.

"Are you squeamish?" Bix asked, smiling.

Bix and Arizona were both edgy, badass women, and watching them go toe-to-toe would normally amuse Rue, but right at that moment she just wanted to crawl under the couch and make herself as flat as possible.

"You're making some assumptions about all the King men being good in bed," Fia said dryly.

"I'm just assuming they all share a genetic predisposition," Bix said. "Besides. I can't commiserate on the biological clock. I'm twenty-two."

"Shut up," Fia said.

Bix grinned. "I'm just saying. It would be practical. He's a good man, you like him."

"I'm not . . . I'm not having Justice's baby."

It made her stomach turn over, made it feel tight. Because . . . just that whole thought sounded intimate. And Bix could talk about turkey basters all she wanted, but it was still his . . . It would be his baby growing inside of her.

She felt vaguely clammy.

"No," she said. "That isn't how I want it anyway. I want a family. Because I didn't have one. And what I want more than anything is a chance to have that." Her eyes started to fill with tears, because she had always imagined raising her kids in her grandma's little house. The place that had become so dear to her.

"Hey," Arizona said, patting her on the back. "It's okay. It sucks. It just does. And there's no jumping forward and making it better."

"I want to, though."

"I get that," said Fia. "And I may not be the best person to give advice either, because I spent a lot of years hanging on to my secrets. I'm not sure that I dealt with my anger in the meantime. I just kind of deferred it." There had been a lot of bitterness between Fia and Landry and nobody had known why. It had all been about the secret pregnancy they'd had when they were teenagers, and Fia subsequently giving their child up for adoption. She suddenly felt uneasy. Both Fia and Arizona had forgiven men that hurt them. She really hoped that wasn't what she was supposed to do, or what they were about to counsel her to do.

"I don't want to forgive Asher," she said. As soon as she said it, a few things felt a little bit lighter. A little bit clearer.

"Oh, of course not," Arizona said at the same time Fia said, "Why would you?"

Bix was just sitting there holding a cheese knife, looking thunderous.

"Well, it's just that you forgave Micah," she said Arizona. "And you forgave Landry for making a really difficult time in your life even harder by not supporting your decision. I was worried that—"

"Neither of them cheated," Fia said. "And listen. Everybody has to make the best decision they can for themselves. I'm not saying there's not a scenario where I don't understand why somebody would make the choice to forgive a cheater . . ."

"I wouldn't," Bix said. "I'd give him a vasectomy with the nearest sharp object."

That was basically how she felt. "I told him I don't want to see him again. And I don't. You know, I think the thing is I can't actually ever look at him again and not see him looking at me and telling me that he lost sight of everything to have sex with somebody else. Because it was just so exciting and thrilling, and they had such amazing chemistry. I can't . . ." She shook her head. "It's the stupidest thing. It makes so much more sense to be crushed about a canceled wedding, about the fact that I'm not moving into the stage of life that I thought I was, but the biggest, rawest wound that I have right now is this painful feeling that I'm never going to find anyone because I'm not, I don't know, *sexy* enough. Like maybe something is broken in me because my parents were so crazed over sex with each other and sex with other people, and it was used as a weapon, and they lost their heads in a way that I never wanted to. Maybe I'm screwed up because the most stable environment I lived in was with my grandma, who told me that good girls needed to wear modest clothing and not let boys get to second base."

"First of all," Bix said, "this is the most patriarchy. That *he* could make a mistake and somehow make you feel like it might've been yours. I reject it. And I hate him for it."

Arizona and Fia made noises of agreement.

"And second of all," Bix continued, "your past doesn't mess you up forever unless you choose to let it. Believe me. If it did, I wouldn't be here. If it did, I might as well give up. Because I got turned into a petty con before I could ever make the choice. Because I coasted down that road and I made a lot of my own mistakes for years. Then I met Daughtry and I fell in love with him. *A cop*. I fell in love with a cop. It doesn't make any sense. But I wanted it. I wanted him. So I did all the rearranging inside myself that I needed to do to be with him. I had to unlearn a lot, but it wasn't stuck learned inside of me forever. I was able to fix it."

"Maybe that's what I need to do. Maybe I need like, sex therapy."

"Why?" Arizona asked. "Is there something you're scared to do?"

She suddenly felt uncomfortable. She'd never talked about sex in detail with anybody before. She didn't even talk about it with Asher. They'd just had it.

"No. I mean I don't think so. Nothing that he asked for that I said no about."

"You're uncomfortable with it," Arizona pressed.

"I'm not uncomfortable. Just like for things to be a certain way. I like for us to have a date beforehand, I like to feel like we have a connection. That we're on the same page. And I like for the lights to be dim, and I like to make sure that I'm feeling good about myself."

"You want to control the whole thing," Fia said.

"Yes."

"Have you ever had spontaneous sex?" Arizona asked.

Rue felt like a light had been shone onto her soul. "We didn't always put it on the planner."

A cracker dropped out of Bix's mouth. "You put it on a planner *sometimes*?"

"He was deployed a lot, and then when he came back he was tired, and we were both busy, so it just made the most sense to sometimes make sure that it was in the planner."

"Oh dear," said Fia. "There's nothing wrong with that. But just so I'm clear to you spontaneous sex is sex you didn't write in a planner."

"Well, yes."

"So no joining him in the shower and jumping him," Arizona said.

"Well, no."

"No watching a movie together and ending up on the floor?" Fia asked.

"No . . ."

"No banging in an abandoned cabin near where your illegal moonshine still used to be?"

Everybody looked at Bix. She shrugged.

"He didn't act like he wanted that either. He acted like he liked things organized and put together and reasonable. He didn't act like he was missing something else. It seemed like things were fine. I never wanted things to be scary or out of control. I never wanted it to feel like a runaway train. There was a rhythm that worked for me, and he made it seem like it worked for him too."

"You don't need to be defensive," Fia said. "I'm not trying to blame you. Far from it. If he had an issue he should've said something to you. He owed you better than that."

"You know," Arizona said thoughtfully, "I would say that the real issue is you didn't trust him."

"I didn't trust him? I was with him for eight years. I was going to marry him."

"Yeah," Arizona said, waving her hand. "I get all that. But you had to keep such tight control on yourself because of all of the trauma you had in your life around the subject, but you would think that the right guy would help you let go. Would make you want to."

"This isn't about him and what he wanted," Bix

said. "Because he never asked you for anything. He just went off and did his own thing. This is about what you want now. Because you're right. You're not moving into your motherhood phase. So maybe you should move into your hoochie-mama phase."

Fia nodded sagely. "I didn't do this myself, but I have heard that it is very helpful for some to have a ho phase."

"A *what*?" Rue asked.

"It's a phase wherein you ho around a little. After dedicating many good years of your life to a man who didn't deserve your loyalty, it seems like a pretty fair reward."

"I don't know about that," she said. But she was thinking about her determination to go down to Smokey's.

You need to trust him . . .

The only person who came to mind that she trusted wholly was Justice. And thinking of him in that context made her want to run screaming out the door into the night. She couldn't stop seeing him like she had earlier that day. Standing on the edge of the cliffside looking rugged and masculine and like every fantasy that any sane woman would have.

She was used to her best friend being beautiful. What she was not used to was having thoughts about that beauty that made her stomach get tight.

Well, not since she was more than a hormonal, emotional teenage girl who couldn't control much of anything.

"Maybe not. Maybe it wouldn't be right for you. Maybe you need to have trust between yourself and the guy you're hooking up with," Fia said.

Yet again, all she could think of was Justice. She felt like the way Bix was staring at her meant that she was thinking of him too. Bix who had jumped right on suggesting she have a baby with Justice like it wouldn't make her feel like her face had been dipped into a bowl of lava.

She had been envious, once upon a time, that those women knew something about her that she didn't.

Now the image of what he might look like hovered at the edge of her consciousness and it made her want to turn her brain off altogether. Made her wish she didn't have an imagination.

"I don't know. I might have to put a pin in that. Right now I'm not really even sure that I could go out and attract a guy."

Which was its own raw-feeling wound. It had just left her not feeling attractive.

"Men do not care about attractiveness." Bix said that with an entirely straight face. "Do you know how many men get arrested for putting their penises into weird things? A man doesn't cheat on you because you're not attractive, he cheats on you because of something in himself. Beginning and end of story. That's the bottom line. Something was wrong with him. He didn't want to deal with it. He was probably running scared from the next step you were taking. Hell, seems likely to me. You know I read a lot of self-improvement books. If you have an issue with your partner, you have to talk to them. So either he had an issue with your sex life and he didn't address it, which is still on him, or he didn't want it all, and he took his own issues and projected them onto you."

They all stared at Bix. An unlikely philosopher.

"I guess so," Rue said.

"I know so," said Bix. "What you do after this should be about you. About what you want. If you want to go out and tear it up, by all means, go out and tear it up. But it has to be about what you want, not about what you think you need to do feel better about yourself."

"I'm planning on jumping in a pond," she said.

"What?" Arizona asked.

"That's my plan for tomorrow. I'm jumping in a pond. I'm facing discomfort."

"I would personally go have sex," said Fia. "But you do you."

She was feeling scratchy and a little bit threatened. "I just feel like sex is overrated. So yes, I am aware that I'm having a little bit of cognitive dissonance. I want to feel pretty, but at the same time I don't think going out and hooking up is going to get me anything. Sex has just never been that fun for me."

All three women were looking at her like she had grown another head. "Well, it's true. I don't, you know, I don't . . . eh . . . *climax* that easily with a partner. Or at least not with the one that I've had."

"Bad form, Asher," Fia said, frowning.

"It's not really his fault. I never talked to him about it. I never said that I wanted anything else. I was happy to give it to him when he was in the mood and keep going through my to-do list in my head."

"No," Arizona said, frowning deeply. "No. I don't like that."

"Well, it's just how it was. I wasn't upset about it or anything. It just works that way for me, so if I go out and I try to make myself feel better by proving that men are attracted to me, I still feel like I'm going to be missing something."

"But you never wanted to find it before," Arizona pointed out, and Rue didn't like that. She felt a little bit seen.

The truth was, she took great pride in the fact that she had never fully lost her head over Asher. That she had never fully lost her head over any relationship. And the idea of doing something to change that wasn't comfortable.

She didn't want to do anything that might turn her into one of her parents. People who followed every random urge that popped up inside of them rather than doing the right things for the people they loved.

"I think that's the real problem. You have to decide what you want. Do you want to feel attractive, or do you want a man to make you scream," Bix asked.

"Nobody actually screams," Rue said.

Fia, Bix and Arizona all shared a look that made her deeply uncomfortable. But she couldn't deny they had a point. If she was going to get out of this pit then she really needed to decide what she wanted. She had told Justice she was curious why somebody would give up what they had for sex. But that was because she hadn't thought of sex as anything beyond an intimacy they shared in their committed relationship. It hadn't been anything wildly pleasurable for her. In fact, it hadn't been about her at all.

Did she want it to be?

She thought of Justice again, and she felt something stir low within her. That was just uncomfortable.

"Well, I guess that is one gift of this," she said. "I really just need to think about what I have to do for myself."

She was unencumbered by a lot of things right at the moment. She didn't have Asher; she didn't even have her own house. She would have the yarn store to go back to soon, but she didn't have to work for a little bit.

She had been obsessed with this external list of things that she needed to do. But she realized now that there were some decisions she needed to make inside. To give the thing she was doing meaning.

Tomorrow would be about discomfort. Something about that made her feel a little worried.

But her whole reality was more than a little unsettling right now. And she was worried she was going to have to be a different kind of brave, the kind that would require her to jump in the icy water.

But first things first. The icy water. Because she was in the discomfort whether she wanted to be or not.

And then she would figure out what to do about herself.

CHAPTER ELEVEN

Rue was dead set on doing her polar plunge today. It was damned-ass cold today. The snow might still be in the mountains but in the morning Justice's breath was visible in the air and there was a bite to it that was impossible to ignore.

He was unimpressed. He also wasn't letting her jump into freezing water by herself. Because it was stupid.

Now he kind of understood how she felt most of the time, and he was a little bit chagrined.

It was annoying when someone you cared so much about seemed bound and determined to do a bunch of weird shit.

So when she came out of her room around noon, layered up and determined, he intercepted her.

"I'm going to drive, in every way. Let's go down to the watering hole."

"Okay," she said.

"How was the party last night?"

Her head whipped around quickly. "Which party?"

"Your girls' night."

She looked oddly guilty, and he didn't know how to interpret that. "Oh, it was . . . good. Probably a good thing to get a little bit of a soft intro back into seeing people."

"So you just ate cheese and didn't talk about Asher?"

"Oh. We talked about Asher."

"Yeah?"

Her lips twisted. "Yeah. So you're coming with me?"

"Yeah, we'll drive my truck and keep it warm and running at the edge of the watering hole so that when you're freezing little ass gets out of the water you can scurry to safety."

"I really do appreciate it." She paused for a moment, then tried to look like she'd just had an idea. Subterfuge wasn't Rue's strong point, and he knew for a fact that she'd thought about what she was going to say long before this moment. "You should do it with me."

Little ferret.

"Hard pass. So what did you talk about Asher?"

"Just . . . about him?"

He snorted. "Come on, Rue. I know there was more than that."

"We just . . . talked about how he was . . . how we . . . I don't want to talk about it."

"Why not?"

"Because it's embarrassing." Her face turned honest-to-God pink and he found himself morbidly curious because Rue never . . . *didn't* tell him things.

"You can tell me anything," he said.

She cleared her throat. "I guess I can, but there are things we only tiptoe around, not jump right into."

It hit him then. They'd been talking sex.

Sex with Asher. Her sex life. Sex.

In spite of himself, he wanted to know.

"Come on," he said.

"It's just . . . I'm realizing we didn't have a great sex life, okay?"

So on top of making her feel bad about herself, on top of giving her a complex, he'd been shitty in bed? Well, that sucked. He didn't like that at all.

He also felt . . . he felt protective and weirdly like he wanted to fix it. His brain got stuck on that. He couldn't figure out what to do with that, couldn't figure out how to move on from that.

Because he would do better for her.

Oh. No. Never. No.

"I should have hit him twice." That seemed like a fair, true and neutral thing to say.

"I appreciate that," she said. "Though I'm forced to take some of the blame for it."

He frowned. "Why?"

'Let's just . . . go to the polar plunge."

"No, hey. Tell me why you think it's your fault."

"I just . . . I don't know. It's me. I didn't realize anything was missing. I didn't realize my sex life was bad until Bix, Arizona and Fia looked at me like I'd grown a second head when I said I wasn't that into sex. I didn't realize we were missing something until Asher told me he had chemistry with a woman he didn't even love that was better than what we had and now I'm forced to conclude that something was off. If I didn't know it was off it must be me."

"That is dumber than wanting to jump into ice cold water."

"How is it dumb? It makes perfect sense to me."

"You can't blame yourself for that. That's not fair."

"Well, I can take half the blame, right? He wasn't

in bed by himself. Something is . . . there's something broken in me, maybe. When it comes to sex. I don't know. Maybe it's my grandma being so concerned with modesty. Maybe it was my parents being so . . . I feel like whatever was happening with him, there's something with me too."

"Do you want to fix it?" he asked.

"I don't know! And I really don't want to talk about it. I want to do my polar plunge."

It was best to let this go. It just fucking was.

He hadn't realized it until right then but his stomach was so tight he could barely breathe.

"Right, your crazy-ass polar plunge. What does this have to do with anything?"

"Because it's a thing people do to like test their mettle and stuff, and I want to test mine."

"I just don't get why this specifically."

"Because. Because it's about doing something that I know will make me uncomfortable, and just committing to it anyway. Because I've been safe for such a very long time, and now I want to . . ."

"Get hypothermia and die?"

This was more comfortable ground than sex, thank God.

"I do not want to get hypothermia and die. I want to try something different. Figure something else out. I just . . . I'm uncomfortable right now. And this is kind of a metaphor for that. I have to submit to the discomfort in order to survive it."

"Or, I could knock off the rest of the workday and we could sit down on the couch and watch one of your favorite movies."

She looked suddenly hopeful. "We could watch *13 Going on 30?*"

"We could. Thirty, flirty and thriving," he quoted.

He knew the movie better than any man should. Because he'd watched it an untold amount of times with Rue over the years. He didn't hate it, he had to admit. Actually, he could admit just privately he kind of enjoyed a romantic comedy. Rue had shown him that.

She made a harassed noise in the back of her throat. "But the problem is I'm thirty-two, I am in no way flirty and you could argue that this is not thriving."

"*I* would argue that," he said. "I would argue that wanting to jump into an icy pond is not thriving."

Neither was having a bad sex life with the same man for eight years but he wasn't going to say anything about that.

She stuck her chin up in the air, looking defiant now. "Support me on my journey or don't, I can go by myself."

"Like fucking hell," he said.

"I need to do this," she said. "So if you don't want to be involved . . ."

Her eyes were full of mischief, and there was something else there. Something that he'd seen yesterday, just briefly, before they'd gone down from the mountain.

It brought him back to that tightness in his gut.

To lines he'd drawn years ago. Lines he didn't want to cross.

She got into the truck and he drove them down the short distance to the watering hole. He had opted for the little spring at King's Crest because he did not want her to parade her breakdown in front of everybody at Sullivan's Lake. And anyway, she had said that she didn't want to encounter too many people right at the moment. She seemed comfortable with him and his family, but there was no need to run the risk of running into other people.

He always got a feeling of unease in his gut when he came down here, though. It was part of the ranch, and he didn't avoid it. It didn't make sense to avoid it. He lived here. He worked here. He made his life here. He might not revisit the exact epicenter of his trauma, but he wasn't going to avoid it like a little bitch either.

They were going to the watering hole anyway. They wouldn't be pushing beyond that.

He pulled the truck up to the water, and just looking at it made his balls want to jump up inside his body.

"Yeah," he said. "Looks great."

True to his word, he left the truck running, and got out with her.

"Come on, Justice," she said, cajoling. "You should do it with me."

Just like that all the words just filtered out of his head. He couldn't think of any intelligent thing to say, because he had gotten snagged on what *she'd* just said. She unzipped her jacket and shrugged it off her shoulders. Then she gripped the hem of her long-sleeved shirt and pulled it up over her head, exposing her bare stomach, and revealing a very small bikini top that gave him a view of her breasts he wasn't sure he'd ever had. Typically, she dressed pretty covered-up.

"I got this for my honeymoon," she said, grimacing. Then she pushed her pants down her legs, and he found the bottom of the swimsuit to be as equally brief as the top.

Do it with me.

Was he in middle school? What was the matter with him?

Why was he standing there staring at his friend's bare skin? Why did he suddenly have the urge to put his hands back on her thighs. Why did he suddenly want to make sure she knew that she was beautiful?

To make sure she knew sex didn't have to be disappointing.

No. Nope. That fell outside of his purview. That was not a friendship task. There were caregiving tasks that fit very comfortably within the borders of friendship. That was not fucking one of them.

"Come on," she said. "Are you really going to make me do this alone?"

He wasn't compelled by the dare. Whether or not she would think he was. He wasn't compelled by the challenge in her voice. It was just her. Which was how he found himself shrugging his coat off and then stripping his shirt off. "I don't have swim trunks on."

This was a mistake.

Her eyes went round. Well, she'd made her bed so she could lie in it. He undid his belt buckle and kicked his boots off, pushing his jeans down his thighs and leaving himself wearing only his black boxer briefs.

Everything slowed down.

She looked at him. *Really* looked. From his face,

down to his chest, his stomach. He watched her eyes skim quickly over his package, and to his thighs, then with an almost panicked speed, go back to his face.

He felt it.

Dammit to hell, he felt it.

When she looked at him like that it was difficult. And she probably didn't even know how she had looked at him. But he had seen a curiosity in her eyes that wasn't going to lead anywhere good.

Would you rather she looked at some other man that way?

That was a shitty thought. And an intrusive one.

What he wanted to do was wrap her up in cotton wool and put her on a shelf until she was able to process what had happened with the dissolved wedding. He didn't want her going off half-cocked with some ridiculous notion that she was unappealing and needed to test herself with some random man to prove she was hot. But he also didn't need her looking at him like she was both curious and hungry. It was just bad. It was all bad.

"Aggghh."

The moment was broken by Rue's plaintive noise.

Rue was hopping from one foot to the other because the ground was so fucking cold.

"The water's only going to make this worse," he said.

"We can do it!" she shouted.

"This is insane. And not only that, it's unnecessary."

"Quit being a baby!" she said.

"I am not being a baby. I am being a reasonable human being who is pointing out to you that this is not going to—"

And then she shrieked and began running toward the water. At full tilt. And he had no choice but to follow.

The minute the icy water enveloped her, Rue knew she had made a mistake. Hell, she had pretty much known it from the moment they had pulled up, but he was giving her such a hard time and she wouldn't allow him to win. Which meant they both had to lose.

And then . . .

Then he had stripped his shirt off, his pants off, and she had found herself staring at a whole lot more of his body then she usually did.

Everything was so tangled up in her head. She was single. So that was a thing. Single for the first time in a very long time, and he was a man and she didn't normally think of him that way.

Well, it wasn't like she had never thought of him that way. But that wasn't what defined him the most. It was all this sex talk. Around him. At him. With him.

And suddenly then she couldn't really think of him as anything else. The most gorgeous man she had ever seen in her life, standing there with her half-naked out in the middle of nowhere, and that was the thing that had got her feet moving. Like she was running away from him.

Only he had followed.

And now she was submerged in ice.

It was like the thought jarred her awake. She propelled herself back up toward the surface and gasped, which actually came out a lot more like a scream as she started windmilling her way desperately to shore.

"That was so dumb!" she screamed as she pulled herself up on the shore.

"No fucking kidding," he shouted, coming out behind her.

She shivered, and then started laughing. "Oh my goodness, I am so ridiculous." She chattered and chattered. "What was I thinking?"

"You weren't," he said.

And then he moved to her and wrapped an arm around her, bringing her close to his body, which was still warmer than hers, in spite of the fact that he had just gone into the same water. Her hand pressed against his bare chest, his skin wet like hers. She felt his chest hair beneath her fingertips. Her ear was pressed against his heart, and she could hear it thundering fast. And it was like everything stopped making sense. Like the world had been turned on its head. Maybe they had hypothermia. Or at least she did. Because this didn't feel like it should have. Like it often did to be taken into Justice's arms. Because he was a man. And their skin was pressed together, and she was really curious about what it was like to lose your mind over somebody. She was afraid to look up at him, but at the same time she was compelled to do it. She tilted her face upward, and he looked down at her.

It was like time stopped. A more heightened version of what had happened to her up on the mountain during their ride. "We've got to warm you up," he said.

She looked away from him then, because she had to. And that was when she saw it. It looked like a cave that she'd never noticed before, nestled just behind the watering hole. You would have to snake along the rocks to get into it, but she wondered if anyone had.

"Is that . . . ?"

"Don't," he said, grabbing hold of her arm and dragging her back, his grip bruising. The look on his face was so unlike Justice. She didn't even know what to do with it.

"I was just looking," she said.

"It's not safe," he said. "It's dangerous."

"To look at a cave?"

"Don't go in there. You can't . . . you can't go in there."

"I wasn't . . . I wasn't going to."

She grabbed her other clothes up off the ground, and held her shoes in her hands as she made her way back to the truck. He followed her, but he didn't get dressed. He opened up the truck door and got inside, still in only his underwear. And he was all *angry*. And everything felt strange.

"It's not you," he said.

"What? I know it's not me, you're freaking out and I didn't do anything. So I assume you don't like caves."

"No. I don't," he said. "I . . . I never mentioned this because it happened before you moved to the ranch. I used to go exploring all around these parts. I went in that cave. There was a cave-in and I was trapped for three days."

"What?"

She was already completely disoriented and his words didn't even make sense. He'd never mentioned this. He'd never even hinted at it before.

"Yeah. I was seven. Anyway. I still don't like closed-in spaces like that."

She had never actually noticed Justice having a phobia of anything like that, but if she thought about it, there were certain things he didn't do.

"Why didn't you *tell* me?" She was still shivering in spite of the heater in the truck. "Why has it never come up in your family? Why—"

"You know how we are, Rue. You know how things were back then. I don't even know what all was happening with my brothers all the time at that point. The house was chaotic. Half the time Denver slept out in the barn and Daughtry was always following after Denver. Landry was already obsessed with Fia—whether she knew it yet or not—and he was always loitering wherever she was to try to catch a glimpse of her. Basically, everyone was just trying to survive. Me being lost for a few days? That was just . . . the kind of thing that happened." He cleared his throat. "So yeah. It's just never been that big of a deal."

"But you got . . . really upset."

"Yeah," he said. "I did. I don't avoid this place. I live here. I would never go back in that cave, and I would never want anyone else to."

"Well, that's why it seems odd you haven't mentioned it."

"My brothers know. And not very many people come down here. I've never had to worry about you being an exploratory little rat because you're usually so cautious. So yeah. I don't normally have to worry about you. But that was kind of a random move on your part."

"I'm not random," she said.

"You're being a little random."

"I'm sorry. I didn't realize."

That added to the weirdness of all of this. There was some major trauma in his life that she didn't even know about? She had witnessed a whole lot of his childhood, so she had always been pretty sure that she just knew about the things that happened to him. Apparently not. It was a strange revelation. As was sitting there looking at his bare chest, his bicep, being this close to him in the truck.

"It was so exhausting, suddenly. She was wet, and it was getting a little bit humid inside. Her best friend was half-naked right next to her and he had just told her about something awful that had happened him. She wanted to reach out to him, but it felt weird to do it because there was something about the way he held her down by the water that had rearranged things inside of her. She felt exposed. Which was strange because he was the one that had told her this new thing about himself.

"Let's go home. I'll get you some hot chocolate. We'll watch a movie."

"No. I want . . ."

He looked at her, his gaze sharp.

"Just leave it. Okay? It's not a big deal. I'm sorry that I freaked out at you."

Was he sorry that he'd held her in his arms for a minute there? Was he sorry that something had shifted between them, and she didn't know how they were going to shift it back? That was what she was really curious about. She didn't care that he had been angry at her. She cared that she had suddenly seen an intensity in him that she had not seen all that often. It had come up at the wedding, when he had gone after Asher.

Intensity. She couldn't help but think about that. She couldn't help but think about it.

"How did you survive that?" she asked while they were driving back.

"It's the simplest thing to survive. You sit in the dark and you wait for somebody to come get you. That's it."

He was being . . . very Justice about it. And she felt horrified.

"You must've been dehydrated."

"Yeah, pretty dehydrated. But there was a little bit of water trickling in a top corner. And I sipped on that a little bit. I don't know. I was a kid. So it's fine. I mean kids are resilient. And you know . . . ?"

They both had been. Because they'd had to be. But she didn't like him minimizing this or writing it off. And she liked even less that she hadn't known about it. It felt like a strange spanner that had been shoved into the works of their friendship, works that had been moving unevenly because their dynamic was all messed up and had been for the last few days. Imbalanced and kind of a mess. Because of everything she had been through, and everything he'd had to help her with.

They were driving back toward the house, and she put her hand over his without even thinking. Because it was what they did. But she was wearing a jacket and bikini bottoms, and he was in his underwear, and the air was thick with something electric, while there were raw waves of emotion she couldn't begin to read radiating from him. It was a mistake, because the normal touch wasn't normal in a moment that contained nothing of what they normally were.

She didn't want to jerk her hand away because it would reveal it. Would reveal her. What if everything inside him was the same?

Her wedding had just been called off. What was wrong with her? Why was she allowing it to reverberate through the solid pieces of her life like this?

She moved her hand away. "I'm just really sorry that you went through that."

"I'm sorry that we went through a lot of things, Rue. You and me. It's not fair. But life isn't fair, and you and I both know that. I had a terrible dad, and I happened to get caught in a cave-in. But you know, I didn't die. I wasn't seriously injured. It was scary. And you know, the kind of scary that gives you nightmares for years when you're a kid. But I survived."

Except she couldn't unsee the rawness in his response in the moment. It was more than just being afraid for a few days when he was a kid. He was afraid now.

I didn't make these decisions to protect myself...

Yes, he had. He did things to protect himself. One of them was not sharing things like this with her. She was so convinced that she knew almost everything about them because they were best friends. Because they had been this whole time. Because they knew each other so well. But what she had said to him the day of the wedding stood. She felt like he knew her better. She had never hidden things from him.

They pulled up to the house and got out. She retreated to her temporary lodgings and got her clothes on. Because what else was she going to do? They had to just keep going. She had to keep going. Because this whole moment was so incredibly uncomfortable. The polar plunge had been the least uncomfortable part. As a metaphor, she supposed it stood.

She got on some sweats and by the time she emerged Justice was also wearing sweats. A pair of gray sweatpants and a tight black T-shirt. She did her best not to do a visual tour of him, and then he took a kettle off the stove and poured some hot water into one mug, then another. "Hot chocolate," he said. "As promised."

Did he really have things like a kettle because of her? Was his kitchen really this orderly because of her?

Suddenly, this man that she had been so confident she knew seemed like a whole puzzle to her. And her reactions to him didn't feel any clearer. Okay. She could be honest. She was feeling attraction.

No. Not attraction to him. It was just a heightened aesthetic appreciation of his masculine form because she had been thinking about sex and she had been preoccupied with it. And what she knew about Justice was that he was an accomplished lover. Rumors suggested this and . . .

She wanted to grip her head and growl. But she wasn't going to.

"Yes," she said.

"I have mini marshmallows."

He was back to being his easy self and it was like none of that had happened. When everything inside of her was scalded red with the fact that it had all happened. His ability to revert right back to form was just annoying.

"I do like mini marshmallows," she said.

"I know."

There he was, that man who knew her so well.

He even knew her favorite movie. And he brought their hot chocolate to the couch for her, and queued that movie up quickly.

"Your favorite movie is *Lord of the Rings*. You pretend it isn't but it is."

He looked at her. "Yes. But I don't pretend that it isn't. Who doesn't love a good medieval road-trip film?"

"I'm just making sure that it's clear that I *do* know you. I know what you like."

That sounded so stupid. She took the mug of hot chocolate from his hand and held it close to her chest.

"I never said that you didn't," he said.

"Well, I didn't know that you had been trapped in a cave."

"I chose not to tell you. It's not a commentary on your observational skills."

"It feels like it is."

"The way that it makes you feel isn't my fault."

"Well. I guess." She pulled her knees up to her chest as he pushed Play on the movie. "Thank you. For jumping into the water with me. It was nice to not be alone."

She hadn't been alone. Not through any step of this. He had been there the whole way. Even when he was annoyed. And somehow things still felt jagged and disconnected between them. When yesterday it had all been fine. Except not really then either because she had looked at him and she had lost her breath.

She didn't like this.

She was beginning to feel panicky. She would rather jump back into an icy pond than contend with this.

The familiar introduction music soothed her to a

point, and she let herself get carried off in this storyline that she knew by heart. The characters were like old friends to her, and she was suddenly deep in her feelings about *this* movie that had been so formative to her.

Maybe because she was a kid who had wished that she could be an adult. Not because she was awkward like Jenna in the movie, just because she didn't like her parents having control over her life. She had wanted to grow up. So that she could be an organized businesswoman and have the life that she created rather than the one that had been given to her.

Of course, things did not go well for Jenna in the film, but there was something about the fantasy that had been the perfect escape for Rue.

Of course there was the romance. When Jenna finally realized that she didn't want a romance with the popular guy, but with her best friend, who had been the right one all along.

Rue felt like she had been punched straight in the chest.

No.

Her favorite romantic comedy was not a psychoanalysis of deep-seated feelings about her life and her relationships. She just liked the scene where they all did the "Thriller" dance. That was it.

She didn't live in New York; she had no aspirations to. She didn't want a big job. She liked her little yarn store in her small town. See. Totally different.

Anyway. She looked to the side; her best friend was not the slightly awkward-looking kid. Her best friend was the stunningly handsome hard-body jock. So to speak. The unobtainable one. Well. He was obtainable. Just in a very specific way. He was hers. Sort of.

She looked back at the movie. She sipped her hot chocolate slowly, trying to make it last, because it provided a little bit of a distraction. But then for some reason she turned to look at him, at the same time he was looking at her.

Her stomach dipped, then hollowed out.

Oh no. Oh *no*.

She couldn't deny what the feeling was. Not anymore.

It wasn't just attraction. She felt . . . attracted *to* him.

She could not let this happen. She could not let her fixation about sex, about her own issues with sex, transfer to her friend and ruin the most important relationship in her life.

Sex was disappointing. Justice never was. If she wanted to go and figure things out . . .

It couldn't be with him.

But what about trust . . . ?

Screw trust. She needed her ho phase, like Fia said. She needed it. It was the only thing that would fix this. She felt that now with a wild-eyed fervor. Because if she was sitting here thinking Justice was viable . . . just no. She needed to get out of her bubble. That was it.

So she said the only reasonable thing she could think of.

"I want to go out tonight."

CHAPTER TWELVE

Rue wanted to go out tonight. He couldn't get the manic light in her eyes out of his head. The way she'd looked at him and then . . . declared she wanted to go out.

Well, much like the polar plunge, he'd be there for that too. And then he had gone off to do some farm chores to try and work the tension out of his system because he was still trying to ignore the thought process that had been dogging him ever since.

Which was how he found himself in the brew works with Bix, Daughtry, Landry and Denver trying to focus on the task at hand, and failing miserably.

"Have you figured out what to do about Rue's house?" Bix asked. "We didn't talk about that the other night."

"You didn't?" he asked.

"No, I felt like it was insensitive. We could only talk about one catastrophe at a time."

He was still angry about this, and the anger about it was much easier to deal with than all the other feelings rolling around inside him. That was for damn sure.

So in the moment, he'd embrace the rage.

He wanted to find her parents and he wanted to . . .

He wanted to figure out if there was a way he could send them to prison.

Poor Rue. She'd earned the perfect life she'd had only a few days ago, the life that was gone now.

Was it all that perfect if her sex life was shit?

Well, he didn't need to go thinking about that.

"Yeah, it's unbelievable," Justice said.

"Poor Rue," said Bix. "Although, there are worse things than being taken in by one of you."

Daughtry looked at her sideways and smiled. "I'm not sure this is the kind of life Rue had in mind."

"Definitely not," he said.

"Well, at least she has you," Denver pointed out.

"Yeah. Great. I'm a great help. Except I can't fix any of it. She did everything right. I do nothing but bullshit, and here I am with a ranch and without a canceled wedding."

"In fairness, you weren't engaged," Denver pointed out.

"Or your wedding would definitely be canceled," said Landry.

"Oh shut up," he said. "Whatever. I'm taking her out tonight. I need to get her mind off of it."

Bix looked at him. "Sounds to me like *you* need to get your mind off of it."

"I already told you, sis," he said to her. "I don't want your husband to arrest me."

"That is fair," said Bix. "I don't want him to arrest me either. And it is often the only thing that keeps me on the straight and narrow."

She looked very grave when she said it, and in spite of everything, it made him laugh.

"So, you told Rue that she needs to live like you." Daughtry asked, "Does that include anonymous hookups?"

That hit Justice square in the chest. It offended him. *Horrified* him.

"Absolutely not," he said. "That is *not* what I meant."

"Well. It is what you said," Daughtry pointed out.

"I think it's fairly obvious that what I meant was she should take a night off and do a little bit of drinking. A little less thinking. Get up late the next morning. She isn't running the shop right now, so she might as well. Might as well take a vacation from trying so hard. That's all I meant."

"Does *she* know that?" Daughtry asked.

"She wouldn't do that anyway," said Justice. "It's not in her nature."

"When your whole world is destabilized, your nature may get shaken up along with it," said Bix, her tone overly sage.

"If I wanted notes from *van life* I would've asked," said Justice.

"And if we wanted philosophy from a drunken man-whore we would've asked," said Daughtry. "In all seriousness, I am sorry. I realize that it was so important to you that she . . . have this."

It was. Because if Rue couldn't get what she deserved, then who the hell could?

"Whatever. If you guys want to head out to Smokey's tonight with us, you're welcome to. Otherwise we'll give you the highlight reel tomorrow."

"We'll let you manage her. She probably wants a

break from having a bunch of people around her to feel sorry for her."

Bix spoke with authority. And he had a feeling that Bix was familiar with pity. Being that she had been an overly poorly creature when Daughtry had found her.

"I'll let you know how it goes."

But he couldn't get what Daughtry had said out of his head. And it haunted him the whole rest of the day.

IT WAS COLD outside. The waning winter season was making it difficult to figure out what she was supposed to wear to a bar. She could recall that there were definitely kinds of women who seemed to just throw a big coat on over a very small dress and call it good, even when you could see your breath outside.

She rooted through her suitcase, and came up with a very short blue dress that came to her midthigh, and had long sleeves and a scoop neck. She had worn it one time to a military social event with Asher, but never in Pyrite Falls or Mapleton, because people knew her here, and she didn't know how she felt about people who knew her all that well seeing that much of her boobs. But they were going out to . . . be wild?

She'd been sitting in this for a week, and for the past few days wrapped in the cocoon of King's Crest, so it had been easy enough to pretend that the only crisis was the wedding that wasn't. And then it had been easy to pretend she was just on a quest to do new things.

But something about last night, and the wild impulse she'd had to turn to Justice and . . .

It was all caving in on her right now.

All of it. And with that, came rage.

She had done everything right. She hadn't been like her parents. She wasn't even like Justice. Who she thought was a good person, honestly—it was just that he didn't . . . he didn't behave. And she did. She was so good. She was so . . . disciplined. Her entire life was in order, and through no fault of her own it was now in utter shambles.

She had *tried*. She had tried so hard and what had it gotten her?

Nothing. Absolutely nothing.

And here she was, trying to deal with the fallout of nearly being left at the altar, being basically told she wasn't sexually appealing and losing her house.

It was too much to bear and she needed to do *something*.

What is it you want?

To stop thinking so damned much.

She put on red lipstick, thicker eyeliner than usual. She fluffed her hair up until she didn't fully recognize the woman that was looking back at her in the mirror. This woman might understand how you could go a little bit crazy over sex. This woman might make a man go crazy over sex.

Maybe this woman could cut loose and not try to choreograph everything.

Except this woman was still Rue.

Except then she felt her confidence crumple, because she wasn't that woman. It was some other woman. A woman she had never seen before. A woman she didn't know or understand.

She had turned her fiancé into a man she didn't recognize. Into a stranger.

The firm knock on the bedroom door startled her.

"Come in."

Justice pushed the door open, and froze. He looked her over, slowly, and she felt her face getting warm.

"What? You act like you've never seen me in a dress before."

"I haven't seen you in one like that."

And she realized that Justice King had just checked her out. His eyes flickered downward, looked at her breasts, then down her legs. Justice had seen more women naked than maybe any man she had ever known, and he had just looked twice at her body.

So either he wasn't discerning, which was definitely one way to look at it, or she looked really good.

Really good.

The thought that he might have looked and seen her as attractive made her feel warm in a way she knew it shouldn't.

"Do I look okay?"

"What kind of question is that?"

"It's just that you *looked*."

"I'm looking *at* you, of course I looked."

"There's no *of course* about it," she said, feeling warm and restless. "I mean did you . . . did you look?"

It seemed very important to know. Because she felt unattractive and sad right now. Because he was . . . Because his reaction to her in her wedding dress had mattered and somehow so did this.

"I . . . Rue," he said.

"What?"

"I don't know how to have this conversation with you."

"But did you?" Danger. *Danger*, so much danger. Why was she doing this?

"Yes," he said, finally.

His face was like granite. She couldn't read it.

She was faltering; that was the problem. She'd come into the room to get dressed all angry and filled with rage and now she felt unsure. She was trying to get a little certainty from the one person she trusted the most.

"I just feel like . . . like maybe I'm not . . . I always felt pretty secure. Because Asher and I were solid. I was okay with us being separate because I trusted him. And I was wrong to do that. I just . . . I'm trying to figure out which way I was wrong. Does that make sense? Because either there's something wrong with me and it's entirely excusable that he had to have sex with somebody else because my boobs are only okay in a generic sort of way. Or there is something wrong with me because there was always something wrong with him and I didn't see it in spite of the fact that I was raised with parents who really weren't great. And it's almost like the lesson wasn't good enough."

Justice sighed heavily. "It wasn't you. Literally no matter what, it wasn't you. You trusted him. And honestly, I thought he was a decent guy. And I'm not very giving. Some people never think about why they do things."

"Who? I think about why I do things all the time. It is literally the only way that I can figure out how to navigate the world. It's the only way that I can make things make sense, and the only way that I can make sure that I don't run around doing the wrong things the way my parents do." She shook her head. "I mean, I get that people like them maybe don't think about their actions . . ."

"No," he said. "A lot of people don't. Rue, do you really think I asked myself why I want to go out and drink? Do you think I ask myself why I like anonymous hookups? I just do."

"It's obviously childhood trauma," she said.

"We're all doing things because of childhood trauma, there's nothing special about that. That's the history of the world. I just mean I don't sit around asking myself deep questions about it. And I bet you Asher didn't either. It felt good. So he did it. And how you look in a dress has nothing to do with it."

There was an intensity in his eyes that pushed her forward, closer to an edge she knew she needed to jump off.

Because this moment in time wouldn't last. This break from her actual life. She would have to figure out her house; she would have to go back to work. She would have to contend with herself. Polar plunges and trail rides and even nights out wouldn't be enough.

But it was all tangling her up right now. Making her feel tense even around Justice.

The only solution was to jump. Like she was leaping off the cliff to escape a fire that was burning out of control.

A fire she didn't set, but one she had to deal with all the same.

"Okay," she said. "Let's go out. Let's go just . . . forget

about all this for a while. Because you know what, being good hasn't gotten me anything. I'm kind of sick of it. You're right. I need to do something else."

"Yeah," he said, "sure."

They got into the truck, and he turned the engine over. "I'll be your designated driver tonight."

"You don't have to do that. I can . . . We could get a car service or something."

"No. Somebody has to . . . It's good. It's fine."

He didn't seem fine.

But she didn't feel fine. She felt reckless. She felt very unlike herself.

Jumping had been what she needed to do.

For the first time in her memory she didn't know where the night was going to take her.

CHAPTER THIRTEEN

JUSTICE FELT LIKE he'd been set upon by a pack of feral dogs, and no amount of running put him ahead of them. The sight of Rue in the dress had been something that he wasn't prepared for. He was even less prepared for her to ask him if he'd been *looking*.

He'd been looking since she'd shown up to the polar plunge in that bikini.

He'd been looking since he'd seen her in the wedding dress for the first time.

He'd been looking for longer than he'd ever wanted to admit, keeping himself leashed whenever he could. Because she was *Rue*.

She was pure and wonderful and his in a way no one else had ever been.

And her body was damned glorious.

It felt like an actual sin to admit to himself that he had looked at his best friend's rack, and thought it was the best he'd ever seen.

Not very much felt like a sin to him. But that had.

At that moment he'd made the determination that he was going to stay stone-cold sober all night, because if he had to protect Rue from other men and from herself while she was in a vulnerable state, then he was going to do it. Because the woman was dressed to make bad decisions. And there were far too many men who were going to be happy to take her up on them.

It was why it had caught him unawares like that. Same as the swimsuit.

Normally there were such clear rules around Rue he didn't even have to think about go and no-go zones.

Tonight, she was dressed like a damned menace— and one thing Ruby Matthews had never been was a menace. But there was a reckless fire in her tonight and Justice couldn't figure out if he was terrified, or in awe.

When they pulled up to Smokey's Tavern the place was already heaving. It was Thursday night, but the cold winter ensured the place was packed out no matter the day of the week. It was about the only thing to do in town, really. Especially when it was still cold as hell and liquor and warm bodies were about the only things that sounded good.

When he and Rue had been kids, their version of that had been to hang out in the barn with a space heater and some blankets, eating snacks they bought from the store with their pocket money.

And speaking of that, Rue was looking very not like a kid tonight. Not like herself really either, which he was sort of relieved to identify because that meant it was a little less appalling that he'd checked her out. The dress was so much tighter and lower and shorter than he was used to on her, her makeup heavier. She was Rue but not Rue, and that had thrown him off for a moment.

His gut tightened. Rue but not Rue. Part of him whispered, *That would be ideal.*

Lord. No. Absolutely not.

One thing Justice would never do was drag anyone else deeper into his shit. There were things not even Rue knew. Things no one else needed to know. Much less have to deal with.

He was the keeper of his own demons. And that was the best thing he could be, he knew.

But he wasn't here to deal with his own demons. He was here to make sure that Rue's didn't get the better of her. And yes, the last forty-eight hours had been interesting, to say the least, but she was going through something. And he was not going to . . .

He looked over at her. She looked beautiful. Any man in there was going to immediately want to take her up on the offer that she was presenting in that dress.

She's Rue. At the end of the day, she's not going to do anything.

Her version of being wild so far had involved going on a trail ride and jumping into a pond.

Granted, her swimsuit had been a little bit wild. And he kept thinking of the moment in his truck cab after. When he had talked about the cave-in and the inside of the vehicle had gotten overly warm. When she had put her hand on his.

He gritted his teeth. That was just a no-go area for him. He had grown up with her. They had survived being teenagers together. He hadn't been completely honest with her when she had asked when he had made the decision to become what he was.

The reality of the situation was he had been sixteen and she had started getting beautiful. In a way that he couldn't ignore. So, it had seemed like a better idea to take the invitation of the seventeen-year-old daughter of a farmhand that had just moved there, who had more experience and sophistication then he did. Who had shown him exactly what she wanted, and hadn't even wanted to get emotionally attached.

It had been the beginning of taking that path every single time. If there was a fork in the road and the option was intensifying one of the connections he already had or staying in the shallow end of the pool, he chose the shallow end. Nobody got hurt. Everyone had a good time.

Rue was sacred to him. A sister, maybe. Or something deeper.

He had a sister, and he loved her deeply, but it was still different than the relationship he had with Rue.

He'd decided a long time ago that he had no more business touching Rue than he did sitting in the front row at a church on Sunday. Sacred things weren't for men like him.

He was a master of the profane, and little else.

He was just going to have to keep walking on the path that he had put himself on all those years ago. Because it was the right thing to do.

He wasn't blindsided by the fact that he thought she was beautiful. He was blindsided by his inability to artfully look the other way. He had failed at that yesterday. The tension between them when they had gotten back to the house had been real. Palpable. The issue was she had looked at him too. And then tonight in her explosion of nerves she had acknowledged something that neither of them had ever verbally acknowledged before. That they both thought the other was attractive.

Which was maybe a silly thing to get hung up on. It didn't have to be that deep.

It just was. Because it wasn't just two friends complimenting each other. It was stickier.

Maybe the real reason he'd been okay with Asher was that it gave Rue what she wanted, and kept her at a very safe distance. Maybe that was it. Maybe that was why.

It made sense. He didn't especially like it, but it made sense.

"Are we just going to sit in the truck forever?"

He looked at Rue, his eyes shining bright. He wondered if she was afraid she was going to lose her nerve if they didn't go in.

"Listen," he said. "No one is going to say anything to you about your wedding and if they do and it bothers you, let me know and I'll punch them in the face."

"No," she said. "You can't keep punching people in the face for me."

"I don't think that's true."

"It is true."

"I'm just saying, you look beautiful." There. He had said it, and it had come out exactly like it ought to. Like a compliment. Free and easy. Exactly like it should have. "You're gonna go in there and you're going to have a good time. However that looks to you. Drink, dance. I'll be there."

He felt squarely back in the position he should be right then. Her protector. Her guide. That was what he was supposed to be.

"Okay," she said. "I've never been drunk before."

"You don't have to get drunk. It's not some magic

portal to having a great night. I mean, some people think it is. And I'm not going to say that I haven't used it as one myself a time or two. But you can have fun in other ways."

"You're beginning to sound like an after-school special."

"Wow."

"Okay. Let's go."

When they walked in, the place was wall-to-wall bodies. Men and women dressed so that they could find a partner to help them stay warm a long winter night. Rue's dress didn't even look scandalous in context. It was funny that it had shaken him so deeply. Just because it was Rue. There were women in dresses that were even shorter, even lower cut, and they didn't stir the faintest bit of interest in him.

He hadn't hooked up for a couple of weeks. He had been entirely consumed by the lead-up to Rue's wedding, and then by the aftermath of the lack of wedding. He just hadn't even cared to do it. That was odd. Because he had been using it as an escape ever since that first time. But he couldn't want that tonight anyway. He was keeping tabs on Rue.

And what if she leaves with some other guy?

Well. That wasn't going to happen. She wasn't ready to do that. She was definitely wanting to spread her wings a little bit in all of that, and it was fair. But she took this kind of thing really seriously, and it would be a mistake for her to hook up with somebody on the rebound.

As if that wasn't human nature.

"I'll order us some drinks," he said.

Rue looked nervous, and it was her mannerisms that made her look out of place, not anything else. She was picking at her nails, her shoulders hunched slightly. She didn't look afraid; she looked excited, but tentative at the same time. This was definitely not her scene. She had been to Smokey's before, of course, but usually with Asher, dressed in something entirely different. She probably felt like she was on display, and she was. He had caught a couple of men noticing her the minute that they walked in.

He was going to keep an eye on those guys.

"Can I get two beers? And . . . how about a couple shots of Jack?"

He wouldn't have any of that. He would have his beer and that would be it. That way he would be good to drive Rue home. But if she wanted to do this, if she wanted to get wild, fine. He would babysit.

He brought the drinks back to the table and she eyed the shot suspiciously.

"No pressure," he said.

"It feels like peer pressure," she said. "My mom and dad warned me about that."

"Did they?"

She laughed. "No. Of course not. They never warned me about anything."

He laughed, even though it was dark. Because it was the kind of dark that they shared.

Dark like getting trapped in a cave. Dark like finding out years later, after years of night terrors and phobias, that you got left there for as long as you did because . . .

"I can drink to that," he said, lifting up his beer.

She lifted hers and took a sip, then grimaced. "I don't know that this is going to be my scene."

"Well, what do you think? You going to dance?"

"Okay. I would like to dance." She looked at the shot. And she picked it up, pressed it to her lips and knocked it back. She grimaced, pulling her teeth back and hissing. "Good Lord."

"You did it," he said, admiring.

"I did. That was awful. How do people do that all the time? For fun."

"I think *all the time* is maybe a stretch if we're talking about functional people who aren't college students."

"That was vile." But she grabbed the other shot and knocked it back too before he could say anything, making the same face and the same noise as she swallowed it down.

She shook her head. "Okay. Yes. I am out. I'm here to have a good time."

"Want to play some pool?"

"Yes," she said. "I do. But let's play for money."

"Sure. Some nickels."

He could tell that the booze was going to her head, and they made their way over to the table in the corner that was mostly unused, because people were primarily focused on who they were going to go home with, rather than whiling away the hours playing games.

She picked up the pool cue, and *apparently* he was so basic that he was held captive by the image. It was such a cliché. A beautiful woman holding a pool cue, running her finger along it, except Rue had no sexual intent when she did that, and his body still responded.

Like she wasn't his best friend. Like he hadn't known her since they were little children.

"Let's do this."

She half stumbled as she bent down.

"Okay. You can break," he said, setting the balls up and moving away.

She did break, inelegantly. "I need more to drink," she said.

"Are you sure about that?"

"Hey, you're my driver, right?"

"And you're still a lightweight, right?"

"Hush, King. I came to indulge."

He turned and headed toward the bar, muttering as he went. "I need to keep you from falling into the deepest recesses of a dark pit, though . . ."

He furnished her with more shots, which only made her a worse player, which might have amused him if he didn't feel so damned tense about *everything*.

She was wobbly, like a baby deer, except her legs were hot, and he couldn't help but think about it when he'd picked her up at the bachelorette party what felt like a whole lifetime ago. And his palm had burned. She'd been engaged. It had kept the rest of him from burning.

She was still Rue, so that ought to work.

It wasn't working.

She went and got herself two more shots before they set up the next game and knocked them back before stumbling into position to break.

She shot the white ball, and it hit the corner of the colored balls at the center as it bounced out of the table and rolled across the room, up against the boot of a guy about their age sitting down enjoying a beer. He lifted up the front of his foot and trapped the ball beneath it.

"This belong to you?" he asked as he bent down and picked it up, holding it toward Rue.

Rue smiled. "Yes. It does."

"I consider myself lucky to have caught it," he said.

Justice frowned. Great. He was going to be in the middle of this guy trying to pick up Rue. It wasn't going to work. She had just said that she wanted to play pool with him so—

"You want to dance?"

Rue's eyes went wide. "I do."

"I thought we were going to play—"

But the guy had grabbed hold of Rue and dragged her out to the dance floor. Justice just stood there feeling like a dick as he watched Rue and that unfamiliar cowboy fast dancing to some honky-tonk. She was smiling, though. Laughing, though. So he shouldn't be mad. Because this was what they were here for. So he abandoned the table and went back to his beer, which he drank slowly in the corner as he watched them dance.

"Hey there, cowboy. Did your girl abandon you?"

He looked down at the petite blonde who had just approached him. She only came up to his midchest even with her platform heels on. "She's not my girl," he said. "She's my best friend."

"Really?" She laughed. "A guy as hot as you can be friends with women? That says a lot about your character."

"I don't know about that. Maybe it says something unflattering about the men you normally associate with if they can't be."

She made a knowing sound. "Touché. Do you want to dance?"

There was no reason to say no. So he told her yes and they went out to the dance floor, which brought him closer to Rue. Who changed partners when the song switched, another guy approaching her and stealing her away from the man she had just been dancing with.

He kept his eye on the proceedings. Guy Number One was looking irritated by what had just happened, and Justice didn't like the look of possessiveness on his face. Rue was just out to dance. Nobody owned her, not even him. He was just watching and paying attention. He was more than ready to jump in if need be.

"She's not your girl?"

He looked back at his partner. "No," he said.

"You look very interested in what's happening with her."

"I am. She just got . . . She got dumped at the altar a week ago. So I'm a little bit worried that she's here to make rash decisions."

"Isn't that her prerogative?"

He frowned. "Yes. But I don't have to like it."

"Would you be that possessive and overprotective of a male friend?"

"Listen, if I wanted to debate gender politics I would be in a classroom not a bar. Also, she is the only best friend that I have, so I don't think we can test the theory."

"Fascinating, though."

If this had been another night, and another situation, this was the kind of woman he would've found himself attracted to. She was self-aware, she was funny. They would be able to have a conversation about concepts, not themselves, and have an enjoyable time until they hit the sheets, where they would have an even better time before saying goodbye.

But tonight it left him cold, and he didn't want to get into the *why* of that.

The song ended and Guy Number One stole Rue back.

"What I don't like is the fact that they're acting like she's a bone they need to fight over," he said.

"Fair," she said. "I can go ask her if she'll go to the bathroom with me and pretend we're friends."

"That's nice of you."

"Hey. Us women have to stick together, because you guys are shady as shit."

He couldn't argue with that. It was, in fact, why he was so bothered by the whole situation. Not because he thought her legs were hot.

"Fair enough."

Suddenly, one of the guys took a swing at the other one, and a ripple of unease washed through the dance floor as everybody tried to move away from what was about to become a brawl.

He let go of his dance partner, and looked over at Rue, who was standing there with a shocked and horrified expression on her face. Guy Number One—who had just been hit—jumped up and tackled the other guy, and they were kicking and rolling around on the floor, when one of them hit Rue, causing her to stumble and fall onto her rear.

He was off like a shot.

He ran over to where she was and picked her up, holding her face in his hands. "Are you okay?"

Her eyes were wide as saucers, her lips parted slightly. "Yes," she said.

"Good."

He moved over to where the two jackasses were still brawling, completely unaware that they'd knocked Rue over.

Justice reached down and grabbed them both by their shirt collars, lifting them up. "Now that's enough," he said, holding them both back. He was bigger than both of them, but wrangling two idiots was definitely being powered by adrenaline.

"Stay out of it," one guy said.

"Yeah. This had nothing to do with you."

"Actually, she's mine. So it has everything to do with me."

He saw a look of absolute terror filter through the other man's eyes. *Good.*

"Well, hell," he said. "She left easily enough when you guys were playing pool over there."

"You made a mistake," Justice said. "That's all right. I'm going to let you off with a warning. But you see, you knocked her down to the ground. You could've hurt her. I don't care if you smash your own dumb faces in. But you hurt my lady and we have a problem."

"Sorry, ma'am," the one guy said, practically tripping over himself to make amends to Rue.

Justice growled, "Go on about your business. Stay the hell away from her."

Then he released his hold on the two chuckleheads before moving back toward Rue. He put his arm around her waist and pulled her up to his side.

Rue looked at him, her eyes bright, her cheeks pink.

"Hey," she said, her words slurred. "Now how am I going to have sex if you scare off the . . . the penis?"

He felt like he had been socked in the gut. "You're *not* having sex with either of those guys."

His rage was beyond irritation. It was a bone-deep, possessive rejection that he had never felt for any woman ever. Even still, he recognized it.

It wasn't about what he thought she deserved or what he thought might put her in danger or anything half so gallant.

She was *his*.

And he wanted her.

Hell. Damn. Shit. All of it. All. Of. It.

"You're not the boss of me," she said. "I can have sex with whoever I want. I could have sex with both of them if I felt like it." Both of them stopped and turned to look at her.

"You fucking can't," he growled, taking her by the hand and dragging her through the dance floor.

"You're making a scene!"

"*You're* making a scene," he shot back.

Suddenly, the woman he'd been dancing with appeared. "I have to go to the bathroom," she said to Rue. "Do you want to come with me?"

He shot her a look. "We're fine."

The woman crossed her arms and stuck her chin out. "I'll let her tell me that."

"He's fine," Rue said, shoving his shoulder. "He's just a dick. He's cockblocking me."

"You can hang out with me for the rest of the night if you want," the other woman said. "I guarantee I won't cockblock you."

"It's fine. We just need to have a talk." Then it was Rue's turn to begin to drag him out of the bar.

He let her; Lord knew she wasn't actually propelling him forward on her whiskey-shaky legs. And then they were out of the loud, crazy bar and into the cold night, freezing air heavy with cigarette smoke, individual strains of conversation that much more apparent than they had been inside.

"What's the matter with you?" she asked.

He knew what was the matter with him. He just hated it. And he sure as hell wasn't going to admit it to her.

He was still pissed he'd admitted it to himself.

"Those guys were making jackasses of themselves, and one of them hit you. What did you expect me to do?"

It was part of what had made him mad.

"I'm not a *child*," she said. "I didn't need you to step in the middle of that. They were two grown men, and they both wanted . . ."

"They were treating you like you were some kind of steak, fighting over you like feral dogs."

"Well, that's what I wanted," she said, outrage pouring through her. "It's what I wanted. I wanted to be fought over. I wanted to feel pretty. I wanted to get fucked."

It was like she'd taken a torch and run it clean through his midsection. Hearing that word on Rue's lips . . . like that. It was enough to push him over the edge. She couldn't give that to *them*.

If Rue wanted it hot, sweaty, dirty . . .

Do you hear yourself right now?

This was the problem. She'd been on her way to safety. Safety from all this, safety from him. Her relationship with Asher had kept his mind from going here, and now? If he had to watch her hook up, it was going to drive him over the edge.

"By one of *them*?"

She stumbled back. "It doesn't matter. I just need to do it. I need to get it over with. I didn't drink all those shots of Jack Daniel's so that you could storm around acting like my angry older brother and ruining my buzz."

"That's exactly why I can't let you behave that way. You're drunk."

It was a good excuse, anyway. It was one he could rally behind, unlike the other thoughts and reasons tumbling around inside of him.

"You knew that I planned to get drunk," she shot back.

"I did. But I also didn't expect that you were going to actually . . . I just thought you were going out to loosen up a little bit."

"So this is only fine for you."

"Dammit, Rue. I know what I'm doing. I am an experienced rake, okay? You can't make these kinds of decisions tipsy when they're not decisions you'd make sober."

"That's stupid. You don't get to be in charge of what I want. Of what I think."

"I'm the one guiding you here. It was time for me to step in. It was obvious that you needed an intervention."

"That girl you were with didn't think so. She was worried about the way *you* were treating me. Even she thought you were being a possessive asshole."

"I'm not being possessive. I'm being protective. You don't know this bar. And this isn't you."

That was a lie. A lie. A lie. But he couldn't tell her the truth.

"I've been to this bar a thousand times!"

"Not like this."

"You're ridiculous! You don't get to say who I am. I'm *tired* of who I am. That boring, responsible good girl hasn't gotten me anything. She hasn't gotten me anywhere. I'm basically the same age as you. Where do you get off treating me like I'm a babe in the woods? I've seen the same shit you have. I had the same kind of terrible childhood."

She hadn't, though. She didn't know. Which was his fault and he knew that. But there were things he didn't like sharing, not with anyone.

Though he knew her trust issues were the same as his. Rooted in the heart of the way their parents had treated them, and hell, she was homeless because of it. But he was just . . . he was just so *mad*.

Mad about the idea that his beautiful best friend would go home with someone who absolutely didn't deserve her because some other guy who didn't deserve her had hurt her feelings.

"You deserve better than this," he said.

"All right," she said, tilting her face up. "I deserve better than random bar guys?"

"Yes," he said.

"Okay then. Are you going to have sex with me?"

CHAPTER FOURTEEN

FOR A FULL thirty seconds all he could hear was buzzing in his ears. Because there was no way, there was *no fucking way she had just said that to him.*

Not when he was trying to keep ahold of himself. Not when he was trying to keep his baser self from winning when he had no real experience with that. He wanted this to stay in the darkest, deepest part of himself and now she'd gone and said *that.*

"I . . . I absolutely will not," he said.

"Why not? You have sex with everything that moves."

"Not you," he gritted.

"Because I'm not good enough?"

She was too good.

"No. No. That's not it. That's not why."

She kept talking, and he needed time. He needed time to let what she had just said settle inside of him, but there was no time, because she just kept going, all drunken fury and boldness courtesy of the shots she had taken and her very low alcohol tolerance. And he was . . . he was all fucking done.

"I do not . . . No. Absolutely not."

"Why not?"

"You're drunk," he said.

"You've never had sex with a drunk girl?"

"Not when I was *sober*." He pinched the bridge of his nose. "Let's get one thing straight. If I'm going to make a bad decision, it's going to be when both parties are on equal footing."

"So get drunk then. Take a couple of shots and have me. It doesn't mean anything to you, you know that it doesn't. You go and sleep with all these random women, but you won't do it with me?"

"No. I won't," he said.

"But that doesn't make any sense, unless there's something wrong with me. Unless there's something so repulsive about me that not even notorious manwhore Justice King will have me."

"No," he said. "That's not it."

"But it doesn't mean anything to you."

"But it means something to you." The words were raw, scraping up his throat, and he was pretty sure that meant that they were the right response. The right excuse. The right way to react to the situation that kept on speeding by him at a rate that meant he couldn't quite grab hold of the train car.

Couldn't find his rhythm.

"It means something to you," he repeated. "You don't have sex with random people. You don't have sex just for the hell of it. You're right. I have done that. I do that. But I can't . . . Knowing what it means to you, I can't."

It occurred to him then that they were standing outside of Smokey's bar yelling at each other about sex. That everybody was probably listening, because they knew who they were. Because that was just the kind of small town that it was. He was outraged. Offended. He couldn't quite untangle all the reasons why, because he was still philosophically living in that first moment when she had asked him to do it, and everything after that only had about half of himself involved.

"Let's go."

"No," she said. "I want to go back inside."

She turned to go back that way.

Absolutely not. This was ending. Now.

"Like hell," he said, bending down and gripping her by the legs, before pitching her up over his shoulder.

"Justice King!" she shouted, and hit him on the back with a tiny fist. "You set me down."

He walked her to the truck, opened the door and dumped her inside. There was a man standing next to the front of the bar who lifted the beer bottle in Justice's direction as if he approved. As if he thought that Justice might be taking home a girl that was *that* drunk. That he was heaving her into his truck so he could have his way with her, and he was congratulating Justice not punching him.

"You're a jackass," Justice shouted at him. "I hope your ass gets arrested."

The guy looked startled, then melted back into the bar.

Asshole.

He got into the truck with Rue and turned the engine over.

"If you think I'm disgusting then just say it," she said, her voice watery.

Fucking hell.

"You are gonna go home and you're gonna sleep this off. And you're gonna realize that you are way out of line," he said, speaking through tightly gritted teeth.

As much to her as to himself.

"Why?" she said, her lower lip sticking out.

"First of all, you sound like a little kid having a damned tantrum, Rue, and that isn't you. If you don't understand why I'm not going to take you up on your offer when you're in this kind of state then I don't know what to tell you."

"I'm not in a state. I'm *furious*. I'm *humiliated*. And you can't have it both ways. You can't try to control who I have sex with when you don't want to do it with me."

"Did I say I didn't *want* to do it?" That burned even worse than the last thing he'd said. "I said I wasn't *going to*. I gave you a damned good reason."

Thank God they were close to Four Corners. Just . . . thank God. Because he really couldn't deal with her right now, and he needed to off-load her little ass into her own bed.

She had no response to that. Thank God. She was quiet and that was what he needed. But then she shifted, and spoke in a small voice.

"I don't understand what your problem is."

"I don't understand what *your* problem is," he shot back. "You are being a little pill. And someday, you're going to be grateful that I intervened. Because you don't actually want those guys. You don't want anything they were after. Let me tell you something about bar guys, okay? If they're never going to see you again, they don't give a shit how good the sex is. All right?"

"Is that your way of telling me you actually suck in bed?"

"I *don't* suck in bed," he said. "Because call me old-fashioned, but I don't see the point in getting laid if my partner's not having an even better time than I am. I get off on that, Ruby. Not that it's any of your business. I want the girl to be having fun. If she's not screaming *something*, probably not *my* name because the chances are she doesn't know it, it isn't a good time. But most of those guys? It just isn't how they are. You have to be realistic about that."

She . . . flailed next to him, her fist hitting the door, her rage palpable.

"I don't have to do a damn thing. And you know what, maybe it's not even about having an orgasm. Maybe it's just about feeling beautiful. Do you know how good that felt? To have two guys fighting over me? Do you know many times that's happened in my life? Basically never. Maybe for me that's all I need. Maybe it's just as good."

"Spoken like a woman who hasn't had very many orgasms."

He regretted that the minute it came out of his mouth. This was too dangerous tonight. Too dangerous with where his mind was at.

"I've had enough," she groused.

"Let's get one thing straight, Rue," he said, right as they pulled up to the dirt road that would take them to King's Crest. He chose that moment to slam his brakes on, the tires sliding over the gravel as the truck came to a very abrupt halt. "If I did have sex with you, we wouldn't be done until you'd come at least three times.

At least. Maybe even more, because we've got time to make up for, from the sounds of it. First, I'd touch you until you were shaking. Until you were begging. And then I'd let you have *one*. Just to be nice. Then I'd lick you until you told me to stop, so you were crying and shaking with it. Then I'd do it again. And then . . . Only then would I give you what you really wanted. After that was done, you would never tell me again that you didn't care about having an orgasm. And you'd never tell any other man that either. You'd *expect* it. Because you'd know how it was supposed to feel. You understand me?"

He was breathing hard, and it wasn't the only thing that was hard.

Hell.

He needed to get ahold of himself. He had made a big mistake saying that. But he couldn't find any regret in his whole body. She had pushed him to this point, so she was going to get honesty. He was going to prove to her that she didn't want it. Not really.

The way she was staring, all wide-eyed . . . And then she doubled over and threw up. Somehow, on his cowboy boots.

For. God's. Sake.

She had just pushed him to his limit. Then she vomited on his shoes.

"You are *so drunk*," he said.

"I'm sorry," she said, her voice small and miserable.

"You silly little rabbit," he said.

"I'm sorry," she said, wailing.

He started driving again, taking them to the house. When they got there, he stepped out of the truck and kicked his boots off. Then he went over to her side of the vehicle and opened the door, unbuckling her and hefting her out, holding her like she was a baby, rather than a sack of potatoes like he'd done earlier.

"I'm going to put you to bed."

"I'm not tired," she said, sounding petulant now.

"You're a mess is what you are, Ruby Matthews." Right then, in the middle of all the anger, and all of the discomfort, something softened in his chest. Because Rue had never been a mess. And here she was, just a whole registered disaster.

"I'm going to tuck you in and then I've got to deal with the truck," he said.

"No," she said, wiggling, her body soft, enticing. He was ignoring all that. Because everything that had just happened was too many things, and he was just going to have to process all of it once he had actually dealt with her.

He kept a firm hold on her and got them through the front door, then carried her straight into her bedroom. She looked at the bed, then at him, her eyes wide.

"Oh, you're safe from me. I'm going to drop you here. You probably need to go brush your teeth, though, but I have a truck to clean. I'll see you in the morning."

That was how he left her. He just wished he could turn off his own brain quite that easily.

Because what he *hadn't* meant to do was dirty-talk his best friend quite so well that it was all he could think about. All he could picture. What he hadn't meant to do was get this far into the whole thing. Get this deep.

The problem was, he could imagine it all too well.

And he had never wanted to. He had never let himself get this far. Yes, he had noticed she was beautiful. Yes, he had moments where that had felt a little more intense than he would like. But he had never let himself imagine it. He had never let himself get close.

Thank God she'd thrown up on him. It had been the reminder he needed that he was turning her down for a reason.

By the time he was finished cleaning the truck up at last he was exhausted. And when he went into the house Rue's bedroom light was off. Everything was quiet.

With any luck she wouldn't remember everything that happened tonight.

And he was left with some pretty uncomfortable truths. About himself. About her.

He didn't want to think of it like he was standing at a fork in the road. He wanted to stay on the same road. He didn't want to feel like he was on the verge of change. Like they were. It just wasn't what he wanted. But it was the only image he saw. The only thing that seemed real. That there were decisions to make. Decisions he didn't want to make. No. There were no decisions to make. Tonight she had been drunk. Tonight she had been . . .

She would want to go out again. Eventually, there would be some other guy. And he would have to decide what he thought about that guy. He would have to surrender her to someone all over again . . .

That was a hell of a thought. Like she was his. Except it felt like she was. It damned well did.

Asher had been safe in a way. Because the guy had

let Rue and him have their relationship. He had been there, and more or less he hadn't disrupted them. He'd been in the military. He'd been distant a lot of the time, and Justice had been able to keep his claim on Rue because of that.

Well. What about a new guy? Would he be jealous of Rue and Justice?

And Asher was crap in bed. So what about if she met a new guy who made her feel more? Who made her feel everything?

No. He didn't need to think about that. Not now. He wouldn't. Tonight had been an aberration. And there was no point digging into his feelings about the whole thing. Tomorrow she would be sober, and everything would be clearer.

Tomorrow, he would just act like nothing had happened.

Because he refused to go down this damned fork in the road.

They had been through too much to let something like this change them.

He would be damned.

CHAPTER FIFTEEN

THIS WASN'T THE first time Rue had woken up disoriented in the bedroom at Justice's house. But she felt remarkably worse this time than she had the first time. She was . . . she was hungover. She'd never been hungover in her life. Actually, until last night she'd never been drunk before.

Last night . . .

Pieces of it started to come back to her. Just little bits. She had gone out with Justice. And . . . that man had asked her to dance. And then . . . there had been a fistfight? She sat up. But that was a mistake, because she was dizzy.

But yes. She was remembering it right. There had been a full-on fistfight over her.

She stood slowly, trying to find her balance, and feeling the ground sway beneath her.

But then Justice had taken her out of the bar. She had been so furious at him and then . . .

She clapped her hand over her mouth. No. Absolutely not. There was no way that she had . . .

She had asked Justice to have sex with her.

And he had *turned her down*.

Oh no.

She stumbled into the bathroom and turned the

light on. No. She had not seriously propositioned her best friend and said . . . said that he didn't care about sex, so he should have it with her. Because it didn't mean anything to him. That was . . . It was a horrible thing to say. It was horrible and mean, and she was humiliated. Because not only had she thrown herself at him, but then she had been mean. And she had . . .

She threw up on his boots. She had thrown up on his boots.

Right after he had . . .

She couldn't remember. She couldn't quite remember what had happened right before she threw up on his boots. She stripped her clothes off and turned the shower on, and did not wait for it to warm up before she got in. Then she howled in indignity as the icy water sluiced over her skin. A polar plunge of shame. One that at least jolted her a little bit out of her groggy state.

First I'd touch you . . .

No.

Then I'd lick you until you were begging me to stop.

No, no. No.

Only then would I give you what you really wanted.

He had said all that to her. In that low, husky voice.

She stood there as the water began to warm up, stood there and let it sluice over her body. Until she felt herself beginning to unravel.

Lick her until she begged him to stop . . .

She had propositioned Justice. And she had *pushed* him. She had pushed him to the limit and then he had said that and she had . . .

She had thrown up all over his boots.

She put her head in her hands and let the water roll over her. What the hell had she done?

What the hell?

How could she have done that to him? And to her?

The bigger question is, do you really want him?

Well. He was the most beautiful man she knew. There really was no competition. He was gorgeous, and he was sexy. And . . . she had gone out last night to let go of that, but instead it had thrown her closer to it. Whether or not he would admit it, he was acting jealous. That behavior that he'd exhibited at the bar was more like a possessive lover than a friend. Either that or he really did think that she was emotionally ten years old and needed to be protected from herself at all costs. She was a grown woman. She had a feeling that if it had been one of his brothers out there making a bad decision, he would've let them go off. So did that mean that he wanted her too?

It doesn't mean anything to you . . .

That had been a really shitty thing to say. She didn't know whether she was more embarrassed by propositioning him, or guilty over having said that. It was very hard to say.

Add in that monologue of his, which was the dirtiest thing anyone had ever said to her—and had come right out of her best friend's mouth—and she didn't know what the hell to do with it. Didn't know what the hell to make of it.

"You have to fix it," she said out loud, her words reverberating off the shower walls.

Yes. She did have to fix it.

But she had to figure out what the biggest offense was first. And she really wasn't sure.

She dried herself, and then brushed her teeth twice, before making her way back out to choose some clothes. She opted for something that covered her head to toe. A black sweatshirt that didn't show off any of her body and a pair of matching sweatpants. Maybe he would pity her. Because she looked soft and vulnerable, and like a sphere. A sad little sphere.

She swallowed hard. There was no use putting it off; he was her best friend. She needed to find him and talk to him and try to smooth it over. It was just right now she wasn't sure what direction she needed to smooth it. Or what way would make it . . .

She opened up the door and padded slowly out toward the kitchen.

And there he was, up and out there making her breakfast. Bacon. And very strong coffee.

"I figured you'd be hungover," he said.

She wanted to cry. Because of course he would know that. Because he'd had his share of hangovers and she hadn't. Because what he'd said about guiding her suddenly seemed a lot more relevant, and made her feel a lot more like a jerk than she even had a few minutes ago.

Because she had been so determined to be insulted by his behavior, and not to be realistic about the fact this was new to her, and she was acting out. From a place of vulnerability and rage and hurt feelings. He was in full control of his faculties when he went out, and suddenly that part of the argument last night made sense. He went out; he got drunk on purpose. He met up with other people who were out there drunk on purpose. Who knew what they were doing. Had decided what they wanted beforehand. While she had just been windmilling her way through the bar, through the night, acting out of character because she felt so hard done by.

"I owe you an apology," she said.

"Oh. You *do* remember last night."

He cleared his throat and turned back to the pan of bacon. Dished several strips onto a plate, along with a pile of scrambled eggs. "Why don't you get some grease in you first? Then we can address that."

She walked over to him and took the plate, careful not to let their fingers touch. "I can talk while I eat," she said. She turned and went to the small table in the nook in his kitchen. "I acted like a brat. And I'm sorry."

"That is a good start," he said.

"I was rude, and I was insulting."

"You were both of those things. You also *never* are those things, so it's pretty fair."

"Yeah. Except it isn't. And I really am sorry. I really am . . . I am."

"All right. Good to know."

"Please don't be mad at me," she said. She knew she didn't really have a right to say that to him. A right to ask it of him.

"Why would I be angry at you?" he said.

"Because I was . . . really insensitive," she said.

"So what? I'm fine."

"You . . . You're fine."

"Did you think that I was stewing over the fact that drunk Rue said something about me being a relentless man-whore? We all know that it's true. Why should I be mad about that?"

"It just wasn't the right thing to say," she said.

"Sure. But you were drunk. I knew you didn't mean what you were saying. That's why I sent you to bed."

"Can we just forget about it?"

"Hell yeah. Let's forget it. I'm not mad, and I'm not thinking about it anymore."

"Good."

She was honestly so relieved. Because she had been out of her mind last night, and if she had ruined her relationship with Justice over a moment of total and complete out-of-character insanity, it would've been the worst thing she could think of.

"I think I'm going to watch TV and knit today," she said. "A little break from my adventure."

"Great," he said, sounding relieved. "Dinner tonight, at the main house. Now you've seen just about everybody, so you might as well."

"That is true."

He smiled. "Don't worry. Your hangover will have faded by then, and I'm certainly not going to tell anybody."

"And you're not mad."

"Of course I'm not."

HE WAS FUCKING livid. He deserved some kind of award for pretending that he had been completely fine with everything that morning. He had decided when he'd woken up, unreasonably early, and outrageously irritated, that it would do him no good to hold Rue accountable for what had happened last night. In truth, he was madder at himself. For letting his own temper off leash. For getting to the point where he was . . . saying those things to her, and putting those thoughts in his mind. And it was all still turning around in his head when he got to his brother's place that night for dinner.

It was freezing, and still, Denver was grilling in the back of the house, his barbecue facing the broad, impressive mountains that flanked Four Corners.

He was drinking a cold beer, and Justice decided to join him.

"We can basically call the big barn done," Justice said.

That at least was a decent distraction. They had put in a lot of good work today getting the place in order. He understood why Denver wanted to do it. Why Denver had gone out and made money, and invested that money back into the place. It was important to him to do something with the King family name. Justice wasn't entirely sure he felt the same. But he worked the ranch. In fact, he did that like he did everything else. It was in front of him, so he did it. But he wasn't sure he really thought the family name could be saved. Possibly because he knew just how dark it was.

"Yeah. Pretty proud. You know, there are things that we'll never be able to make up for. There are . . ." Denver's eyes looked haunted. "There was just a lot of shit that Dad did. It's why I took Penny in. It's why . . ."

"Yeah, I know. It's why you do a lot of things."

"Sometimes I think the only way to avoid paying for the sins of your father in perpetuity is to try and atone for them. Other times I think maybe there's just nothing that can be done. I'm not sure if it's even really Dad's sins I'm trying to atone for."

Understanding passed between them. He had never talked to Denver about the things he'd done for their dad, and Denver had never talked to him about his own place in all of it. Neither had Daughtry, though he knew Daughtry carried around some pretty heavy demons considering the guy had gone into law enforcement like it might wash all his sins clean to outright join a different team.

"I don't have any advice for you," Justice said. "Mostly because I haven't figured out how I feel about any of it. I worked the ranch, Denver. Because you love it, mostly. Because it matters. Because this is where we managed to make a little something that looks like a family. But I think it's atonement I'm after."

There was something that made him angry. Viscerally angry for the young boy he'd been. That boy hadn't hurt anybody. That boy had been hurt by the people who were supposed to take care of them. It was noble, he supposed, Denver's quest for atonement. But it just wasn't the same for Justice. He didn't feel guilt. He felt rage. He felt like he had been used. Like his childhood wonder and trust had been crushed before it ever had chance to really take root.

"You know what I resent? That we never really got to have a childhood. Because everything centered around Dad." That was a simplistic way of saying it, but it was close enough to the truth.

"Yeah. I resent more being recruited to . . . to hurt the community."

"I get that. Maybe that's why I don't want to grow up. I want to get something back for that kid. Doing what feels good . . . it's definitely not something I got to indulge in back then."

"How's that going for you?"

"Just perfect," he said.

He thought about last night. Was that his problem? When he got seized with the urge to do something that felt good he couldn't just turn it off? Was that why he'd said those things to Rue? Lord Almighty. He hoped not. He hoped that he was better than that; he just had a suspicion he might not be. Was that his real thing? Was he running around acting like a giant man-child because when he was a kid he had been full of fear and uncertainty? Because he hadn't had fun?

Well. Maybe. But then, there were other things about him that he supposed flew in the face of that. He also liked his house to be in perfect order. And he liked to limit the traffic in it. Except for Rue, of course.

Though . . . the King household certainly had not been in order during his childhood. Which made him wonder how much of that went straight back to control now.

A freak in the sheets, a control freak on his home turf.

It all painted a picture he didn't think he liked very much.

It made him wonder how much of a right he had to be angry at Rue. Most of it, to be fair, was already directed at himself.

But she put up with a hell of a lot when it came to him. A lot of his own issues. A lot of his broken pieces. The last couple of weeks had been devoted to her, and he didn't think he was doing that great of a job.

"These done?" he asked, gesturing to the steaks.

"Yep," said Denver.

"For what it's worth," he said to his brother. "You've done a good job."

"I'm not Daughtry."

"You're handling it the way you see fit."

"Yeah. For whatever that's worth."

"I think it's worth a lot, actually."

"Thanks, little brother. I appreciate it. Even if I am pathologically averse to showing it."

"Well. How the hell would we know how to show any kind of appreciation?"

He took a plate of steaks into the house, and Rue was standing inside the living room, talking to Bix and Arizona. Fia and Landry weren't coming tonight, because they had gone down to the coast for the weekend with Lila. Of course Lila was thrilled to be having a sibling, but Landry and Fia were now working overtime to make sure she didn't feel sidelined. After all, she might be their daughter, but she was still relatively new to living with them. They didn't want her to think she was taking second place to the baby they were going to raise from day one.

It amazed him that his brother thought of things like that, given their own terrible parenting situation.

Maybe that was the perk of being the youngest. Not that Landry hadn't had his share of struggle. But their dad was more or less identified as the hideous narcissist he was by then.

At least, that was how Justice saw it.

"They invited me to the next town hall," Rue said.

"Do you need an invite?"

She shrugged. "I'm not Four Corners people."

"You've been plenty of times."

She wrinkled her nose. "It's a special thing. Everybody's making cookies."

"Am *I* making cookies?" he asked, lifting a brow.

"I'll bring cookies if it's okay for them to have bacon in them," Denver said, walking in.

"Nobody wants your cookies, Denver," Bix said.

"Speak for yourself, Bix," Denver said, grinning. "Many ladies like my cookies."

"Ew," Arizona and Bix said at the same time.

"Not the prevailing opinion," Denver said.

Rue, for her part, was silent. He wondered if the double entendre was less amusing to her given their whole situation last night. He knew that made it less amusing to him.

"I'll happily make your portion of the cookies," she said to Justice.

"Seems sexist," he said.

"Sexist, or is it in the name of good taste?"

"I couldn't say," he responded.

"Somehow I think you can," Bix said.

"All right. That sounds like a deal, given that you

would have been completely invited to go either way. With or without an invitation from these two sprockets."

"I don't want to freeload," she said. "I've been on my extended vacation here at the ranch, and it isn't like I'm doing any farm chores."

"You aren't invited to do farm chores," said Denver. "Because the question becomes whether or not you have the credentials to do farm chores."

"She doesn't," said Justice.

"That's just mean," she said. "I could knit leg warmers for the cows."

"Yeah. I'm sure they would appreciate it."

Bix's eyes suddenly went round. "Please do that. It would be the cutest thing I've ever seen."

"I mean, I could."

"You do not need to knit anything for the cows. You might as well knit a turtleneck for that steak over there."

All three women looked indignant about that, but Denver howled with laughter. And that was when Daughtry came in from his work out on patrol, still dressed in his uniform. They caught him up on the joke as they all sat down to dinner, and this at least felt somewhat normal.

This was why he was here. This thing they had made. It had nothing to do with the King family name. It had to do with getting something back. This family life they never had. He hadn't realized that about himself before, but it was true. He wanted this. Genuinely. And it felt good to be back on even footing. The whole thing with Rue would blow over. It had to. Because she was one of the most important people in his life. She was part of this family that he created.

He wouldn't let anything disrupt that.

She looked up at him from across the table, her blue eyes shiny. And he felt something grab hold of him, low in his gut.

Hell.

CHAPTER SIXTEEN

RUE HAD SPENT the next three days making cookies. It was overkill and she knew it. She also knitted four cow leg warmers just for Bix. She figured if anybody could find a way to get them on the animals it would be her, and she knew that it would make Bix's whole month.

She felt like she was trying to atone. For everything that had been done for her, and for her own somewhat vile behavior that night at the bar. Even though Justice was acting like everything was normal, there was an unbearable tension in her stomach. And at the worst possible moments it was his monologue that played in her mind, over and over again.

First I'd touch you . . .

She squeezed her knees together. This was outrageous. He had been mad at her. Furious, honestly. He'd been pushing her the way that she'd been pushing him.

And yes, for her, dirty talk like that felt like a revelatory experience, but it didn't mean anything to *him*. It was probably a script. He probably said that to all the women all the time.

Do you really think so little of him?

No. She thought so little of herself. He couldn't have actually meant that. She was Rue. She didn't inspire that kind of raw animal magnetism in him.

She was . . . cute if anything. And also, they were Rue and Justice. Their friendship was the most defining relationship in her life. And . . .

She looked across the counter in his kitchen, at all the cookies there. Was that an appropriate apology? *I'm sorry that I made things weird and was dismissive and insulting to you, have a bunch of cookies.*

It made her frown deeply, even to herself.

She had been such a brat. She reflected, for a moment, on the way he had picked her up. Picked her up and carried her to the truck, then picked her up differently to carry her into the house. He had *definitely* pitied her by the time she had gotten around to vomiting on his shoes.

He was so strong. The way he'd held her had made her feel like she didn't weigh anything. She realized that was how she felt about their dynamic usually. The way he carried her, even if it wasn't physical, actually made her feel like she wasn't a burden at all.

It was why he mattered so much.

He really did matter so much.

Her stomach was a tangle of feelings, and she found it best to just focus on the cookies.

She carefully packed all the cookies away for easy transport, then went into her temporary bedroom to try to find an outfit. She opted for some thick tights, a pair of boots and a sweater dress she had knitted a couple of years ago. It had taken forever. She could remember feeling lost in the endless repeats of color work, and she thought of it every time she put it on. Knitting was a great way to spend a ridiculous amount of time on something you could've bought for half the money. But it was a hobby that her grandmother had taught her to love. One that had shaped her life. She had imagined sitting in that house where she had once knitted beside her grandmother on the couch, watching old movies, sitting with Asher and . . .

Except when she imagined it now it wasn't Asher she saw. It was Justice, with *13 Going on 30* playing.

She shook her head. Violently.

She emerged from the bedroom right when Justice arrived.

"You're bringing all these?" he asked, gesturing to the trays of covered cookies.

"Yes. It's been my sole focus the last couple of days."

"You're definitely making me look good."

"I try."

They had worked so hard to pretend that everything was normal. They almost managed it sometimes. But it felt different, and she was angry with herself about that. She didn't want to acknowledge that.

She didn't want to let them know that she still felt wrong.

"Well, let's get it all packed up. Denver is going to be asking for more funds today, so that should be fun. But he's also got some more business opportunities up his sleeve. A couple more buildings he wants to renovate."

"Why are there so many buildings on King's Crest?"

"Oh, because our great-great-grandfather was involved in illegal gambling. Among other things. So I believe some of them were brothels, and rooms where people could go get busy. There was a lot of gold rush activity out here in the day, so there were temporary swells of people that would come out to mine. He was good at taking advantage."

"No way. So you guys are outlaws from way back."

"Yep. Kind of cool, though. I mean, the facilities, not the rest of it. Though, I think giving minors a good time is maybe different still than being a loan shark."

"Yeah. Definitely. Is your dad just off doing the same things now that he used to do here?"

"I don't know. We're all totally no contact with him. There's no point trying with him, because he sucks you in if you aren't careful. If he was cruel, outright and obviously cruel, it would be easier. But he's charming. He can be, anyway."

"Is that why you never really let me come around your family?"

A fierce light entered his eyes. "Yeah. I never wanted you to be anywhere near him."

She let that settle between them. That little thing she hadn't known mingled with their shared history. She was beginning to realize there were pieces of himself that Justice didn't share with her. But there was also such a breadth of shared experiences there. She wondered if it mattered.

If they needed to know every little thing about each other.

She wanted to. She just didn't think she needed to.

"Well, thanks for including me."

"Of course," he said. And she felt that carefulness again. Like they were dancing around what had happened the other day. Trying to pretend that it didn't matter. That it had been written off as something silly she'd said when she was drunk. But the fact of the matter was she had introduced the idea of sex between the two of them.

You couldn't unhammer a nail. That was the thing. She had decisively hammered that thing.

Which was a little bit of an unfortunate metaphor when she thought too hard about it.

Lord.

They started heading toward Sullivan's Point, to the big barn where they had their town hall meetings.

"Do you think you'll start having the meetings at King's Crest now that you have the big event space done?"

He shrugged. "It would be an interesting thing to float, and now that our families are linked by marriage, we may not get the resistance from the Sullivans we might have otherwise. But I have a feeling the McClouds and the Garretts won't necessarily want to have meetings on enemy territory."

"You're not enemies. You're all part of the same collective."

"Sure. But you know we're different. We always have been. Just more separate. But you know, that's part of the whole thing with my dad too. He could only maintain his facade to a certain point, so a little bit of distance was a necessity. Anyway, it's not like the other heads of household were much better back then. I guess we'll figure out how to rally around each other, but never really how to integrate with everybody else."

"Landry is pretty firmly integrated at this point."

He chuckled. "True."

"Anyway. You guys took care of me. You took care of your own, really."

"I guess that was all we could manage," he said.

He was so weird about compliments. He was, in general, a cocky guy who seemed eternally confident in himself but he didn't like anything too deep or serious. And he never wanted anyone talking about him being good, heaven forfend. She didn't get it.

"It's more than most people. I mean, family, sure. But you took responsibility for Penny, and for me. When Bix showed up on the property, Daughtry immediately took care of her. I guess my point is you've all done better than your dad."

"Thanks."

"And I really shouldn't have said what I did to you the other day."

"Yeah, we don't need to bring that up."

"It's sitting there between us. Whether I say something or not."

He looked at her and lifted a brow. "I haven't thought about it."

"You're a liar."

"Well, I like that. You tell me I'm better than my dad and then you call me a liar."

"You're being a liar about *this*."

If he wasn't lying then she felt really stupid.

"Maybe so. But what's the point in telling the truth?"

Right at that moment they pulled up to the barn. Her jaw went slack. She had been to many town hall meetings at Four Corners Ranch, the big gathering where all of the ranch hands and the four families got together to discuss the moves they were making, the state of the collective and where things might need to improve and where things were going well.

They hadn't had meetings like that back when she'd been a kid because the collective hadn't functioned the way that it did now.

But still, over the past few years she had gone to quite a few, and she had never seen the place decked out like this. There were lights strung everywhere, the trees out front, including a glorious weeping willow, all lit up like they had been at Christmas. The bonfire was already going, and the tables were laden with food, and candles.

There was hot cider, and everyone was milling around, talking and laughing.

The meeting commenced quickly, with Denver putting forward his pitch, to be voted on at the March meeting. After that, they dispensed with any business, and decided to move on with celebrating.

For a minute, she forgot about her problems. For a minute, she just felt happy. Because here she was, in the middle of her found family, at this place that felt like home, with hot cider and cookies, and it really did feel like everything was going to be all right. Nobody treated her like she was sad or a pariah. Granted, a lot of people at the ranch may not know what happened, but it helped soothe a lot of her fears. And it was different than going out that night at the bar, because she wasn't trying to prove anything. She was just herself.

The makeshift band, which was made up of different rotating ranch hands, began to play music out by the bonfire, jingle bells adding a festive flare to the sound.

Couples began to make their way to the dance space in front of the fire, spinning and twirling and laughing.

She watched, wistful.

She and Asher had never gone dancing. It wasn't something he was into. That was something she had enjoyed when she was at Smokey's. The dancing. At least until it had erupted into a fight.

"Come on," Justice said, his tone long-suffering.

"Come on what?"

"Dance with me," he said. "It's clear that you want to."

"Really?"

"Rue," he said. "I'm your oldest friend. Who else are you going to dance with?" She looked at him, his outstretched hand, his blue eyes sparkling.

And what she couldn't figure out was if this was an offer from an old friend, or an invitation to the kind of temptation she was trying desperately to pretend wasn't there.

She took in a sharp breath, and took his hand, because at this point hesitating would only make it weirder.

They touched casually. This wasn't extraordinary. Except it sure felt that way. The fire was warm, and everyone around it was laughing. Spinning and dancing. There were children out there. It wasn't the kind of sexually charged dancing that happened at Smokey's Tavern. Groups of women danced together, and kids spun in circles alone. A lot of the dancing couples weren't couples at all, and there was no reason for her to feel scalded. Except that she did. Except that when Justice spun her around and then brought her back to him, his arm strong around her waist, she couldn't keep her feelings neutral.

First I'd touch you . . .

There had been so much resistance, so much panic inside of her since these moments between them had first started. And for some reason, right there by the fire, she let go. As he spun her away again, it was like she stopped plugging the hole in the dam. She just let it all wash through her. Justice King was a man. And she was a woman. It was like letting out a breath she had been holding.

What would it be like to kiss him? What would it be like to feel those strong hands over every inch of her body?

He was her friend. But he was a man. He was her friend, and they had so much shared history. But also so many things she didn't know. Like how he kissed. How he looked naked.

How his hands would feel on her bare skin. What it would be like to be beneath that warm, muscular weight. So she let herself think about that. All of it, and when she spun back into his arms, she couldn't breathe.

When her eyes met his a spark flared there. Like he knew. Like he heard her thoughts. The music slowed, and some of the people on the dance floor cleared out. But Justice brought her close, his hand low on her back. She closed her eyes for a moment, and he brought her a bit closer, her breasts brushing his chest.

It was like everything made sense. For the first time. Maybe the only time. The reason things felt weird and tense was that she was denying the truth of it.

The box had already been opened. And the nail

had already been hammered. Somewhere. She wasn't rightly sure quite when. Maybe when she had seen him in his suit. Or when she had been in her wedding dress, and they'd linked arms, and she'd seen the two of them standing there in the mirror. This acknowledgment that there was something else between them.

She'd suppressed it and suppressed it. Had pushed it down, down, down. And it was only now, with him holding her, like he wasn't trying to pretend, that things felt good.

"Justice," she whispered, his name barely audible with all the noise surrounding them.

He shook his head, just a fraction. She didn't know why. Didn't quite know what he was saying no to. But the song ended and he released her. But he didn't rush her away like she had thought he might. Instead he stayed and talked to everybody. Everybody. He never did that. He stayed and helped put everything away, and so did she. They stayed until everyone else was gone. All the chairs in the barn put away.

It was completely silent. He was on one side of the barn, and she was on the other. Then he started to walk toward her, every step purposeful.

"I'm sorry," she said.

"For what?"

"I'm sorry that I said it wouldn't mean anything to you. It was the wrong thing to say. It's us. Of course it would mean something. That's the problem, isn't it? What I said was dumb. And it devalued us. Our friendship."

"It's the kind of wild thing people say when they

want to make excuses. So they can give themselves permission to do something they know is wrong," he said. His eyes were hot on hers.

"Yeah," she said, nodding. "That's exactly right." He kept on walking toward her, each step punctuated by a breath. By her heartbeat. What were they doing? She didn't know the answer, but there was no question they were both doing it. They had stayed this late. They had danced. They were . . . They weren't pretending that it wasn't happening.

Then, he did something he'd never done before. He turned to her and reached out, cupped her cheek, his hands rough on her skin. He smoothed his thumb over her lips, down to her chin and up her jawline.

She was utterly captivated.

This was how he did it.

How he got women to take their clothes off with reckless abandon and give themselves to him for a night. Who could blame them?

She'd known this man forever and it still made her want to give him everything. Anything. Whatever he asked for.

His movements were slow and deliberate, unmistakable.

This was not friendship. This was a seduction.

She wanted to say something. Anything. Maybe his name. But she didn't have words. She didn't have anything but feelings. Far too big to be contained. Too big to be turned into language. She knew a moment of terror, her stomach clenching fiercely. This was the last moment to turn away.

You're lying to yourself if you think this is the turning point.

That voice, that insistent, overly honest voice, was right. She didn't know where the turning point had been, but it wasn't here. Not kissing him now wasn't going to set them back to where they'd been before. It was just going to draw out what now felt inevitable. What felt essential. So she didn't move away.

She didn't know what she expected. A claiming, maybe. Or something questioning. Seeking.

She didn't get either one.

Instead, with certainty, with confidence, he closed the distance between them, his mouth soft against hers.

If he hadn't wrapped his arm around her waist then, she would've collapsed. Because her knees gave out. Entirely. And that was when the kiss became firm. That was when it became an exploration. He parted her lips beneath his and slipped his tongue inside, the friction of it sliding against her own so delicious she could hardly stand it.

It was all so deliberate, all so controlled, and then suddenly, it got away from them both. Suddenly, she wrapped her arms around his neck, and both of his arms went around her waist as the kiss became all-consuming. As it spread between them like a wildfire. At no point was she unaware of whose mouth she was devouring. At no point was she unaware whose hard body she was being held up against.

Justice.

Justice King was giving her the best kiss of her life.

It all made sense.

Because he was the best of everything. So why wouldn't he be the best of this too?

Someone was saying yes. Over and over again, and it took her a moment to realize it was her, whenever she could come up for air. Whenever their mouths weren't fused. They were breathing hard, like they had just run a race.

Like they were on the verge of collapse.

Her heart was beating so hard she was dizzy with it, the instant, throbbing need between her legs like the works of fiction, and not of any sort of arousal she'd experienced in reality.

She clung to his shoulders, and she felt herself being propelled backward, and then suddenly, stopped.

"Dammit," he said, moving away from her, the exhalation that happened in the moment leaving her weak, barely able to stand.

"Can we just not . . . ?" Her eyes filled with tears. She just didn't want him to pull away and act like it hadn't happened.

"We need to talk," he said. "I didn't mean . . . I didn't mean for that to happen."

"Well, what did you mean to happen?"

"I meant to kiss you. I just didn't mean for it to get that out of control. Five more minutes and . . . I'd have had you against the wall."

The admission was raw, made her throat go dry. Made her body liquid.

"And that would've been bad?"

"Yes," he said. "For the same reason you just said. Between us it's never going to be nothing."

"I know."

"Let's . . . let's have a conversation about it."

That was how she found herself back in the truck, driving toward his house.

Deeply uncertain as to whether or not a conversation was what she wanted. But one thing was certain. They wouldn't be able to go back.

CHAPTER SEVENTEEN

HE WAS SHAKING. He was so hard it hurt. His whole body was on high alert, everything in him pushed to the brink.

He had known that he was lost the moment he had led her out to the campfire. Hell, he had tempted it. He had told himself it was to prove they were all right. That without the bar, without her tight dress, without the alcohol, things would be like they'd been before.

And this was where it had gotten them.

He had known that he was lost when she had looked up at him and whispered his name.

You made a huge mistake.

He had.

He was no stranger to mistakes.

He made mistakes with people.

With feelings.

He followed the wrong instincts.

He'd done it now. It was too late to turn back.

He'd known it was a risk, so had she. Still, they'd lingered. Lingered until they were alone, tempting this inevitability.

Looking at her standing there, illuminated by all the glimmering string lights, there hadn't been another choice. He'd had to kiss her. Because he'd never seen anyone or anything more beautiful than Ruby Matthews in that moment.

She was right. It would never be nothing.

He could also never go back to pretending he didn't see this. To pretending he didn't see *her*. It was impossible.

Equally impossible was taking her against the side of the barn where anybody could walk in. Equally impossible was taking her, *his friend*, who'd confided in him that her experience of sex had been lackluster so far, in a way that would satisfy his base lust, and little else.

"Well . . . that really sucks," she said.

"What?"

"That this was so . . . good."

"Excuse me?" he asked.

"It could've been bad."

He huffed a laugh. "Did you think it would be?"

"I tried not to think about it. Until tonight."

"Bullshit," he snorted, "you thought about it before tonight."

"I did," she said. "But I didn't let myself really imagine it until tonight, you know?"

If only he didn't. "Yeah. I do."

"I haven't been keeping this a secret. It's not like I've been secretly waiting to jump you," she said. "I made a decision. When we were teenagers. That *this* wasn't you and me, not when I needed us to be *us*."

He nodded slowly, looking straight ahead. "So did I, Rue."

She looked away, her cheeks turning pink. "We chose the same path."

"Yeah. We did. And it *was* a choice. Because with hormones and everything. I never was as close to another girl as I was you. We could've been the Fia Sullivan and Landry King of our grade."

"And no thank you," she said.

"A big *no fucking thank you*. I didn't want the drama."

"Me either."

It wasn't that simple. He and Rue had never been drama. But they had been sure. Certain. They had been and he hadn't wanted to do anything to disrupt that. They trusted each other. And introducing anything else into the mix had seemed like a bad bet. Especially then. Especially when they'd been young.

"I wasn't ready for sex," she said. "Back then."

"I probably wasn't either. But I ran out and had it so that . . . I didn't want my hormones fucking with you and me, okay? The minute I started looking at you differently I did something about it." The words sat uneasy inside him, like they were a lie. But they couldn't be.

"What?"

"I just thought it was the better choice."

"You had sex with somebody because you wanted *me*?"

"It's not that simple. I had sex with somebody else because I could feel myself beginning to be attracted to you. I wanted to firmly remind myself which camp you were in. Our friendship survived so much already. I didn't want it to collapse because you were beginning to become a woman and I was becoming a man, and that was changing things. It used to be comfortable for us to sit together in the barn, with our heads together.

And then it wasn't. It used to be comfortable for us to hold each other when it was cold, and then it wasn't. You know what changed."

"I got boobs?"

"Yeah, that's what I would've said when I was fifteen, but we know now it's a little more complicated than that. Our bodies started to recognize how we could fit together. We *both* decided not to take that path, so don't be wounded about it."

"I can be wounded about it if I want," she said, sounding angry.

"You chose something different too. You chose Asher."

"Yeah. I did." She was silent for a moment. "I really don't want to mess us up," she said. "But I realized earlier tonight that the ship kind of already sailed."

"Yeah, it did."

"Because this is the thing, isn't it? Acknowledging that it exists. That we . . . that we have chemistry."

"I've always been honest with you," he said. "And I didn't want to stop . . . being honest with you now but it would have been easier. You know I have always admired the way that you did the right thing. The way that you've always been so measured and sweet. Why the hell couldn't you stay that way?"

"It is me, isn't it? I jostled myself out of the position we were both used to me being in. I wanted something different. It turned everything on its head."

"It did that."

"When you think about it," she said, "it actually makes sense. Because we've been a lot of things to each other. And we tried to be rational and reasonable at the beginning of all this."

"The beginning of what? We just established that this actually started a long time ago," he said, looking out his windshield at where the headlights fell on the road. Where they bled up the sides of the pine trees.

"Right. But we put it in its place. Now it's bubbling up because of what happened with Asher. And you've always been there for me, Justice, and I think it makes sense."

She let out a slow breath, and continued. "Fia said something to me at our girls' night. She said I probably needed to be with someone I trusted. In order to get out of my own head. I realize I never actually trusted Asher to the degree that I thought I did. I wanted Asher to be my husband. I was desperate to shoehorn him into a husband-shaped mold, because there was something easy about him. There was something easy about the two of us together. But I wasn't in love with him. Of all the issues that I had since the wedding got called off, heartbreak really hasn't been one of them. Disappointment, yes. Profound disappointment. But about the life that I thought I was going to have, not about the man who wasn't going to share it with me. Because he was never the one that I trusted. He was the guy I had to keep control with, even during sex. You . . . I trust you."

"So you think that you want to do this."

"I never canceled my room at that resort. I never got to go on any nice holidays when I was a kid and I really haven't done it as an adult and I thought I deserved it. You should come with me."

"I don't know . . ."

"It's a week. Away from here. It won't be at your house, it won't be at King's Crest. Nobody has to know. I wouldn't want anyone to know."

"Because it embarrasses you?"

She shook her head. "No. Because everybody already has opinions about us, and you know that."

He laughed then, maybe to dispel some of the tension that was gathering in his chest, or maybe because it was funny. "You don't want to admit that they were right. That we couldn't not have sex."

"That's half of it. Probably actually a full half."

"For me too," he said, because hell, why lie?

"The other part is I just don't want anyone else to make comments or have opinions in general. I want for us to be able to figure this out, you and me. Because that's what we do. This is a part of myself that I need help with. And I . . ."

"You have to want me," he said. "It can't just be about wanting to feel attractive. It can't just be about you thinking I know what I'm doing. You said it earlier. It's never going to be nothing, because it's us."

Few things scared him. At least at this point. A little PTSD here and there, sure, but he was a man who had lived a lot and done a lot of things. Certainly when it came to sex it didn't feel like there were a lot of novelties left in the world. But she was his friend, and much more than a novelty. She was the most important person in his life. And she was trusting him with her body.

More than that, it was like someone had delivered a fantasy so forbidden, so secret that he had never even let himself acknowledge the desire existed inside of him.

Now that he had the idea introduced to him he didn't want anything else. Didn't want anyone else.

No woman had ever been forbidden to him. No woman except for Ruby.

That was making him feel a lot of things. Most of them illicit. But he needed to hear her say it. He needed this to be more than just her looking to feel good about herself. He didn't know why the hell he needed that. He had plenty of sex he didn't interrogate. But she was different. He knew her. He cared about her. And that would always make her singular.

"I do want you," she said. "I've been trying . . . I've been trying not to. But it isn't working. There's a reason that when I got drunk I flung myself right at you. Because that was when I forgot. I forgot why I wasn't supposed to say that to you. I forgot why it was a bad idea. And that's just part of the whole thing. I want you to show me. I want you to show me what it can be like when it's good. Because I know that with us it would be."

"You expect me to go inside," he said, pulling up to the house and killing the engine, "and go to bed having just had this conversation with you?"

He could see her pulse throbbing at the base of her neck, even in the low light of the truck, and he knew that if he leaned in and kissed it, he would have her naked in seconds.

"I just think we need rules," she said.

"That's one thing you're gonna have to learn," he said. "Sex needs less rules than you've been applying to it."

"Maybe," she said softly. "But . . . we need to be able

to come back here. We need to be able to come back to King's Crest, to come back to our lives. To come back to each other. Because . . . I have lost everything in the last few weeks. I cannot lose you. The lead-up to the wedding was hard, because I would look at you and it felt like I was losing something. But I think I wanted you then. And it just felt like a terrible loss, a terrible waste that I never kissed you. That we had all of these things, but we never had that. You know how angry it made me that there were women out there that knew what you look like naked and I didn't?"

Her words, though they were not carefully practiced seduction speeches, were the damned hottest thing he'd ever heard in his life. There was no doubt about it.

"I was just happy," he said.

"You were?"

"Yes. Because you were safe from me. Because you made it. Yeah, I was really happy that you were gonna make it." He let that sit between them.

"Do you not want this?"

"I want you. If that wasn't damned clear, I don't know what is. And I know it's hard for you to believe that for me this isn't meaningless."

"It's not. I'm sorry."

"It means more. I want you to know that. Because I don't have sex with women I know. I don't want to know their names, I don't want to know where they live, I don't want to know what they want to do with their lives. I don't want to know what issues their daddy gave them, and I don't want to be responsible for easing any of it. I don't want to be involved. But I can't say no to this. To you. That's how much it matters. It is everything that I don't want, with one thing I desperately do. So when I tell you it means something, you best pay attention."

"Okay."

His heart was pounding hard; his hand still hadn't stopped shaking. "You should go into the house."

"You want to come with me?"

"I'm going to drive a loop. I'll be in later."

"You don't trust yourself."

He shook his head. "I do not trust myself. No."

"You would never . . ."

"Oh, I know I wouldn't do anything you didn't want. But the trouble is, I'd have you wanting it in seconds."

She laughed. "That isn't how it works for me."

"Were you not just in the barn with me?" Her cheeks turned pink. "Yeah, I thought so."

She got out of the truck, and he watched as she walked into the house. He sat there in the truck, then he drove back out toward the main road, and just parked his car in the middle of it. He took his phone out, and dialed Denver. "Hey."

"It's late?"

"Yeah, I know."

"You need me to pick you up?"

He laughed. "No. I just wanted to tell you . . . I'm going to go away for a week. In a couple of days. Sorry that is short notice. I hope you guys are covered."

"Yeah. That's fine. Where are you going?"

"Rue still has her honeymoon booked."

"What?"

"Yeah. She doesn't want to go by herself."

"You're going on your best friend's honeymoon with her?"

"Yep."

"Is there something you're not telling me?"

"Yep," he said.

"Well . . . Good luck, I guess."

"Not that kind of luck."

"Don't close yourself off to it," Denver said.

"What would you know about it?"

"I know that if you can have something like that, you ought to."

"Let me guess. I can, but you don't think *you* can," Justice said.

"This isn't about me."

"Right. But you're going to tell me what to do even though you're not actually going to ever do it."

"She's your best friend. You could do worse," Denver said.

"I also don't need it to be anything other than what it is." He needed that to be true. For both of them. "It's just . . . I'm just helping out a friend."

"Oh yeah, helping out your friend and getting laid in the process. Aren't you a regular superhero."

"I didn't ask your opinion. And please don't say anything to anybody else."

Denver snorted. "Yeah. I won't."

"I'm serious. I need this to stay between us."

"Are you going to tell anybody else that you're going away with her? Because you know people are going to wonder."

"I'm okay with them wondering. I don't want them to know."

There was a short pause. "All right. Be safe."

Justice rolled his eyes. "Yeah."

He went back to the house, went straight to his room and locked the door. Then he got into the shower and turned it on cold, bracing his hands against the wall. And he started planning. Because if he was going to do something so damned dangerous, then he was going to do it so good that it made it all worth it. He started thinking about all the things he would do to her. All the ways he would make her scream. And the cold water didn't do a damn thing to keep his hard on at bay.

But he didn't touch himself. Didn't let himself have any satisfaction. Hell no. He wasn't giving himself that. No. He was going to wait. Wait until the honeymoon. And then, he was letting himself off leash.

Just for the honeymoon.

Then it was back to the way things had always been.

The way they had to be.

CHAPTER EIGHTEEN

SHE AVOIDED HIM the next two days, and she felt bad about it. It was also a real feat considering they were staying in the same house.

She couldn't avoid packing anymore, though. Which meant thinking about something she had also been deliberately avoiding.

She went to her lingerie drawer and opened it. She had bought quite a few things for the honeymoon. She didn't know why. It wasn't like they had been super into lingerie in their regular old sex life.

But because of that she hadn't really bought it with him in mind. It had been more about what she thought a honeymoon was supposed to be. So when she looked at all the pieces now it was with a different view.

She remembered the way that Justice had looked at her when she was wearing the bikini. When she was wearing the dress. He liked her in clothing that was a little bit more daring. What would he think of something like this? She held up a black bodysuit that had felt completely out of character when she had added it to her online shopping cart. But she had wanted to be the kind of woman who could wear it. Right in the moment when she picked it. She thought, wouldn't that be great. To just strut out in something that daring.

Designed to showcase all of your most private areas, rather than conceal them.

Thinking about wearing it in front of Justice made her mouth dry. And it made her heart beat faster. Made that space between her thighs feel aching and swollen.

That kiss had been the single most erotic experience of her life. And maybe it should've been weird that it had come from her best friend, but weird had never even crossed her mind when his mouth had touched hers. It had been right.

Like his was the mouth she'd been meant to kiss from the beginning.

She had just been too afraid to do it.

Giving herself permission to think of him that way was revelatory.

It had also been why she had to avoid him, because it was her own rules that she was following by not touching him here in the house, but they were very hard rules to follow. She wondered if he thought it was hard.

They were leaving tomorrow. It couldn't be that risky to send him a text about it.

Would that count as sexting? She'd never even considered such a thing.

She opened up the text box quickly. Are you thinking about tomorrow?

He never texted. He never did. So he wasn't going to . . .

She saw three little dots appear. Then disappear. Then reappear.

I haven't been thinking about anything else.

I had to avoid you because otherwise I doubt I could've kept my hands off of you.

Don't say that.

Why?

Because I'm close enough that I can be back there in two minutes and make us both forget what we're waiting for.

I want to be in the bridal suite. In the bed I was supposed to share with him.

That's naughty, he said.

Is it? Or is it just petty?

I don't care. I think it's hot either way.

Her midsection bloomed with heat. It felt so strange and so freeing to be talking to him like this. To Justice. To just say whatever she wanted.

You're so hot. I can't wait to touch you.

Damn. You're getting me hard.

She sat down on the edge of the bed, her breath coming in short bursts. I'm packing for the trip. I have a lot of lingerie.

I can't wait.

IF THERE WAS one thing Justice King had no prior experience with, it was pleasure deferred. Except perhaps when it came to Rue. But he had never let himself really sit in that. In the last few days, it was all he had done. Let himself turn over every moment that he hadn't allowed himself to examine at the time. Let himself think about when he put his hands on her thighs at her bachelorette party.

Shit. She had been about to marry Asher. She would've married him. And he would never have gotten to taste her.

The things he wanted to do to her . . . It was why he had avoided her last night after she had sent him those texts. They had been so bold for her. At least, bold for the Rue that he knew. Maybe she liked dirty texts. Maybe it was in her wheelhouse. He didn't think so, though.

And now it was finally time to leave. The place was three hours away, and he was hoping that if they showed up they could get an early check-in. Because he . . .

He stopped, standing still right where he was in the middle of the barn out on King's Crest. He was desperate for her.

He was trying to tell himself that it was all right playing by these rules.

Maybe that's what she was doing too. She was right, though. It made sense. They made sense. They had known each other forever. He didn't like that it was all about him doing something for her, when he felt like the reality was he was getting a fantasy in return.

Maybe this is the real thing you can give yourself. The real thing you were denied.

That insidious thought came up out of nowhere and gripped him by the gut.

But maybe if their lives had been different, maybe if he had a different family, something functional, it would have been different. He would've met her. They would have been friends, but maybe they wouldn't have *needed* each other the way that they did when they were kids. Maybe their relationship could've grown into something different organically. Maybe there was a version of himself that didn't get left underground for days. That didn't get lied to, tricked by the people that he trusted most. Maybe that version of him would've wanted a wife. Children. Would have known how to share himself. Share his life.

Maybe if he were different he could have had that.

Just thinking about that made him feel like he'd been stabbed. So maybe that was the gift. Maybe that was what he got. A moment. Like it was his honeymoon.

That was kind of sad. But, he was kind of sad. That was the truth of it. He let out a breath and went toward his truck, heading back to his house. Rue was sitting out front with a little pink suitcase next to her. He had thrown his own black duffel bag in the back. He had a couple sweaters, a couple pairs of jeans, one nicer outfit in case they wanted to go out to dinner at the resort and about five boxes of condoms. He had priorities.

She picked up her little suitcase, and started to walk toward the truck. He put it in Park and got out, moving to her and taking the bag from her. Their fingertips brushed, and his whole body went rock hard.

Her face turned pink.

"I hope you've got all the stuff in here that you promised me," he said.

She looked down, then back up. How weird, to have an interaction with Rue that was uncertain.

It was almost exhilarating.

"I brought some things," she said, holding her hands primly as she lifted herself up in the truck and sat.

"Tell me about it."

"I don't know if that's a good idea," she said.

"We have a long drive ahead. I wouldn't mind something fun to think about."

He rounded to the driver's side and got in, closing the door, leaving them well ensconced in the tight space.

"Did you tell anybody about this?" he asked.

"No!"

"I didn't mean about our plans, I meant that we were going."

She shook her head. "No. I mean, I mentioned to Bix that I would be gone for a while."

"I told Denver, because I needed him to be prepared for the fact I was taking the time off. He guessed."

"He what?"

"He guessed. He knows what we're doing."

"Oh," she said, frowning.

"It's okay. He certainly is not going to expect it to have any long-lasting ramifications. It's not like Denver has any long connections in his life."

"That's sort of sad."

"He'll be glad to know you think so."

"That must make you mad, though. That he guessed."

"Less him than anyone else. Mostly just because he never gave me a hard time about you. Denver is the kind of guy who has his own secrets, so he certainly doesn't pry overly much when it comes to other people's."

"Right."

"Tell me about it," he said.

"It's embarrassing," she said.

"You were talking a big game over text last night."

"I've never done anything like that before," she said.

"It wasn't *that* daring."

She sniffed. "That's mean. It was the most daring thing I've ever done."

"You would've had to send me nudes for it to be real daring."

"No," she said. "I am not sending pictures of my naked body to go flying through the ether to hopefully land on your phone."

"Do pictures often get stuck out there in the air?"

"If any did, they would be pictures of my boobs."

"That feels a little narcissistic." He looked at her sideways, and caught the toothy, menacing smile she was giving him.

"Don't threaten me," he said.

"You're acting like a man who wants to be bitten," she said.

"I'm not opposed to biting." He let that sit for a second, because it brought up some things that they needed to discuss. The kinds of things he'd never had occasion to think about with his best friend before. He cleared his throat. "On that topic, do you have any . . . hard nos."

"What . . . what?"

"Things you *won't* do"

"I . . . I mean, I feel like there are probably some things, but I would have to google them, and they would take me to corners of the internet I don't want to be on."

He gripped the steering wheel a little bit tighter. "There was nothing that you did with him that you didn't like."

"I don't know that I want to talk about him."

"He's the only man you've been with, right?"

"Yes," she said, looking ahead.

"So he's your reference point. Comparison is going to be natural."

"You already sound smug."

"Oh, I am not worried."

"I am. What if it's me? What if I can't . . . ?"

"Go ahead. You don't need to be embarrassed. I'm your best friend. And if I'm going to get naked with you, then I need to know everything. I need to know the things you've held back before. I need to know the things you're afraid would hold you back with me."

"You know my parents were just overwrought. All the time. It was like they loved and hated each other so much they couldn't stand it. They loved sex with each other so much they would shut themselves away in the middle of the day, but somehow at the same time they also loved to have sex with other people. So they could fight? I never understood how they could act like they wanted each other so badly, but then also be with other people. I never understood how they could be such a registered mess all the time with each other. I never wanted to be that way. I wanted my life to be different. But I think I gave myself a complex about passion. Because I could only ever look at it as this two-edged sword. And if you wanted one edge of the sword you had to take the other one. I get that that isn't really true. At least I think I do. But it made me feel like I always wanted to be present during sex. I can never lose myself. I was always halfway in a spreadsheet and I just got used to thinking about other things. It seemed like it was easier to just not worry about my own orgasm because that created pressure between us and I didn't want pressure. I didn't want to be work. And I also didn't know how not to be."

"Sex with a beautiful woman's not work," he said.

"You haven't had sex with me yet."

"I'm aware of that. But believe me, if it takes me an hour to get you to come, it won't be work. If it takes me two hours it won't be work."

"Who has sex for an hour?"

"Well, now I'm going to take that as a challenge."

He could definitely fill an hour exploring her body. He started to drive a little bit faster.

"It's supposed to be a really nice place," she said. "There's a spa and an indoor pool, but all the windows are glass so we could look out at the view. I got us the honeymoon suite."

"Is there early check-in?"

"I don't know if the room will be ready."

"I'm going to need it to be ready."

"It's the middle of the day."

"I'm not opposed to sex in the middle of the day."

"I'm not . . . overly familiar with that as a concept," she said.

"You gotta understand something, Rue. You're playing with me now. And I do things a little different."

CHAPTER NINETEEN

She was completely strung out by the time they got to the lodge. Justice had been so frank and exacting in his conversation. Asking her if she had any boundaries that he couldn't cross, talking about the sex they were going to have in such a casual manner. Well. Maybe it wasn't casual. But he was right; she had been more comfortable playing with him over text. When they were sitting next to each other in a truck it felt risky. Far too risky.

But what was the risk? They were going to have sex. That was the whole thing. It was what they were there to do.

It was a natural evolution of their relationship, honestly. She had taught him how to read. He was going to teach her how to come.

Seemed like a pretty fair trade.

It took her a minute to realize that they had been sitting in the check-in spot in the hotel, under the broad overhang that was just in front of the grand lobby. The windows stretched from floor to ceiling, and the view of the mountains and green pines dusted with snow was glorious.

And she'd been sitting there spacing out thinking about sex.

"I guess I have to check in. Since everything is under my name."

"I'll get the bags," he said.

A man in a suit came up and asked for Justice's keys.

"Valet," he said. "That's fancy."

She was sort of surprised when he surrendered the keys. It was out of character, but she supposed it spoke to the honesty behind the comments he made about urgency. Her hands were sweaty. She went into the lobby and walked up to the wide, highly polished oak front desk. "Hi. I have a reservation under Matthews. Ruby Matthews."

"I see that. Yes. Checking in for a seven-night stay."

"Yes. That's it. Seven nights. Seven of them."

"Honeymoon suite. And the other guest on the reservation is . . ."

"I need to update that actually," she said.

The eyebrows of the woman behind the desk shot upward.

"It's just . . . I . . . The wedding ended up not actually happening. But I'm here. And I have . . . My friend . . . Just add Justice King to the reservation. If it matters."

"It probably doesn't," the woman said.

"I just didn't want the other name on there."

The woman met her eyes for a moment, then she nodded. "Understandable," she said, typing quickly on her computer.

"And I was won—What *he* was wondering . . . is there any way we could check in early?"

"I'm not sure if the room is ready . . ."

At that moment, Justice came in, carrying the two

bags they had brought. He grinned at the woman behind the counter. And then looked at Rue. "Getting checked in okay?"

"I'll see what I can do about the early check-in," the woman said, looking at him, then looking back at Rue.

Rue's heart started to beat a little bit faster. This was actually going to happen.

She felt her face getting hot.

"I didn't see the other guy," the woman whispered, reaching into a drawer and taking out two key cards which she put into a machine that was obviously programming them. "But all I can say about who you brought with you is . . . nice work."

"Yes," Rue said, her breath coming out in a gust. "I think so."

Usually, in these situations she felt slightly awkward. All these years, people had been assuming that Justice was her man. He hadn't been. He had been just a friend. But now . . . Well. Things were a bit more complicated. And the woman's assumptions weren't wrong. They wanted an early check-in so . . .

She was starting to get nervous. Very nervous.

"You'll be room 605. Sixth floor, and you're going to take that third elevator bank and go up. Then all the way down at the end of the hall. You have a view that overlooks the mountains, and the most spacious accommodations available."

"Thank you," she said.

The whole place was done up in a sort of rustic fanciness, glossy wooden beams and antlers adorning everything. There were also a lot of touches of new technology. A beautiful haven out in the middle of nowhere.

She was focusing on those details because if not she might actually hyperventilate and pass out. And that wasn't what she was trying to do. Justice for his part was a silent, strong figure behind her, and her throat was dry, her body achy.

She might've thought she had a fever, or was catching some sort of illness if the malady hadn't come on as soon as they approached the room.

He had bags, so she was the one that took the card out and unlocked the door, pushing it open so that they could let themselves in.

The room was . . . It was gorgeous. The back wall was entirely glass, nearly invisible sliding doors leading out to an expansive balcony that overlooked the mountains.

They were covered in snow, a winter wonderland right outside.

Not a person or residence anywhere in the view. A lovely feature, because that meant windows that size didn't compromise privacy.

She pushed open the bathroom door, and saw that it was nearly as big as the bedroom. There was a massive tub, freestanding, like a giant white bowl positioned next to a window, and then there was a big glass shower with two showerheads positioned opposite each other. Definitely for a couple to enjoy it together.

She swallowed hard, then looked back at the room. At the bed, which she had been trying to ignore.

It was huge. The bedding all white and plush. This

room wasn't quite so rustic as the rest of the hotel. It had more of a sleek, modern design to it, but still seemed warm and soft. But most importantly, the bed had a sort of minimalistic quality that seemed to announce that its real and only true function was for two people to be on it, exploring each other.

Not sleeping.

There was nothing in the way of extra pillows or other accoutrements that might get in the way. No. It was all about having an expansive playing field.

"I can hear you thinking," he said.

She turned to face him, and she must've looked like a terrified squirrel. Because he looked at her like he might look at a poor animal that needed quieting. But then he moved to her, and cupped her chin. He didn't usually touch her like that. Intimate. Knowing. Firm. "We don't have to do this. If it's not working for you, or it's not something you actually want, I'm okay with that. Rue, you are the most important person in my life. Nothing is ever going to change that."

She wanted to thank him for that, but the words got jumbled up in her throat. And mostly, she didn't want to think that meant she didn't want this. She really wanted it. Really. She was terrified that he was looking for an excuse. An out.

But she was also just plain terrified.

Not because she didn't want it, but because she did, and because of how much.

"I want this," she said. "But I'm nervous."

"Then let me take the lead. If we were knitting, you would have to be in charge, wouldn't you?"

"Yes."

"I *have* knitted before, you've shown me. But what I've come up with is just a lumpy mess. I just don't have the experience. But you do. You're a good teacher. So I could trust that whatever you told me would be the right thing. And that you wouldn't be upset at me if it was imperfect, right?"

"Right," she said.

"So think of this as knitting class. But it's sex. And I'm the one that knows what they're doing."

She shivered, and looked around. Needing a barrier between them. Because this. "It's bright in here."

"Good," he said, his voice rough, bringing her focus back to him. "I want to see you. I want to see every inch of you. Ruby Matthews, I have known you for most of my life. But I don't know the secret of what you look like under your clothes. I'm a curious guy. I like knowing that the mystery is going to be solved. What do you think?"

"Yes," she said, the word coming out breathless.

"Meaning you want to see me too?"

"Yes," she said. "I . . . I want to see you."

"Good. So I'm going to take the lead. And if there's ever something that you don't like, you just tell me to stop. I will. But trust me. Trust me that I know what's going to make you feel good, okay?"

She nodded. He wrapped his arm around her waist then, bringing her flush against his body. Then he dipped his head and pressed his mouth to hers, and it was like those dark corners inside her all lit up. And all the fear just melted away. This was like the moment in the barn. When their lips had met for the first time.

So slick and hot and perfect. So glorious.

His large hand moved to her lower back, and a small moan escaped her lips. She didn't even know herself in the moment. Maybe that was a good thing. She didn't know herself, but she knew him. He was solid, his hands strong. He was Justice King. And there could never be any doubt about that.

He paused their kiss for a moment, and looked at her, and she knew a solid forty-five seconds of pure panic.

Once they did this they couldn't go back. She would never be able to not know what Justice looked like naked. She would never be able to not know what it felt like to have him surge inside of her. She had convinced herself that they had passed the point of no return a long time ago. But this was *really* it. These were the things that would never be a mystery again.

These were the things that would take their friendship, this thing that they'd cultivated and protected for years, and put it in a different space altogether.

Then he kissed her again, and there was no more room for panic, because need filled her, drove her.

Made her into something she didn't even recognize.

The way his hands moved over her body, creating a web of tension inside of her, that each new touch vibrated. So that when he touched her lower back she felt it between her legs, so that when he slid his fingertips up her spine she felt it in her breasts, which had grown heavy and sensitized.

Her lips felt swollen, hot to the touch. He just kept on kissing her. On and on. He moved his hands through her hair, and she let her head fall backward as he kissed down her neck.

Then he moved back, and stripped his shirt up over his head.

Her throat went dry and the place between her legs went liquid. His chest was broad and muscular, his stomach muscles shifting with each hard breath. She had seen him shirtless countless times. But that was different. It was different, because even though she had been able to tell that he was aesthetically beautiful, she had been intentionally not looking at him as a sexual object.

Now she was.

She wanted to touch him. And she realized with a jolt that she could.

She took a step forward, and reached her hand out, putting it flat on his chest. He closed his eyes, a masculine grunt sounding hard at the base of his throat.

"Justice," she said, watching as her fingertips moved over his muscles. Watching herself touch him.

It didn't feel wrong. It felt right. It felt like it was a long time coming. It felt like everything. She moved her fingertips over his pecs, his abs, down to his belt buckle. And a slow, wicked grin crossed his face. "Getting impatient?"

"Is it impatient when you've waited more than twenty years for somebody?"

She realized how true it was once the words were there, sitting between them.

It was more serious than she meant to be, but she saw a spark of agreement in his blue gaze.

He felt the same way. He understood.

They were adults now. So it was safer. If they had

done this when they were teenagers they might've broken everything.

Just trying to imagine taking these feelings, these feelings that felt too big for the adult woman she was, and transferring them to sixteen-year-old Rue . . . ? *She* would've combusted.

Thirty-two-year-old Rue was about to combust.

Teen her would've been terrified of this. It would've been the sure and certain sign that she was going to turn into her parents and that she needed to run far away from Justice King. No. There was no way they could've had this before. There was no way she could've had it before. It was only now. Only now that she could begin to grab hold of this.

"You're beautiful," she said. And maybe it was a foolish thing to say, but it was the only thing she could think to say.

He was just the most gorgeous man she'd ever seen in her life. And she was awestruck by his beauty. But more than that, by the reckless, wild feeling that was beginning to stir up in her stomach. Like a herd of mustangs galloping across the high desert. A part of herself that she had never tapped into. A part of herself she had always been afraid of.

Then he did it. He reached down and started to undo his belt slowly. Kicked his boots off as he got rid of the belt, got rid of his socks, unsnapped his jeans and unzipped them slowly.

"Justice," she said.

A plea, she thought maybe. Definitely not a warning. Her hands were shaking as if she was the one undressing him as he pushed the denim down. First, she looked at his thighs. The muscles there. And it was only after that she let her eyes go to that hard masculine part of him that hung there.

She was not being dramatic to say that it felt as if the wind had been punched straight out of her stomach.

He was like art. If a person asked an artist to create the perfect ode to masculine beauty, the result would've been Justice King. All heavy muscles and thick masculinity.

She shouldn't have been surprised to learn that her best friend was well endowed and then some, especially not when the rumors about him and his sexual prowess verged on legendary. Still, she hadn't known what to expect, and her expectations were blown somewhat all to hell.

"Well," she said.

He moved to her then, and she could feel the shift. He'd been patient.

He was letting her see exactly what she was getting into, letting her see him. Letting her warm up. But when he wrapped his arm around her, and gripped the bottom of her T-shirt, pulling it up over her head as he growled, that was when she knew his patience was at an end.

He kissed down her neck as he reached behind her and undid her bra with one practiced hand. His hands cupped over her bare skin, and the feel of his rough palms against her skin was such a revelation she could scarcely breathe.

She had been touched like this before. But it was like it had been an entirely different activity.

It was like she couldn't think. Because Justice's

hands were everywhere. Because he pinched her nipples between his thumb and forefinger and made her cry out, spots blooming behind her eyes.

He kissed down her collarbone, to her breast, sucking one nipple deep in his mouth. And all the while he made that magic he was dispensing with the rest of her clothes. She was dimly aware that she made all the right movements to help him. But only just. She only became highly aware of the fact that all her clothes were gone when he cupped her ass with his hand and drew her firmly against his body, completely naked, every inch of her bare skin pressed against every inch of his.

The need that was growing between her thighs was so intense it was foreign. It was an ache that she was entirely unfamiliar with. She was slick with need, and he hadn't even touched her there. She would've said that her breasts weren't all that sensitive, but Justice was making a mockery of that. Teasing her, toying with her.

First I'd touch you.

He claimed her mouth, plunging his tongue deep, and right at the same time he moved his hand between her legs. His finger slipped through her slick folds, stroking that sensitive bundle of nerves there, before he pushed it deep, sliding it in and out of her until her knees began to shake.

"Justice," she breathed.

There was no way. There was no way that she was this close this fast. It was one thing to think that he might be more practiced. More skilled. But this was something else. Something entirely new. The way that he was bringing up pleasure in her body so far surpassed anything she'd ever felt before. This knife's edge felt better than any climax ever had.

Maybe she was making things up. Maybe she was exaggerating it.

But she didn't have any time to think about that, because he was still touching her. Stroking her.

He had two fingers inside of her next, his thumb swirling around that most sensitive part of her. They were still standing in the center of the room, completely naked, the windows open to the mountains. She looked up at him, at his blue eyes, and she saw the view behind him. It reminded her of that moment up on the mountaintop, when she had been sitting on the picnic blanket and he had been there fully clothed.

She had felt something. A pull toward him. Her friend. Justice. Who had his fingers buried inside of her now, who was feeling how wet she was, who was *responsible* for how wet she was.

It was that moment, that image, then patched together with now, that sent her over the edge. She cried out, her knees going weak, and just like he had done the night she was drunk, he scooped her up into his arms. But this time, when he laid her down on the bed, he didn't step away.

"I told you," he said. "I told you just how I was going to do it. And I meant it.

He moved to the edge of the bed, and then, he put his hands on her knees and forced her legs apart.

She hadn't been embarrassed to be naked in front of him, not until that moment. Because this was . . . this was an intimacy that felt a little bit too far. She tried to close her legs, and he forced them apart again. "Don't hide yourself for me. It's been too many fucking years, Rue. I want to see you. All of you." He shook his head. "Damn, you're so pretty."

"I'm . . . I'm pretty? There?"

"Hell yeah," he said. "I could come just looking at you. Do you know that?"

She had never particularly thought that a person was pretty right there. But he seemed to think so. So maybe it was true.

She looked away from his eyes, down at his masculine member. Well. He was beautiful there. It made it easier for her to believe him.

But then she couldn't think, because he kissed her ankle, the inside of her knee. Her inner thigh. And then closed his mouth over her center, licking and sucking and kissing her deep.

She swore, her hips coming up off the bed, and he took that opportunity to move one hand beneath her, and pull her ass, lift her up so that she was in even more intense contact with his mouth.

"Justice," she moaned.

"That's right," he said. "Give it to *me*."

She was panting, too turned on to be horrified.

"I've never . . . He never . . ."

"Fuck that guy," he growled against her skin as he kept on licking her, pushing two fingers inside of her as he did.

And that was when she found her next orgasm, blinding and glorious, squeezing his fingers tight as she found her release.

"Please," she said. "I can't breathe." But he didn't stop.

Justice King was a man of his word. And the degree to which this was going exactly the way he had told her it would was both terrifying and exhilarating.

The idea that this man could know her body so well that he had been able to map out a path to her pleasure before he had ever seen her naked was like a miracle.

It probably spoke to the sheer volume of women he had sex with before, but she was choosing not to think of it that way. Because this was them. He had told her that it could never mean *nothing*, so she was going to hang on to that truth. It could never be nothing.

It also couldn't be everything. It was just a fact. She could never allow it to be everything.

But that thought evaporated in the recesses of her mind as he continued the pleasurable assault on her system, licking, stroking, driving her higher and higher.

"Justice," she said his name again.

"Come for me," he growled.

"I don't know if I can," she said.

This was already practically six months of orgasms thrown at her in one day.

"You will," he said, stroking her firmer, faster, his tongue working overtime.

"Ruby," he said, her name a plea on his lips, and that was what did it. That was what pushed her over the edge.

Her hips arched up off the bed, and she felt herself dissolve yet one more time.

She was gasping for breath, when he moved up to

kiss her mouth, give her a taste of her own pleasure on his lips.

Her face got hot, some of her thoughts returning to her now that her pleasure had a chance to subside.

Then he moved over to his duffel bag, and took out a box of condoms.

She felt embarrassed that she hadn't thought of that.

But thinking was an unavailable skill right now. She couldn't say that had ever been the case before. Typically, she was all thought, with a determined lack of access to her feelings. She was okay with having feelings; she just wanted to stay in control of them. And there was no control. Not here. Not with him.

There was nothing but this driving, relentless need. He was beautiful. Just so beautiful.

And he was *hers*.

It was the sudden swamp of possessiveness that surprised her. That grabbed hold of her like a feral thing she had never known was part of her.

He was hers.

Her best friend.

And he had just done things to her that no man had ever done before. That made her feel unequal in a way, because what could she do? When a man was so experienced, what could she give him that hadn't already been given? Maybe that was the wrong way to think.

"I want to hear you beg," he said.

He looked at her then, and there was a dangerous light in his eyes. An edge to him that she had never known before. It was like magic. Like one of the doors that had always been locked to her inside of Justice was finally open.

Not just her safe space. Not just her friend. But this man who had a sort of sensual edge to him that had never been hers to harness. And now there it was.

"You want me to . . ."

"Tell me what you want," he said. "Beg for what you want."

She wanted him. Inside of her. She ached for it. Was desperate with the need for it.

But it was . . . embarrassing.

"This is you and me," he said. Like he had read her mind. "There's no reason to be embarrassed about it. There's no reason to be ashamed. Just tell me what you need."

"You," she whispered. "I want you inside of me."

"That's what I want too," he said, opening up the condom box slowly.

Maddeningly slowly.

Then he took out a packet, and tore it open, positioning the latex over the blunt head of his arousal and rolling it down. She had never been so fascinated by the act. Never. But then, she had never found a man's body quite so beautiful.

He moved over her then, kissing her deep, and she could feel the blunt head of him pressing against the entrance to her.

She wanted him. But right then, she nearly panicked. Nearly pushed him away. Because it felt too big. Too significant. Because it felt like it would be too much for her to handle.

This change. The shift in who they were.

But she couldn't deny her need any more than she could deny him. And as he began to sink inside her, inch by agonizing inch, it was like she understood something that was both basic and complex that had always eluded her. Something deep and raw and honest.

This was what sex was. She'd had sex. More times that she could count. But it had never been this.

The feeling of this man deep inside of her surpassed everything.

Their connection was more than just physical. Physically, he was a gloriously attractive human being; physically, he appealed to her in every way. But there was something deeper, something more real. A rawness that burned between them when he pushed his way into her.

When he was buried all the way to the hilt, he looked at her, intense fire burning in his eyes, and she felt undone. His breathing was fractured, and her own need was so intense that she could barely breathe.

Then he began to move. A pained expression on his familiar face, the action between them so new, so intense that it was like they were strangers. But they weren't.

Because it was Justice. Her Justice, and she could never unknow that.

You couldn't unhammer a nail.

She would never be able to go back to the way things had been before. To not knowing this. To not knowing that he fit perfectly inside of her. To not knowing that when he thrust deep, he reached parts of her that no one ever had.

When the pleasure started to build inside of her it was a deeper, richer pleasure than what had come before. It was beyond sanity. Beyond words.

They were both breathing hard. She put her hand on his chest, could feel his heart thundering.

She could feel her own need mounting into something impossible. Building and building until it was like a skyscraper of desire that she didn't think she would ever be able to reach the top of.

But failing to do it might kill her.

She wrapped her legs around his lean hips, and he began to drive deeper, harder. Her name was a prayer on his lips, the desperation there fueling the need inside of her.

Justice.

She rocked her hips up against his and he reached beneath her hips, holding her up against him as he thrust down. Like they couldn't get close enough, like he couldn't go deep enough. Like there would never be enough.

"Rue," he said, against her mouth, and that was when she shattered. Every other time had been waves. Rolling and rolling within her, making her cry out. But this was something else. Like she had been reduced to a million crystal pieces, undone, but more beautiful than she'd been before.

Justice.

She was saying his name over and over again, wouldn't have been able to stop herself if she tried. *Justice.* This man destroyed her. In every single way.

And yet she felt reborn. Remade.

New.

He pressed his forehead to hers, and he kissed her. And that was when she knew it would be okay. That was when she knew that he was as undone as she was. And maybe there was no first that she could give them, but it was something.

It could never be nothing.

He'd said that. She believed him. Because she trusted him.

They held each other, breathing hard.

"I didn't know," she said. "I just didn't know that it could . . . I really didn't know."

"Me neither," he said.

She looked up at him, and she didn't know what to say to that.

She touched his face. "Thank you."

His smile curved, just on one side of his mouth. "You're welcome."

She wasn't sure what he felt about that. She wasn't sure where to go from here.

"I'm going to go run a bath," he said.

His decisiveness, yet again, saved them.

She lay there on her back, staring at the ceiling. She was supposed to be here with Asher.

That made her laugh. Because not a single part of her felt like that was true. Not a single part of her felt like that was actually meant to be.

No.

This, Justice, felt a whole lot more meant to be than anything else could. She didn't know what was going to happen next, but she knew that he was going to take care of her. And that was no small certainty. In her life, the certainty that somebody would take care of her was the biggest thing she could think of.

CHAPTER TWENTY

THE WATER WAS running, and had been for several minutes before Justice came back into the room.

"You good?" he asked.

She realized she was still lying on the bed like a starfish, breathing heavily. Her heart rate still hadn't returned to normal.

"I mean, I think you might've killed me."

"Don't be dead, Rue. I'm not finished with you yet."

"I know. That's what scares me.

He came over to the bed, still completely naked, and every last brain cell went dormant as she took in the sight of all that perfect male flesh.

Then he bent down and scooped her up. "You have to be careful," she said. "I'm going to get used to this." She had meant for it to sound funny and lighthearted, but she was afraid it had sounded a whole lot more loaded. She was afraid that it actually might be.

He carried her easily into the bathroom, where the tub was three-quarters full. And then he set her down slowly into the warmth.

She sighed, suddenly becoming aware of some muscles that were sore. She had been tensing up more than usual. Then Justice got into the tub with her, and it was just so . . . strange and terrifying and sort of wonderful, to be naked in a bathtub looking at him.

"Do you still think orgasms are overrated?" he asked, with no small amount of smug amusement in his voice.

"I . . . I don't even know how you did that."

"*You* did it."

"But I . . ." She scrunched up her face. "It is really silly to be embarrassed after we did all that, isn't it?"

"Nothing is silly," he said. "You can feel however you want to feel."

"Well, I don't want to feel embarrassed."

She chose right then to just stop. To stop being embarrassed. There was freedom in this. In being able to actually talk to him, talk to somebody about the way she felt about all this. She had never been able to talk to Asher about it.

That was a problem.

"I've always been afraid to let go. But with you it felt easy. But no one's ever . . . no one's ever actually . . ."

"He never went down on you."

"No," she said. "I didn't want to ask, because I accepted a long time ago that stuff with sex was *my* issue. I think right at first when I slept with him I was a little bit frustrated. I wanted something more out of it. Something different. Well, at first, I was just glad that I felt the same after the first time we slept together."

"How do you mean?"

"I think part of me was afraid that I would forget who I was. Because it seemed like my parents were possessed. I was kind of afraid I'd lose my head. But instead, he was this really nice guy, and I liked him.

I dated him for three months, and then we slept together. It was very planned, very controlled. I felt the same. When we were done, I felt like myself. I didn't lose my head. I didn't suddenly want to race out and bang somebody else. I didn't want to get in a fight over him. I just felt like *me*. I didn't feel it had been turned inside out."

She felt a little bit inside out now. But it was Justice. So it had to be okay.

"So . . . you had sex finally and it was lame."

She laughed. "I guess."

"You know, I've never thought much about what it means to be a woman trying to navigate this stuff as I have since you told me about you and Asher. It's important to me that my partners have a good time, but I *know* I'm going to have an orgasm. Could be memorable, might not be. But a minimum amount of pleasure is a certainty. That's why I do it."

"I did it because I wanted to be in a relationship. A good one. A healthy one. And to me, that meant needing a nice man and having a nice house and having nice sex. You know, nice. Companionable. I wanted all these pieces of normal. But I don't even really know why I wanted them except to just have the opposite of what I had growing up."

"Sometimes I think . . . I was trying to give that poor kid the stuff he didn't have. We have this version of family that's different from anything we had with my parents. I go out when I want, I don't deny myself anything."

He believed that; she could see it. But there were actually a lot of things he denied himself. Because while she had been determined to make herself a family, while she had been dead set on finding a way to normal, finding a way to give herself something that she never had, he avoided it. Avoided emotional connections as far as romance went.

But then, she could see why. Part of her still believed that the ideal existed. Part of her still believed that there was something good out there. The kind of good that she might never have experienced, but that she believed, bone deep, had to be real.

She didn't know why she believed it.

Her parents hadn't exemplified it, her grandma had been single since long before Rue was born. She'd never mentioned Rue's grandfather, which had made Rue assume it had ended badly. Asher had betrayed Rue.

But she believed that love existed.

Maybe she was the idiot. Maybe she was the one that was wrong.

"Maybe that's what I'm doing. I'm trying to give that kid who never had a well-ordered life the life that I wanted. And more than that, the one that I believe my parents could have had if they would've cared enough to try. I just knew that I wanted something more. Something different. But it kind of became its own cage."

"Are you afraid that you're going to be like your parents? Because nothing about you is like them," he said.

"Yeah. I am." She lifted her hand up out of the water and watched some drops fall back in, leaving ripples on the surface. "I've always been a little bit afraid that I could be. Because I don't know what they were like before. Part of me wondered if they transformed each other. Into these kinds of uncontrollable monsters they were."

"Well, you're not them. And there's nothing wrong with you."

"I don't think I could've had that with him," she said softly, letting her hand drift down beneath the surface again.

"Because he wouldn't lick your—"

"*No*. Because it wasn't the same. It wasn't a matter of trying to stop myself from getting lost. I just was."

"Thank you," he said.

"For what?"

"For giving that to me. All the trust. It's not a small thing."

She shifted so that she sank a couple of inches lower in the water, then looked at him. Hard. "What was your first time like?"

He tilted his head, a crease between his eyebrows. "What?"

"I wanted to ask you back when it happened. Kind of. I also didn't want to think about it, which is why I never asked you."

"And you want to think about it now?"

"Yes. Because I feel like I finally get to know all of this about you, so I want to know it."

"Uhhh . . . I was young. I was horny. I looked at your boobs."

"You looked at *my* boobs?"

"Yes. It was summer. You were fifteen, I was sixteen and you had really what was quite a demure swimsuit. But I just looked at them. They were growing, and I was a guy, and I remember thinking your body was so pretty. And then there was Chelsea, and she was seventeen. She was wearing a bikini. She wasn't younger. And innocent. I just knew that I didn't want to screw up what I had with you over that. So . . . I redirected my focus to her."

She frowned and looked at the surface of the water, then back up at him. "I don't know how I feel about that."

"You don't have to. It just is. I met up with her at the bonfire by Sullivan's Lake that night, we had some beer, her dad was cleared out of the cabin for the night, she had condoms, we had sex."

"And did you make her come four times?" She knew she sounded salty. She *felt* salty.

"No. I didn't make her come at all. I felt like a dick. I told myself that I needed to figure out what I was doing before I ever did that again because it didn't seem right or fair that I got to pump a couple of times and have the *best time*, when the girl I was with might not. So . . . There you have it. It was a shitty first time, actually. I wish it would've been with someone that meant something to me. But then, until today, I don't think I'd ever had sex with someone who meant something to me. But at least I was better at it."

Rue shifted in the tub. Their legs tangled. A bolt of arousal hit her between her thighs. "I was so afraid. Not that it would hurt. That it would be *too* good."

He laughed, threw his head back and laughed.

"Yeah. Well. I was naive. It wasn't. Obviously. But that was actually just right for me. I found my comfort zone. I stayed in it. For eight years. It isn't just you and your sexuality that I opened the door to, it's my own. I'm still me. A little bit inside out, but still me."

She scrunched her eyes, trying to keep the tears at bay.

"All right, chickadee. Let's get you out of here before you turn into a prune."

"You're a lot more solicitous after you've had sex with a woman."

"Am I?"

"Yes."

But she was being lifted out of the tub, so her commentary didn't seem to make much difference.

"Tell me about it."

"Only that when we were friends—I mean we are friends—but when we were friends who'd never had sex, I don't think you would worry about the amount of time I was in the bathtub."

"Not a fair statement. Because when we hadn't had sex I wouldn't have been in the bathtub with you. I wouldn't have been able to see these." He moved his thumb over one of her nipples.

Shock, arousal and embarrassment lanced her. "We just . . ."

"I want to again."

"Justice!"

"Come on, Rue, it's three in the afternoon. It's the perfect time."

CHAPTER TWENTY-ONE

IT FELT ESSENTIAL that he stop talking to her and start making love to her. It was weird to have found himself in this situation. Rue was the one woman he was better at *talking* to than anything else.

Now suddenly, they'd had sex.

It had blown his mind. The feel of her under his hands, the taste, the way it had felt to slide inside her, it had nearly destroyed him.

He didn't know how to categorize it, or where to put it.

But *this*, he knew what to do with this. With her body. He knew how to make her scream. He was so damned good at that.

And she was tempting.

That was the main thing. He had lost his control somewhere back there. He had pushed her, and he wanted to push her even harder. Wanted to undo her completely.

You don't have the right . . .

She wanted him. She wanted this. He was doing it for her, and yes, he liked it. But it wasn't about his own pleasure. If Rue hadn't asked, he wouldn't be here.

Hell, he'd done a good job of keeping himself occupied with other women all these years. She was the one who'd led the change, and there were boundaries on the change, so it was safe.

And anyway, it would be over after this week.

Natural light poured into the room, and with the backdrop of the snow, that white light all over her glorious pale skin had him all messed up.

He was already hard, like he hadn't just come less than a half hour ago.

He set her down on the bed, and she looked at him, her eyes greedy.

"I'm going to tell you something," she said, her expression almost comedically grave.

"Okay."

"I think I probably *do* have a gag reflex. I don't want to disappoint you."

He laughed, because his brain was sort of tripped up. On the implications of all that. On everything. *"What?"*

"I didn't understand it before." She looked at him meaningfully. "But I do now. I get it."

"Oh?"

He still wasn't entirely sure he understood what she was saying, because he was still too strung out on the whole implication of the moment. "You're so much bigger," she said.

"Dammit," he said, the words like a punch to the gut.

It was *fucking hot*. Hearing those words come out of his best friend's mouth. It shouldn't be. Damn, it probably made him the worst kind of pervert. But it was just so damned hot.

"Let's get you on your knees and test that, shall we?"

Her eyes never leaving his, she slid off the edge of the bed, and got to her knees. He never prayed for forgiveness in his life, but he was close. Real close, just so he could relax and enjoy the rest of it. Because there was no way this wasn't a sin. But damn. He wanted to drown in it.

She wrapped her hand around the base of him, before leaning in and taking him into her mouth. "Shit, Rue," he said, reaching back to take hold of her hair, guiding her lips along his shaft.

The sight of her, her, doing that to him pushed them too far too fast. It was just too good. And he didn't . . . he didn't want to end this way. She tried to take him. All of him, but she couldn't. And it was wrong that that satisfied him. Made him feel like beating his chest. But it did.

It nearly finished him off. Nearly undid him. He pulled her head away, needing to get ahold of himself.

"But I want . . ."

"I want you," he said. Because he couldn't think of anything else more eloquent to say. Because there was just nothing more in him. He was used to being the one who had the control. Used to being the one that did the pushing. Hell, he'd done that a bit with her earlier, but there was something more to it. A bite. An edge that he'd never known before.

That was a big part of why he liked to make his partners boneless with need. It gave them the upper hand.

He lifted her up to her feet and crushed her against him, walked her back to the wall and flattened her against it, kissing her hard.

"Justice," she whispered against his mouth.

"Yes," he said. "Say my name. And don't forget

who's taking you."

"I can't. I couldn't."

"Good."

He was wild with it. This need inside of him. He was completely undone. And he wanted her to join him.

He put his hand between her legs and found her slick with wanting for him.

It was all he could do to separate from her for a moment to get a condom.

He had her against the wall again, her wrists pinned above her head, her breasts arched out toward him. He bent down and took one nipple into his mouth, sucking hard, until she cried out.

Then he reached down, gripped her hips, moved his hand on her thigh and lifted it up over his hip before testing her, sliding deep inside of her.

"Oh my gosh," she said, gripping his shoulders, arching her hips forward.

He almost could've laughed. Her saying such a sweet thing in such a gloriously filthy moment. But he couldn't laugh, because he was too overwhelmed. By the feel of her. The reality of her. He had wanted to do this because it put them back on solid ground. Because it put them back in his comfort zone. But nothing about this was comfortable. It was explosive. And nothing less.

She clung to him, and he urged her to wrap her legs around him, as he pounded home, gave no quarter, gave no mercy. There was nothing but this. But this race to satisfaction. He had forgotten to make her come before he got inside her. But she was panting, desperate, rolling her hips against his as she clung to him.

He buried his face in her neck as he thrust home. As he gave himself over to the thing between them.

And then, he was at the end of his control. He was desperate. Desperate for her to go with him. For her to go before him. But she didn't. It was like they were barreling perilously close to the same cliff. And then, something happened that he had never experienced before.

They went over together. Shaking and clinging to each other as their climax took hold.

And it was the closest thing to a perfect moment that Justice King had ever experienced in his life.

CHAPTER TWENTY-TWO

When Rue woke up the next morning, she felt . . . warm. Hot even. It was like a furnace had been plugged in right behind her. Then she registered the weight of a heavy arm thrown over the top of her, and deep breathing coming from behind.

Justice.

That's right.

She was on her honeymoon that was no longer a honeymoon, with Justice.

And last night . . .

Images from last night flashed through her mind. That second time against the wall . . . She didn't even recognize that woman. That woman that had so effortlessly lost herself. Who had given herself completely over to the experience. They had climaxed at the same time. It had been so intense. The most altering experience.

They had gotten room service at some point. They had eaten naked in bed. And now it was . . . morning. The snow was falling outside. They could go snowshoeing. They could rent a snowmobile There were any number of activities to be done at this place. They could get a massage. She had a voucher for a couples' massage, actually. Nothing seemed that interesting. Not when they could just stay together.

The thought sent a worrying pang through her system. That moment when they had both come together . . . It had been like a vow. And it wasn't supposed to be. This was supposed to be about her learning to cut loose, kind of. But it didn't feel easy. She felt safe. She felt like she could relax and feel. Except relaxing was the wrong word. Because there was nothing about it that was casual; there was nothing about it that was loose.

It was all just . . .

It's happening. Can't you just live in the moment?

That was something else she didn't know how to do. She had all of her binders, all of her planners. All of the things that she seemed to believe were going to insulate her from life. From being overwhelmed by the things her parents had been held captive by.

That was the real lesson she hadn't learned. That no amount of organizing the wedding had made it go forward. No amount of Asher being good on paper had actually made them marry each other.

Maybe what she needed to do was figure out how to exist in the moment. Not be afraid of what she felt. Not catastrophize about what it would mean in the future.

She rolled over and looked at him. He was still asleep. The lines on his face more relaxed, that wicked grin turned down as he snoozed. She reached up and touched a lock of his hair that had fallen into his face, and pushed it back.

It felt like a deep privilege, to be next to Justice while he was sleeping.

Another thing that they had never done before. Another thing they hadn't experienced.

"Good morning," he said. His eyes opened, the

white light from the snow highlighting what a startling blue they were.

"Good morning."

He breathed out, heavy and filled with meaning. She laughed, butterflies rising up in her stomach. "You know we used to talk."

"Yeah," he said. "We did."

He rolled her onto her back and spent the next forty-five minutes or so showing her exactly why he was the best man to have been brought on this trip.

After that, they ordered more room service, and she got out a pamphlet with all of the activities they could do.

"I think I want to zip-line," she said, taking a sip of coffee.

"Why?"

"Because we're here. We're here, and we need to do something."

He lifted a brow.

"I'm not going to be able to walk," she said.

"Oh, don't be dramatic."

"Saddle sore is *a thing*, Justice. Some of us don't ride like this all the time."

"Yeah. I guess," he said.

He didn't look repentant or convinced. She just thought it would be a bad idea for them to sink entirely into a 100 percent sex situation. Yes, she wanted to live in the moment. She didn't want to catastrophize. But she had only been sort of kidding when this morning their gazes had collided and the only thing they could think to do was come together again. They had too many years of friendship behind them to let it turn into that.

"What else is there to do?" he asked, so skeptical that it flattered her, even if it shouldn't.

But what woman wouldn't want to be the sole focus of the desire of a man that hot? She paled in comparison to zip lining. Perhaps that was a strange thing to be complimented by but after her most recent experience with a man—she was.

"Oh, there's all kinds of things. You can take a dog team out. I mean, guided. You can't just grab the dogs and *mush* all around the place."

"You would be kind of a cute musher."

She sniffed. "I have no desire to be a musher."

"I'm shocked."

He didn't sound shocked. He was wearing nothing but low-slung jeans, and she couldn't help but admire his body.

"You keep looking at me like that we are not going to make it out to zip-line."

"It's going to be very cold."

"Are you having second thoughts? Because if we stay in I can keep you warm."

"I'm not having second thoughts. I think it's something we should do."

"Would you have done it with Asher?"

"No. It's pretty safe to say that 90 percent of what we've done so far I wouldn't do with Asher."

He smirked. "A man does like to hear that. If he's going to be compared it might as well be favorably."

"They do have an ice cave," she said, pointing to the brochure. Then she blinked. "I'm sorry. I forgot."

He looked tense. And a little bit angry. "It's fine,"

he said. "But yeah. I might skip the ice cave if it's all the same to you."

How had she not known this? She'd stepped on it twice now in the past week and it just . . .

She cared for Justice. She'd known him for so much of their lives. It meant they didn't have "getting to know you" conversations, though. She'd known him since he was eight so she figured she knew it all, but she'd missed this glaring trauma that had happened to him.

He was her tall, handsome, confident friend.

How had she not seen the depth of his vulnerability?

He was her brave, larger-than-life surrogate, who lived life in a way she was too timid to.

"What happened?" she asked.

"I told you. I got stuck in a cave-in."

"You were just down there playing?"

"More or less," he said, shrugging.

She knew him, though. She knew it wasn't a casual gesture. Knew that his muscles were tense. That he was upset.

"More or less," she repeated. "What does that mean?"

"Let's go zip lining. I'm fine with zip lining."

"What happened?" She knew she was being persistent, but she just felt like all the doors between them had opened last night, and he was still keeping things from her. And it just seemed silly.

"I got sent on an errand, okay?" He shook his head. "I was doing something for somebody. I went into the cave, there was a cave-in. Nobody was looking for me. Or maybe they did, but they didn't look in that spot. It was a long, shitty few days. But I survived it. But no, I don't go back in the caves for fun."

"*Somebody* sent you?"

"It's not . . ." He let out a long breath. "You really want to have this conversation now?"

"When else can we have it?"

"Maybe when the focus of the week is not us . . . doing this. Why do we need to talk about personal stuff on top of that?"

"I know that you're in a little bit of a different space with this kind of thing than I am, but for me, what we just did is personal. So it all seems compatible."

"My dad used to give me . . . packages. To put in the cave."

"What?"

"He told me it was important, and that he could only trust me with it. Not even Denver. And Denver was . . . He was the oldest, and I always thought he was Dad's favorite. If you knew . . . if you knew how magnetic my dad was. How fun he could be. How much I looked up to him. He told me it was a special job only I could do and I wanted to be special." His eyes went vacant. "I didn't understand what I was doing. I . . . I thought I was doing something good. Helping the family. Helping my dad."

"What was it?"

He looked away. "Drugs. I found that out later when Denver finally started talking about some of his own experiences with Dad. I used to take them out there and stick them in the back of the cave. Because only a kid could get back there. I have no idea who was picking them up. Probably some other kid that was acting like a mule. My dad told me the most important thing was keeping it secret. So when the cave-in happened, and I was trapped in there with the package I . . . I was terrified to be found. Terrified not to be. I knew . . . I knew if someone found out I'd have failed my dad. It could have ruined everything. They'd have found the drugs and . . . and he'd have been arrested."

"Why haven't you ever told me this?"

"Because it doesn't matter. It's a thing that happened when I was like seven years old."

"You were a child." Her chest hurt. She could barely breathe. "Why didn't your dad come for you?"

"He . . . he had to make sure if he did that his secret wouldn't get out."

"Justice, you were a child. Why didn't you ever tell me this happened? It's horrifying."

"It was a long time ago. And the only lingering issue is really the fear of caves. All things considered, I got out pretty well unscathed."

"Are you serious? You think you got out of it unscathed? You think that all you have is a *slight phobia of caves*? You don't think that any of your other issues—"

"What other issues?"

"Your need to control your environment, your desperate need to pretend you aren't affected by anything, your fear of commitment . . ."

"You don't have a fear of commitment. Does that mean you don't have issues?"

She sputtered. "No. But this isn't about me. This is about you. And you know what, you know all of my stuff."

"That's bullshit. No, I didn't. I didn't know about all the sex stuff."

"That was personal."

"This felt personal to me. It's not any different. You choose to keep certain things to yourself. You're a liar if you think you don't. Were you attracted to me when we were teenagers?"

"Justice . . ."

"Were you?"

"I thought you were good-looking. But I wasn't where you were at as far as all the physical stuff goes. So I don't know if I would say attracted . . ."

"You had feelings that you didn't share."

"Yes," she said finally. "I did. Okay?"

"So don't stand there and act like you share everything. Don't get angry at me for not giving you transparency. There are certain things that I choose to keep to myself. I've never even talked to my brothers about that situation. I mean they know what happened. Because they remember it. The older ones do anyway. But the whole thing, the drugs and all that, I never talked about that. I just . . . It's stupid but I couldn't talk about it."

"But it's not stupid."

"Plenty of other people have been through way worse things. There's no reason to be all traumatized about something like that."

"But you are. And that's . . . Your father used you. He manipulated your love for him. Why are you trying to undervalue what happened to you?"

"Because there's no point to marinating in it, is there? What good does it do? What good does it do you to try to avoid all of your parents' trauma? It didn't do you any good, did it? That's the point of this whole quest. You lost the house anyway. Their stuff still reached you even though you tried to be better. And yeah, I think that's messed up, but it's the way of things. It didn't do you any favors in your relationship with Asher either. I just try not to hurt other people. That's it. That's all I want. I don't need every single thing inside of me to be healed or fixed or whatever. I was raised by a narcissist. I had some things happen. But so what? It doesn't make me special."

"Then maybe there are some things that you should talk to someone about."

"I just talked to you. See? Am I healed now?"

"Why are you acting like this?"

"Because you're pushing me."

"Why shouldn't I push you sometimes?"

He pushed her all the time. And even though the sex had been amazing, why was she the one that had to change? It wasn't like she didn't want to change; she did. She was the one driving this. But why was he so convinced that what he did didn't require change? Because he wasn't hurting people? Didn't he care that he was hurting himself? Limiting himself?

She took a breath. And let her own discomfort reverberate inside of her. She was upset because he'd been hurt. She hated that he'd been hurt. It didn't seem fair. He was one of the most important people in the world to her, and this terrible thing had happened and she hadn't been able to be there for him. It added to her sense of inadequacy. To the idea that she had missed things with him. That she hadn't earned her place.

So yes. Some of it was wanting to push him, but some of it was feeling upset about what she hadn't done for him, and that was about her.

She was upset that he was hurt.

Because she cared about Justice. More than just about anyone in her whole life.

He was her best friend, and now he was her lover. And he . . .

What is it that's really bothering you?

He'd been hurt. That was it.

"I'm sorry," she said. "I'm honestly not trying to start a fight. I'm just really sorry that happened to you. I'm so sorry your dad was such a . . . such an asshole."

She closed the distance between them, and hugged him. She pressed her cheek to his bare chest, let the hair there scratch her cheek. It took him about thirty seconds, but he returned the hug, his heat and his strength enveloping her. She had hugged Justice countless times. But not like this. Not with this sensual knowledge between them. This acknowledged desire. It was like she could feel their heartbeats melting into one, like it had done when they had raced over the edge of the cliff together, their hearts thundering.

Even in this still, painful moment, they were the same. Together. United.

"I don't need you to feel sorry for me," he said.

"If I can't feel sorry for you then who can?"

"I don't need *anyone* to feel sorry for me."

"*You* feel sorry for you," Rue said. "You feel bad for that kid you were. And you should."

"It's not the same thing. I'm just trying to give back to him."

"Why can't I want that too?"

"Because I think our idea of what I need is different."

"Can't you accept that maybe I know you as well as you know yourself? Maybe even a little bit better?"

"No."

That made her heart twist painfully. Why was he being so difficult? Or maybe she was being difficult.

"You can't stop me from feeling sorry for you." She kissed his chest. Then she stretched up on her toes and kissed his lips, just quickly. A little zip of desire raced through her.

"Let's get dressed."

He put his shirt on, and she was regretful.

But then, they went out together. She still felt raw and sore from the conversation, from the revelations. But she wasn't going to let her own discomfort poison the day. Her desire to push, and to get everything in the little boxes, was only going to make it so he was more distant. She didn't want that.

She wanted to spend this weekend being present.

So that was what she was going to do.

CHAPTER TWENTY-THREE

HE DID HIS best to banish the dark shadows this morning had built up inside his soul. He didn't like talking about that shit. But there was a point where *not* telling her built it up into something bigger than it was.

He just didn't like it. It made him feel like he had then. Young, stupid. Vulnerable. He'd thought that his dad loved him because he'd been doing things for him. He'd thought it made him important. It was foolish to be angry at a six-year-old who didn't understand narcissism. But sometimes he was.

Over the years he realized his dad would never love anyone as much as he loved himself. He would never care about anyone else's feelings, comfort or safety like he did his own. He also wanted admiration and loyalty and that meant manipulation was his stock-in-trade.

But Justice still hated it. Because it wasn't like it was the end of his wishing his dad cared for him.

No, that had happened later.

I shoulda let you die in that cave, boy. You're no good to me at all.

That was how he found himself harnessed and standing up on a platform fifteen feet up a tree. At least, the two things seemed connected. Rue was crouched down, like it was spreading out her center of gravity, her eyebrows locked together, her expression one of furious concentration.

"May I remind you," he said, "that this was your idea."

"I know," she said. "I'm happy to be here."

They were safely harnessed in, but it was clear to him that Rue didn't entirely trust the harness. Of course, neither of them had a great reason to trust much of anything. He thought a network of cables, rope and steel clips was infinitely more dependable than people. But that was him.

"Do you want me to go first?" he asked.

"Yes, please," she said.

The whole rest of the crew had already gone, one of the guides having already demonstrated the way that they were supposed to go off the platform, with another remaining to handle the timing, and the clips on the different cables.

He got up onto one of the boxes, and stood there while their guide adjusted the clips. And then, just like he'd been told, he lifted his feet up, and gravity did the rest of the work. He went sailing off the platform, picking up speed as he went, watching as Rue and her round eyes got farther and farther away while he went hurtling easily through the trees.

It was like being weightless.

He hadn't expected to feel much of anything doing this. It wasn't about him; it was about her.

And yet.

And yet he felt his own heart lift somewhere it had never been before.

Just for one moment, the only thing left inside of

him was all the lightness. Was Rue. Kissing her, holding her. Making love to her. Her lips on his chest in the hotel room, and then again on his mouth. Sweet and casual, like they were a couple. Like they had all the time in the world.

But the shadows existed. Even if this moment of weightless wonder suggested that there could be only this.

He was too many years into living like he did.

To living like a man who didn't know where the right hook might come from.

He had been burned out on high stakes when he was seven years old. Where things had felt like life and death and he couldn't trust anybody.

Then she had come into his life and she had changed everything. Given him something to hold on to. Given him hope.

Much like now, Rue had given him wings. A way to fly away from the reality of being a king. A way to transcend.

Just like now.

Too quickly, his feet connected with the next platform. His legs were less steady than he had realized, and when he got unclipped and moved back to the platform his heart was thundering like he'd just finished running a marathon.

He turned just in time to watch Rue lift off the platform back where he'd begun and start screaming.

Then he watched as her expression of terror transformed into one of joy. He wished he could experience it with her. He wished he could be weightless with her.

He had never felt quite so desolate in his life as

he did standing on that platform watching Rue. She spread her arms wide, and let her head fall back, her hair flying out behind her.

Then she lay out flat on her back, a technique they had been shown earlier. It was like watching her surrender. Like watching her truly fly.

But she wasn't near him. She was getting farther and farther away.

When she landed on the platform, the instructor caught her, and she opened her eyes. An expression of wonder on her face. She unclipped, and then got reclipped to the line he was on, and he couldn't help himself. He pulled her into his arms and kissed her. Her face turned pink, her eyes shining bright. "It's like flying."

"Yes, it is," he agreed.

The whole rest of the day was like that. As they sailed through the snowy woods, lighter and freer versions of themselves.

When they got back to the hotel they couldn't keep their hands off of each other. Their dinner out had to be deferred again, because once they were in bed, they didn't get back out.

And that was how the next few days went.

It was the closest thing to zip lining, the closest thing to flying. Like they had both surrendered and let go, just for these moments. They left heavy conversations behind, and they forgot that there was any other world beyond the one they made in bed.

But on Friday night, he knew that he needed to take her out. She dressed up in the prettiest red dress that came just above her knees, showing off those legs that had been driving him crazy. Then he noticed that she put on the blue necklace.

"Something borrowed," he said.

"And blue," she said. "I thought it went with the dress."

He had given her that to marry another man, and looking at it now made his chest hurt.

He felt like he was standing on the edge of something. Much like he had been when they had gone zip lining. But he couldn't put a finger on it. Or maybe he didn't want to.

So instead he took her hand, and let her out of the hotel room, down to the lobby restaurant.

"At Christmas time all this gets decorated," she said, gesturing around the lobby.

"I bet it's great," he said.

"Yeah. I'd love to come up sometime but . . ." A sad look crossed her face. "This is so beautiful," she said, sitting down at the table. There was an elaborate five-course meal for dinner, so they didn't have to look at a menu or place their orders. He realized he didn't much care what he ate. He just wanted to watch her.

"Yeah," he said. "It is."

"Do you remember the Christmas that we spent in the barn?"

He let out a hard breath. Of course he remembered it. He remembered it every year. But with feelings more than specific, clear thoughts. Because sometimes thinking back to when they were kids was painful. And not for the reasons that thinking about his childhood often was, but there was something about them that he missed sometimes, and he had never been able to say what that was.

Possibility.

He pushed that aside.

"Yeah. I remember."

His dad had decided that he was too stressed out to have Christmas. Hadn't had a Christmas tree. He had been subtle about it, but he had somehow shifted the blame to something Justice's mother had or hadn't done. The details didn't matter. Only that he was somehow responsible for the kids being disappointed, but he had managed to lay blame on their mother.

He couldn't remember if they had been angry with her. He hoped not. Because the next year she had been gone, and sometimes he did wonder if their own behavior had led to that.

But then, it was just another reminder that you couldn't trust anyone. That the people who were supposed to care didn't.

At least, not in the way they should.

Except for Rue.

She reached across the table and took his hand, the way that she had done always, even before this. Even before they had become lovers. "You got me the best present."

"I didn't *get* it for you. I made it for you."

Her eyes went glittery. "You made that?"

It had been a necklace that he had fashioned out of a leather strap and some sea glass that he had found.

"I thought . . . I mean I guess I don't know what I thought. I was only nine. So, I guess I didn't really think it through." She took a shaky breath. "You got me my only present. My parents were being so volatile that year. We didn't have any money, because they spent it all on alcohol and . . . I don't know. Whatever else they spent it on. I've never fully understood them. Not what they did with anything, not what they wanted out of what they did, I just never understood. I still don't. Because they just keep on living that way."

"Maybe it makes them feel alive. Being that angry."

What he hated was that he almost understood her parents then. Because he had decided not to care about anything, and the years passed without much to mark them by. When life didn't have intensity, it was like a smooth stretch of water, endless and unchanging all around you.

No wind. No movement.

No purpose.

He would've told Rue or anyone else that he didn't need things to change. That he had found his spot in the middle of the lake and he was happy with it. With the lack of resistance. With the way things worked.

But right then, he envied the way that her parents could try, explode, cling together. He envied that passion.

He looked at her, his chest clenched tight, and he tried to ease it by taking a deep breath.

"All I know is we had a Charlie Brown Christmas tree and we sat in the barn and sang carols. And I've never been so thankful for anything as I was for you that Christmas. Because you made something so awful feel magical. Justice, what you and I had, never even felt like second best. It felt like real Christmas magic."

That was like a glass shard cutting his chest. It was painful. Damn, it was painful.

Because sometimes he thought she was right. That had been the best. He had wanted the real best for her. With someone else. He had been sure that was the only way she could get it, and then he had let her down.

And now she didn't have what she deserved and...

Everything hurt. It just hurt.

But dinner started to come out, and they talked about that. The food in front of them. And he watched the candlelight flicker over her face, and he knew without a doubt this was better than their barn Christmas, it contained more magic than any holiday ever could. Looking at her by candlelight, at the beautiful woman she'd become. Knowing that he was going to touch her later. Kiss her.

"I still have that necklace, you know," she said. His eyes flicked down to the blue stone she was wearing.

"Not that one," she said. "The Christmas present. It's in my Justice box."

"What's that?"

"My box. Of everything you've ever given me."

Everything he'd ever given her? All contained in one place? Kept. Treasured.

He gritted his teeth. But it was a damned thing to realize in that moment that no one had ever loved him half so well as Rue Matthews. They had wonderful bread and filet mignon, perfect mashed potatoes and the best cheesecake he'd ever had in his life.

But he could remember other meals with her, other times. When they'd cobbled together cheese and crackers and huddled in her room, or in the barn.

The past and the present had never existed quite so intensely together, that necklace she wore shifting between the blue stone and that sea glass.

And when they were through, they went back to the room, and she closed the door behind them. She reached behind her back and unzipped her dress, letting it fall to her hips. The breath got sucked from his lungs. The lingerie she was wearing was . . .

"You gotta warn a man," he said as she took the rest of it off, her gorgeous breasts just barely covered by two silky strips of black fabric that created a V down between her legs, dipping dangerously low, barely offering coverage. "I'm liable to have a heart attack."

"Don't be dead, Justice," she said, her eyes sparkling with need and humor. "I'm not finished with you yet."

They had two days left of this. This was his present for all the bullshit he'd endured in his life up till now, and he was set on unwrapping it.

Two days.

He took her into his arms and kissed her. Moved his hands reverently over the curves of her body, then kissed her mouth sweet and slow.

He had never wanted to find the reverence at the center of his own debauchery quite so much. But he wanted to give her both. The profane and the righteous, because this was real, and it came from deep inside of him. And if they were this close to going back to not being able to touch each other like this then this had to be special.

He was good at living in the moment. He was not good at facing the reality of losing something he cared about. And he did care about this. This new dimension of their relationship, not just because it felt good, but because . . .

He didn't let himself think anymore. He just kissed her, touched her, lost himself in her. Over and over again until she cried out his name.

He had said to her once that the women he was with didn't do that, because they usually didn't know who he was. But she did. And he knew her. Across time. Across dreams and fears. He knew her.

Not just her name, but the substance of who she was.

They had made love countless times this week, and he realized that after the first time it hadn't been about helping her let go, because she simply had. She had held on to him and let go, and every time it was like that. Every time, it was just that real. Just that perfect.

And this time, when he gave himself over to his pleasure, he said her name too.

She held them, brushing his hair back from his face. "This isn't done, you know that," she said softly.

"What?"

"When we get back. I've been thinking this from the beginning. But trying not to think about it, you know? You can't unhammer a nail."

He closed his eyes. "Okay. So what does that look like?"

"Do you feel like you're ready for this to end?"

"No. But even though things have changed between us, I haven't changed."

"That's okay," she said. "I don't need you to. I just need . . . more of this. I can't keep staying with you knowing what you look like naked, sleeping down the hall from you, trying to stay in my own room. I can't."

He couldn't do it either. She was just one that was brave enough, honest enough to admit it. She was the one that had faced the terrifying reality that they couldn't go back. Maybe that was why thinking of them as children made him ache. Because back then they hadn't crossed this line. Hadn't complicated things.

That's not it, and you know it.

"You're my best friend," she whispered.

"You're mine too."

She was supposed to be here with someone else, and she wasn't. She was here with him. She'd been here with him for a long time.

Part of him wanted to trust her, with everything.

But he found that he couldn't speak. Couldn't breathe. So he just held her. It was the closest thing to that feeling he had the other day. The closest thing to freedom.

But one thing he knew for sure about things like this. The line didn't hold forever. Eventually, it would break. Because in the end, there was very little that you could trust to last. Very little that you could trust to be true. But for all this time she had been one of them.

He didn't know why, but it filled him with a sense of dread.

So he just held on to her tighter.

CHAPTER TWENTY-FOUR

THE REST OF the trip passed in a blur. And before Rue knew, it was time for them to go home. The real risk had been on that night they'd gone out. When she had told him she didn't want it to be over. Ever since the zip lining she had realized that she needed to tell him. Ever since she had given in, done the terrifying thing. Lay back and spread her arms and truly let go.

She had known that they couldn't be done.

Because she couldn't . . . She couldn't go back.

They had to go forward. It was the only option. Anything else would be dishonest. Anything else would be a disservice to them and who they were.

Who they had always been.

But she had been doing a disservice to herself for a whole lot of years.

She had been so afraid of big feelings because she had seen them play out in such a toxic way. But she had denied herself. She had denied herself true passion. She had denied herself what she really wanted.

She wanted Justice.

What she had *always* wanted was a life with him, and she had never been willing to let go of him entirely, but she had wanted to take those feelings, to take that pain and divide it. Asher was for romance, to marry, to have children with.

She had determined she was never to fling herself against Justice and his issues, because she would only get hurt.

As they drove back toward Four Corners, she looked at him, at his profile, and for the first time in her life she finally let herself admit the truth. The truth that had lived inside of her since she was a little girl. The truth she'd spent years trying to ignore, suppress, and minimize.

Justice King was the love of her life.

When he'd bent over that textbook, unable to sound out the words, he'd been the love of her life. When he'd given her that necklace in the barn, he'd been the love of her life. When he'd given her the blue necklace, the day she was supposed to marry another man, he'd been the love of her life.

It had been him. Always him.

With the deepest, truest part of herself, she loved him.

It had taken her until now to realize it. Because she had never seen love. Not like this. True and enduring. Selfless. For years their love hadn't been based on romance or sex; it had just been there. Real and as bright as the sunrise.

It had evolved and shifted. They'd let themselves add this level of intimacy to it. And that was when she had realized it had always been there.

This one man had the capacity to be everything. She hadn't wanted that. She had wanted to spread it out, to make him less important, as if that were possible.

He had agreed to see how it went at home. So there was that.

At least there was that.

Her heart thundered, so hard it was painful.

She swallowed, her throat scratchy. She didn't know what to say.

She let her head fall back against the seat. "We really did use to spend all of our time together with clothes on," she said.

"Yeah, we did," he said.

After only a week it was so hard to imagine. That she'd spent years not knowing his body like this. Not knowing his taste. Years with this barrier between them.

"I'm glad that we're doing this," she said.

Except, she hadn't been brave enough to ask what they were really doing. She hadn't been brave enough to try to find out if this meant that they were something more than the friends they had always been, or if to him it was friends that had sex. For her, it was accepting that he was the man she loved, now with sex. It was just so hard.

All of it.

But it was wonderful too. All of it was like a metaphor for the zip lining. For the polar plunge. Or maybe, they were the metaphor. She had been looking for what she really needed in her life, and she had told herself that maybe it was bravery, so she had done all these things that weren't what she actually needed to do.

What she needed to do was stop hiding from herself. What she needed to do was realize that he was what she wanted. That she had tried to give herself something easier so that she could maintain control. But she didn't want control anymore as much as she wanted to be happy. Really happy.

She had to lose everything to figure this out. That was all.

Just the carefully crafted life she had built, just her home, just all of the crutches and excuses and hiding places that she had ever put up between herself and her feelings for Justice.

Maybe she should write her parents a thank-you note.

Well. No. She wouldn't go that far.

"Are we going to tell anyone?"

"I don't . . . I don't see why we need to. Yet."

The way he said that, the way he hesitated, she didn't like it. It made her feel scratchy and uncomfortable. It made her feel precarious.

Maybe that was just something she was going to have to accept. That this wasn't going to be entirely comfortable. That this was going to be a little bit terrifying. That this was going to be bigger than she could handle, that it was going to be a risk.

She had her fill of risk when she was a kid, and she had done her best to avoid it ever since.

Because she had lived around people who had taken risks, made big emotional leaps that she hadn't consented to being a part of.

So this was hers, she supposed. And she couldn't hide from it.

"Okay," she said.

She needed to come up with a way for them to talk about the cave again, because for some reason, she felt like it mattered. Because for some reason, she felt like it was one of the locked doors that Justice still had inside of him that she couldn't access. Yes, he had told her about it, but there was just . . . There was something else. And she could feel it, when she got close to things that he didn't want to deal with, things that he didn't want to talk about. She could feel the resistance.

She just didn't know what to do to get through it.

"Can I stay in your room?"

"Yeah," he said.

There had been a moment where she had felt so free with him. Free to actually talk about things they never had before, and now it was like she was facing the reality of what they still weren't able to discuss. What he wasn't willing to share. And because of the other intimacy it felt more pronounced, not less. She touched the blue necklace the way she had wanted every day since their fancy dinner. Because she had decided to hang on to it like he had said. Until she was building a better life. Like his grandmother. He didn't seem to notice that was the symbolism of it, but she supposed that was a very male thing.

This was the better life. As far as she was concerned, this was the better life.

But she was finding her footing, and she wasn't quite sure how to go forward.

Talking used to be the easiest thing. Now it seemed to be sex. Maybe that was fair because it was still new. Maybe that was why they were burying themselves in that for now. Because it was something they hadn't been able to do for so long.

Still, she wished talking was easier.

Physically, things couldn't be better.

She never spent a night in her room, though she felt compelled to keep her things in there. It was just that he hadn't fully invited her to move into his room. Sleep in it, yes. But not actually move her things into it.

"Had you ever spent the night with a woman before?"

She asked him that over dinner one night.

"No. But I've spent the night with you plenty of times, so I guess it doesn't seem different."

That bothered her. Because it felt like he was downplaying, even though she supposed it was a fair thing to say. She was special, either way, because it wasn't like he had actually spent the night with other women. It was just he felt the comfort of it being her. She shouldn't be salty about it.

In spite of little moments like that, the next three days went well. And then finally, he decided they should have dinner at his family's.

He kept such a healthy distance between them when they went inside, and it was silly that she was offended by it because she had been so adamant that they keep it a secret when they had first left for the honeymoon. Denver knew, but she didn't know about anyone else. And now it seemed like it was Justice who was more concerned with still keeping lines there. Even though they had erased the other boundaries that they had put up, he seemed to be heavily concerned about this one.

Everyone was purely and truly themselves during dinner, and she was having trouble. Everyone was here tonight, Landry and Fia, Arizona and Micah, their children, Daughtry and Bix, and Denver.

"We missed you," Arizona said.

"Thanks," Justice said. "We didn't miss you, since we were busy enjoying the fancy-ass amenities at the place we were staying at."

Everybody knew they had gone, so Justice acting casual about it was really the only way to make it so they weren't announcing that something intimate had occurred.

"You should take *me* somewhere fancy," Bix said, grabbing hold of Daughtry's arm.

"I'll take you wherever you want to go," he said. "Paris?"

Bix's eyes rounded. "Are you serious?"

"Of course. Name the place you want to go for our honeymoon and I'll take you there."

Bix's eyes were shiny. "Would you really take me to Paris?"

"Yeah," he said.

"He'll take you *fancy*," Denver said. "In fact, that will be my wedding gift to you."

Daughtry made a scoffing noise. "I don't need you to pay for my honeymoon."

"I know you don't need it," he said. "But I really want to give Bix the fanciest thing she can get."

Bix glowed with pleasure, and for a second, Rue could only marvel at the similarities between Justice and Denver. They were caring, even if Denver was more reserved than Justice in general. But they both seemed like they were happiest—if you could call it happy—when they were isolated. Alone. They had people in their lives, but did they really?

There was just this big wall around parts of Justice. And Denver was much the same. She had known this whole family for most of her life, and yet with a lot of them, she couldn't say she actually knew them deeply.

They ate, and talked for a while, and then the men took their home-brewed alcohol outside, which left Arizona, Bix, Fia and Rue alone.

"So," Bix said, her sharp gaze pinning her to the spot. "How was the honeymoon?"

She didn't know what Denver had said to them. She suspected nothing, because she had a feeling the man was a locked box when he wanted to be. And of course they were women, and intuitive. She thought about lying. But really, there wasn't any point. And she wanted some advice. Because each of them had someone. Really had them. Fia and Bix had managed to snare Kings. Arizona was a king. Normally, Rue would talk to Justice. But she was realizing that when you had romantic feelings entangled with somebody, when the stakes felt this high, and that person was your best friend, it was difficult to go to them directly.

She couldn't turn it over inside of herself anymore. She had spent the last three days doing it.

"I need help," she said.

"Oh good," Fia said. "I love telling people what to do."

"Well. It's your lucky day. Because I really need to be told. I'm in love with him."

It felt like all the air had been sucked out of the room. It was the first time she'd said it out loud. The first time she'd admitted it to herself like that. He was the love of her life, but for some reason, that felt easier than admitting she was in love with him. It felt a little bit more all-encompassing.

"I knew it," said Arizona. "I *knew* you were going to marry my brother."

"Well, I don't think he wants to marry me."

"Why not?"

"I don't know if you've noticed this, but he's a little bit commitment shy."

"You slept together, though, right?" Arizona pressed.

She felt her face getting hot.

"That's a yes," Bix said, gesturing to her face. "You're the color of a boiled beet."

"Charming," Fia said, then turned back to Rue. "So you slept together. That must mean that he has feelings for you."

"He does have feelings for me. I don't have any doubt about that. That's not the issue. The issue is . . . something has kept us apart this whole time. For me it was being afraid of how powerful my feelings for him could be. I'm not less scared of that now. It's just . . ." She laughed. "You can't unhammer a nail. And I hammered this one a little bit ago. I was fussing around it trying to figure out how to pull it out. Then I just finally gave in. I accepted that there was nothing I could do to go back on all this. He and I are a done deal. For me. Sleeping together was just part of it. It wasn't *the* thing."

"I get that," Bix said. "I fell for Daughtry before he ever kissed me." It was a soft, sweet admission coming from spiky Bix. "By the time that happened there was just no more pretending."

"Yes. That's exactly what it is. It was finally letting myself in fully on how I already felt. It explained so much. Why things with Asher were never amazing. Because Justice has always had my heart. He's always had the most of me. I wanted to keep him in my left hand and Asher in my right hand. It feels somehow related to two birds in the bush? To a bird in the hand? I don't know. It just felt like I wanted to double my odds. Or split my emotions. Because this is so damned painful."

"So what's the problem?" Fia asked.

"I can feel him pulling away sometimes. He wants this. Well, he likes sleeping with me. And he cares for me, but he's never been in a relationship. And he claims he never wants one. But it feels an awful lot like that's what we have."

"In fairness," Arizona pointed out, "that's what you've always had with him. You've kind of been his wife for years without actually being his wife. He's doing the same thing you were. He has you. But not all of you. And you get to have him, but not all of him. It keeps both of you safe. They are the defining relationship in each other's lives, it's just that . . ."

"When I used to make moonshine," Bix said, sounding so sage it was almost funny, "I used to bury some of my batch in different places. Because I didn't want to put everything in one spot in case it got raided, right? It's a way to protect yourself when resources are thin. That's what you and Justice are doing. You're protecting your emotional resources by burying your moonshine in multiple places. But in this case moonshine is your feelings. For him, he's got sex moonshine all over the place. His *heart* moonshine, that's you. But now you're both kinds of moonshine mixed together in one shot, and his heart's having trouble taking the wallop that packs."

"That's very deep," Fia said.

Bix smiled. "Thank you."

Really, Bix made more sense than she had a right to.

"So . . . What am I supposed to do about this? How do I convince him to bury all the moonshine in one place?"

"Well, the reason you don't do it is because you're scared. Scarcity. All that. It would take a hell of a lot of trust."

"I trust him," Rue said.

"It's hard for us to trust anything," Arizona said. "Our dad was such an asshole. And our mom left. To protect herself, but still. She left her kids behind. My dad was a smooth narcissist to the boys, but he really let his true colors out with me. Because I disappointed him. He was so mad when I scarred myself up in my accident. Because I think he was afraid he might actually have to take care of me, and there was no way in hell he was going to do that. So he was just ugly to me. Angry and horrible. We were taught that love was very conditional. That everything was conditional. Our childhood was confusing and erratic. Our dad was a manipulator, yes, but he was also primarily a giant selfish toddler. He did what felt good to him, and when you're in the care of a man like that, you never know what's going to happen next. It's hard to trust anything."

She thought about the cave. About the way he felt abandoned. How no one came for him. Of course he didn't trust anything.

"So what do I do? Do I tell him that I love him with no strings attached?"

"Do you want more from him than that?"

"I do," she said. "But I don't want to be another person holding something hostage."

"But you can't keep being his emotional surrogate either," Fia said. "He's always had you, and he's never had to give you everything."

Both were good points.

"Maybe there's not a right answer," Bix said. "Because people aren't math problems. And life is just a confusing shitshow. Believe me. I know."

"We all know," Fia said. "And I guess that's the one piece of wisdom we all have. In the end no matter how you handle it, if it's right, you'll find your way together."

Arizona smiled. "Remember you asked us if that meant you had to forgive Asher? Because we had forgiven Landry and Micah. But that wasn't the lesson. The lesson is that the right man is the right man, even if it doesn't come together for thirteen years."

"And sometimes the right man is the right man even if you've only been sleeping with them for a month. But it changes you forever," Bix added.

"I guarantee you that sometimes the right man is the right man even if you've known him since you were seven years old and it took all that time for the two of you to find each other," Fia said.

"I just love him so much," she said.

"Show him," Fia said.

"Love is a risk, there's no way around that. But it's the best risk I ever took. And sometimes it is a fight to get there. But in the end, it's worth it," Bix said.

Bix was so young, but she had a world-weary spirit about her, a fighter's attitude. She wasn't a romantic. Hell, none of these women were. They had all lived, and had scars. They had all seen their share of hardship.

And they were all saying that love was worth fighting for.

She wasn't entirely sure it was what she wanted to hear.

But the pursuit of comfort was what had seen her nearly marrying Asher. And it had been the wrong thing to do. If it was the right one . . .

Asher hadn't been the right one. She hadn't been heartbroken, not for one moment. In fact, all of it had only driven her closer to Justice. She thought back to when she had tried the wedding dress on, and they'd linked arms and looked in the mirror. She knew then that it was right. That that was the life she was supposed to be moving toward. But it was too scary.

It wasn't being good that had landed her in this place. It was being scared. How had she not realized that until now? She hadn't been well-behaved; she had been terrified.

Terrified had only ever gotten her half of what she wanted. Half of what she deserved. She wanted everything.

Oh, she wanted it all.

It was getting close to auction time. Her house would be sold. But the house didn't matter any more than Asher did. Not anymore.

She hatched a plan, then and there. One that was all about who they were now. Lovers, and friends.

One that was about sex and talking and sharing.

She might take a little while to tell him that she loved him, but in the meantime, she was going to show him exactly what she wanted. She was going to figure out a way to give him all of her in a way she hadn't before.

Because she couldn't be afraid. Not anymore.

Not now that she knew.

Now, she had to take what she wanted, once and for all.

CHAPTER TWENTY-FIVE

SOMETHING HAD SAT uneasy in his gut for the last few days. And he realized that it was the way the lines were getting so blurred with Rue. She texted him, but he didn't look at it. Instead, he picked up the phone and called the bank. "When exactly is the auction for the Whippoorwill Road property?"

"It's at 9:00 a.m. on Tuesday."

"And it's actually at the property?"

"Yes. Cash only."

"Got it."

He called Denver right after. "I'm going to need a big favor."

"How big? Are we burying a body or . . . ?"

"It's about money."

"Oh. That's easy."

"Well, you did just offer to pay for Bix and Daughtry's honeymoon."

Denver laughed. "Yeah. I'm not worried."

"I need enough money to buy a house."

"What caliber of house?"

"Rue's house."

He paused for a moment. "Right. Well. Yeah. I can do that."

"I'll pay you back."

"With what? Money you make on the ranch? It's all my money."

"I have my own investments, asshole. I might not have all the cash you do but—."

"Fine. I'll wire you the money."

"Thanks."

And he told himself that it was about doing something good for her, rather than getting space from all of this. Rather than regaining control of his life.

This shared space, the shared bed.

He had lied to her. He told her it wasn't a big deal that they spent the night together. It was. It had seemed convenient when they were staying in the hotel. It seemed intense back at his place. In the bed he had never shared with anybody else. Yeah. There, it seemed damned intense.

In fact, all of it did. Waking up every morning and having her there, going to bed with her at night. It was almost like it was becoming everything.

And he didn't know how to have her in his life that way. He didn't know how to do much of anything that way.

Then, he looked at the text from Rue.

Dinner, tonight. Meet me in the old barn.

His stomach went tight, and he imagined them again as young kids.

He didn't know why that was becoming so painful. So much harder to reflect on.

Maybe it was because he was closer to thinking

about the cave. Maybe because he was closer to thinking about the truth of everything.

But he had no reason to tell her no, so he told her yes, and when he was done with work for the day he drove on over to the barn.

The doors were closed, but he could see light flickering from the inside. When he walked in, Rue was sitting down on the floor on a blanket, candles in lanterns positioned all around. There was a picnic basket next to her. It reminded him of the picnic they'd shared up at the mountain after their trail ride. It reminded him of countless picnics they'd shared in here.

"I hope you don't mind," she said. "But it's bologna."

His stomach clenched.

"I don't mind," he said.

"I know those kids didn't have everything," she said, and he knew exactly who she meant. "But I'm glad they had each other."

"Me too," he said, his throat scratchy.

He moved closer to her, and that was when he noticed that she was wearing not just the blue necklace he'd given her the day of the wedding, but the necklace he made for her all those years ago. A leather strap with sea glass clumsily attached.

How had she ever thought that was store-bought? It was so clearly made with inexperienced hands. And yet . . .

He suddenly felt the strangest swelling of affection for the little boy that had made that for the girl that he . . . The girl he cared about more than anything in the world. That little boy that had spent days in a cave, but had still looked at Ruby Matthews and seen some kind of magic.

She was the only magic that he had been able to see in the whole world for a really long time.

That poor kid. That poor damned kid.

"There's nothing to hide from anymore," she said as he sat down. "Isn't that the craziest thing? Your dad's gone."

He huffed a laugh. "Yeah. I guess he is."

They opened up the picnic basket, and took out the sandwiches. There was more than just bologna. There was potato salad and macaroni and cheese. Some nice-looking rolls. But they both took a bite of the bologna first.

He didn't do nostalgia all that often. Mostly because his childhood wasn't a lot to write home about. The only nostalgia he had centered around her. This place. Bologna sandwiches.

It felt particularly intense and bright now.

"I really can't believe you still have that," he said.

"I can't believe you think I would've thrown it out."

He hadn't, she realized. He hadn't thought that she would've thrown it out. On some level, he knew that he could trust that Rue would've kept it.

That was a strange and terrifying feeling, and he didn't know why it should be.

"It means a lot," he said.

She ducked her head, and looked up at him, taking a bite of the sandwich. Right then, he saw the girl she'd been. Like she was sitting right in front of them. Like no time had passed at all.

Then she wrinkled her nose and gave him a more

mischievous look, and he remembered being sixteen and thinking she was the prettiest damned thing he'd ever seen. And running from it.

He'd stopped running. He might as well kiss her.

So he did. He leaned in and cupped her face and kissed her, because that was really what he wanted to do then, and he hadn't let himself.

Maybe the boy he'd been had always wanted this.

You denied him this. Not anyone else.

And suddenly, the deepest anger that he felt was at himself.

But there was no point being angry at himself. Because even now, Rue had to go back to her own house. She had to go back to her own life. He needed . . . he needed space. As wonderful as it was to have her in his life, in his house, there was something deeply uncomfortable about it. And he just . . . He couldn't.

But he could indulge in this. Tonight. Now.

He kissed her like he might die if he didn't, because right then everything felt like dying. He didn't know what the hell you were supposed to do with that. With every outcome feeling impossible. Feeling like the wrong one.

Yeah. He didn't know what the hell you were supposed to do with that.

But he kissed her anyway in their sacred spot. Kissed her like his life depended on it.

Kissed her for all the years he hadn't. For all the times he hadn't even let himself want it when deep down he understood now that he had.

He kissed her for every one of those wasted years she had spent kissing Asher.

And he kissed her for all the years after this when . . . he wouldn't.

It was getting to be too much. That was the thing. And it tore them apart to recognize that, but it was just the truth of it. He couldn't.

He would get her house back. He would put her back in her rightful place. He would . . .

He would send her off with both necklaces. The one he'd made her then, and the one he'd given her at her wedding. For that good life that she was supposed to have. The better one. The future that would involve another man who could give her everything. One who didn't feel like he was always waiting for the other shoe to drop, then get picked back up so he could be beaten with it.

And as he stripped her bare there in the barn, he realized exactly why he hated thinking of them as kids. It wasn't because it had been simpler back then. It was because they had a whole life ahead of them. To make different decisions than the one they'd made.

A whole life to figure out how to be okay. For him to figure out how to have her instead of how to give her away.

But he hadn't taken that path. There had been a fork in the road and he had taken the easy one.

Damn him.

He thought he was indulging that kid, but he was protecting him. From ever having to be afraid.

And Rue didn't need to wait for that. For him to figure it out. Because God knew it was all still a mess. Jumbled up inside of him.

He was a good friend. Because he could hide parts

of himself. Because it didn't mean staying, because it didn't mean opening up his house, his life, his whole heart.

He had thought because he was so good in bed that meant it would be easy for him to keep it all about the physical. Because that's what it had always been about for him before.

But never with her.

Never with her. And as he entered her, as he found himself drowning in desire, he knew that it had never been that. It had been a mistake. Because it had brought all the pieces of them together. Everything that they'd ever held back.

She had taken off everything except the necklaces. The sea glass and the glimmering blue sapphire sat heavily between her breasts. This tangle of everything they were.

Of everything he wanted.

It made him feel like he was being cut into.

His orgasm cost him. Took something from him. Left him raw and ragged as he held her, her own breathing fractured.

She'd come. But for the first time in his memory he hadn't worked at that. Hadn't made a performance out of getting her off as many times as he could.

Because he'd been lost.

In this, in her, in a way that he never was.

The way they went over together wasn't like anything else in his experience. She wasn't like anything else.

They lay there in the barn, no sound but their own breathing, but the beating of their hearts.

He closed his eyes, and he could see them as kids, sitting in this barn.

But they weren't those kids anymore. And he was even more determined about what had to happen next.

RUE REALIZED THAT things had changed when the day of the auction rolled around and she wasn't upset. In fact, she didn't even think of it until what would've been the middle of the auction.

Someone else was going to buy her grandmother's house, and live in it. But her life wasn't there anymore. She had memories there. She would always love the time that she had there. She would always be grateful for it. It had been her other refuge. But Justice was the biggest one.

She felt like she had been a little bit wimpy since that night in the barn. In that she hadn't told him yet that she was in love with him. It almost seemed silly. Because it seemed so obvious to her that what was between them was so much deeper than anything else. So much deeper than anything they'd ever been. Than she'd ever been.

But as scary as it had been to think about how sex might upset things between the two of them, the idea of introducing feelings that she knew Justice wouldn't be comfortable with was terrifying. Because it was the unknown. There were very few things about him that were unknown. But the deepest part of him, the way that he held himself at a distance, was something she didn't have all the answers to. Didn't know the intricacies of. Because of that, it was just a terrifying prospect. Putting herself out there like that. She really didn't know what he would do. He was her best friend, and she knew so much. But she was reminded of the way he had reacted when he'd seen that cave.

She had never known that fear existed inside of him. And if anything had ever spoken such loud volumes about Justice, it was that.

She'd been friends with him for most of her life, and she didn't understand that.

She sighed, and looked out the window, just as she heard the sound of tires on gravel. It was Justice.

She assumed he had been out working. His whole schedule had changed since she had moved in with him. He didn't stay out all night. He didn't get up quite so late. It was a very different experience of Justice King.

He was dressed up this morning, black pants and a button-up shirt. It was strange.

He opened up the door and took his hat off, which was even weirder. He was acting like he'd just walked into a church.

And for one second, her heart lifted. Because maybe this was it. Maybe he loved her too. Maybe he was going to ask her to marry him. It made sense. They made sense. She had never really loved anyone else, not in her whole life. She had never really wanted anyone else. It had just taken years for her to be brave enough to see the truth of it. But maybe he was brave enough now too.

She moved toward him, not even thinking, and reached her hands out.

"Hey," he said, leaning in and kissing her cheek.

His lips were cool, which was strange. Or maybe not, because it was winter outside. But it did feel weird. It made her heart sink just a little bit.

"I've got something to tell you," he said. But he smiled. So it had to be good.

"What?"

"I went to the auction this morning."

She frowned. "You did?"

"I bought the house."

For a minute, her head went completely fuzzy.

"You bought the house. *My* house?"

"Yes. Because you're special, and you didn't deserve what happened. And after everything . . . I wanted to get it for you."

She was fighting to get words out, fighting to breathe. "You can't do that."

"Yes, I can. I don't have a mortgage here. So, it's fine to pay for that."

"But *how*? You had to pay with cash."

He shrugged. "Yeah. Denver fronted me the money. It isn't a big deal."

"*Six figures* isn't a big deal?"

"No. Not between us. Anyway, I have it. I have some investments of my own. I just needed time to access the accounts, sell a few stocks, so I'm going to pay him back."

It was such an amazing gift, really it was. He had given her her grandmother's house. But she didn't feel happy.

Because she didn't want to leave. She didn't want to leave this life here. She wanted to get closer to him, and this was him moving him farther away.

His grand gesture was lovely in so many ways. But it was also ending them.

Ending this.

"I don't want the house," she said.

"What?"

"I mean, I do. Don't get me wrong. I'm grateful. I am. But I . . . Justice, I want to stay here with you."

His shoulders went rigid, and that was when her heart tightened like a fist. He wanted her somewhere else. This wasn't just about buying her the house; it was about getting her out of his. He hadn't come to tell her that he loved her. Quite the opposite.

"Justice," she said, tears filling her eyes. "Don't you know that I love you?"

She hadn't meant to say it like this. She hadn't meant to say it all weak and watery like this. She hadn't. Everything just felt so tenuous and fragile, and it had never felt like higher stakes. Because she really might lose him. She had no idea how he was going to react to this, except she already knew that he was running scared. But she had to say it. She had to.

He started to speak and she could already tell she wouldn't like what he had to say. She knew him. Right now she wished she didn't know him quite so well.

"Rue, you know I care a hell of a lot about you too. But you have a plan. A plan to get your life back on track. I want you to have the house."

"Are you pretending you don't know what that means?" she choked out. "That I love you? I'm *in* love with you, Justice."

"Please don't," he said. "I can't give you what you're asking for with all that. I'd . . ."

"You bought the house so you could break up with me."

"No," he said, emphatic. "I fucking didn't. There's no *breaking up*. We're us. We're us, just the same way that we've always been. But I thought that you would want your own space back."

"You wanted to go back to being just friends?"

"We *are* friends. Whether we're having sex or not. What difference does it make?"

She couldn't take it anymore. She exploded. "Are you this big of an idiot?" she asked. "Are you *really* this big of an idiot. Like sex didn't change things between us. Because it's actually harder to talk about some things now. All the mysteries that make you *you* are just more amplified. I'm more aware of the differences between us. You're a man, and I'm a woman. And there are pieces of you that you hold back from me." She paused. "Not just me. Everybody. You do this, you take care of me instead of being honest about what you're actually doing. You bought me this house so that you could be my hero. And you would rather do that than admit that . . . There's never going to be anybody else for me. Just like there's never going to be anybody else for you. Why do you think we're like this? And why do you think . . ."

She took a deep breath, put her hand on her chest and tried to keep on talking without faltering. "Asher was like my stand-in. I couldn't get love and marriage from you, and I got it from him, keeping you with me, I liked you best the whole time. I think you know that. I think you liked it. You got to be the most important man in my life, and somebody else was going to marry me and give me kids. And you *knew* I never loved him as much as I loved you."

"I don't know what the hell you're talking about. You are the most important person in my life. Hands down. But I can't do this thing that you want me to. I can't do a shared life. And shared feelings. And shared everything. I can't . . . I can't love you the way that you deserve to be loved."

"How do you think that is?"

"You want that beautiful house, you want that beautiful life. That gorgeous wedding, and I'm not the guy that can give you that."

"No. I wanted all that because it made marrying Asher feel right. Because I could plan it and organize it and put everything in its place, and that made me feel good, because the emotions weren't there. But if I have you . . . I don't need a wedding. I don't need the perfect dress. I don't need anything but *you*. You and me together. I just need you to love me. The way that you already do. I just want you to hold me, and be there for me, and admit what we are. What we have always been."

"And what is that?"

"Running scared, I think. Because I think we fell in love when we were two kids who didn't know what the hell it was, and we chose to run away from it rather than deal with it because that was easier and we were scared."

"Rue, there was a time when I might've been able to do it. But it has been a long time past. A long fucking time. And you grew into the woman that you are. All the shit you went through, it made you better. Maybe if I would've dealt with it back then I would've figured out something different than what I did. I just shut everything down. I don't know how to fix it. I don't . . . It's uncomfortable. Even having you in my space sometimes. Because I just . . . I want to be in control of everything. Okay? Because you can't . . . you can't trust anyone with anything. Not really. Not when your feelings can be manipulated any which way as long as a person has the power to use your love against you."

"You can trust me."

"I can't trust myself. That part of me is broken. And I know, because I broke it on purpose. Because I never wanted to be as scared or hurt again as I was when I was a kid and I was in that cave and . . ."

"It's not the cave, though, is it? That was scary and it was horrible. But there's more."

"It doesn't matter."

"It does. Because this is the wall. It's the wall I can't kick down, the one that I can't scale. It's the thing that I can't be enough for. And I need to know why. I need to know what it is."

"He left me there, Rue. After I did what he wanted. Do you have any idea what a mind fuck that is? I thought my dad was a good guy back then. He was my hero. After that everything just felt terrifying. Like a cave that could collapse at any moment. If doing everything he asked me to didn't make me matter, then what could? And I don't know what to do for that kid. So I just became the man that I am."

"But we met after that," she said. "And you still let me in. You still cared for me anyway."

"Yeah. I did. You're the one person I ever trusted,

the one other way I've ever found to trust love, and if it changes, Rue, if we change.... I need you to be the person that I made you in my life. And I can't risk losing it."

"But we did change. We changed. Or maybe more accurately we were finally real about what we wanted."

"I trusted you," he said. "To be my friend. And now you're changing..."

"Don't you dare," she said, anger fueling her now. "Don't you dare turn this around and make it about your trust issues. I love you, you dick, *I* didn't leave you stranded in a cave. I am sorry that your dad is a hideous narcissist. I am sorry that he hurt you. You have no idea how much. And I would spend the rest of my life trying to make up for that for you."

"I don't want you to do that. I wanted you to have that perfect life. I wanted you to have that with him. Because that's what you deserved. You have any idea how fucking relieved I was when you found somebody else." His voice broke. It broke *her*. "Do you have any idea?"

He meant that. With every fiber of his being.

Her eyes filled with tears. "I . . . Give me the keys to the house."

He reached into his pocket, and took them out, and she grabbed them.

"I'm going to go," she said.

"You don't need to leave," he said.

"Are you kidding? Yes, I do. You . . . you broke my heart, Justice. Asher didn't break my heart. He didn't have the power to do it. Because I know the difference. I know the difference between a thwarted plan and heartbreak. God. I thought that I did before. I thought I knew. But now I really do. And it hurts. I can't be with you right now. I can't stay with you like things are fine."

"We're friends, Rue. Lifelong. We've weathered all that stuff, and—"

"I don't know if we can weather this, Justice."

"You're acting like my dad," he said, the words stinging her. "You know, he told me years later . . . He asked me to do another delivery for him when I was fourteen and I said no. Because I was scared, sure, because of what had happened before but also because I couldn't stand how disappointed you'd be if you found out I did a drug delivery. I told him no, and he said he wished he would have let me die because I was useless. I did that for you, and now you're leaving me?"

That made her feel like she was being stabbed right in the chest.

She had been afraid of this. Terrified, and part of herself had decided that no matter what she would stay his friend. But now she didn't know. Just like she had said to Arizona and Bix and Fia, she didn't know what the right thing to do was. To demand everything, to demand what she wanted, to not be another person who abandoned him, or who loved him conditionally. She didn't know what would be possible. And she wouldn't know for a while. She was certain of that. She was also . . . You couldn't unhammer a nail. They could never take this and make it something that it wasn't. They could never take it and make it whole again. And it was up to her to decide if she was okay with the shape of the new relationship they were left with, or if she had to walk.

"I'll pay you back for the house," she said.

"I don't want you to."

"I'm not sure that I can be beholden to you, Justice."

"You're going walk away from our friendship over this? Over sex?"

"It's *not* over sex. I don't know if I can stand being with you knowing what we could be. Knowing what you won't let us be. You had really awful stuff happen to you. And I am so sorry. Of course you don't trust people. You're so worried about the way you think you can love me, why don't you think about the way that I loved you. For all those years. The way that I earned your trust. You're entitled to your trauma. Because it is really bleak. But *I* deserve better. I've been the best friend. I've been loyal to you. I stayed. I'm everything that I've ever said that I was. You felt so sorry for me when my behavior didn't get me what you thought I deserved. But what about *this*? I've earned the right to be loved. I've earned your trust. You not giving it is about you. It's a choice."

She stood there for a moment, then walked into her room and opened up her Justice box. She took the borrowed necklace out and she went back to him.

"Take it," she said, holding it out to him.

"Ruby . . ."

"Take it, Justice." She shoved it into his palm. "I don't want it. It doesn't mean anything now."

She stormed out the door and stood in the driveway, her world spinning.

She decided then that she would call Bix, Arizona and Fia to have them help her move, even though she knew the two pregnant women would only be able to lift light things. She knew they would understand what she was doing. She knew they would understand.

She clutched the keys in her hand and went out to her car, her whole world dissolving around her. "Bix," she said, dialing her first. "I need help moving."

"Is that code for committing a murder? Because if so, I'm in."

CHAPTER TWENTY-SIX

HE COULD REMEMBER well what it had been like when that cave had collapsed. The rock shifting, his fear that he would be crushed to death. And then, when he had survived that, the fear that no one would ever come for him.

The fear that he would die alone in the dark.

It was a fear that had never left him. It was one that he had been running from for his entire life. That he was so weak he could be used like that. That he was so insignificant he was a tool that could be left to die when he didn't serve his purpose.

And so he had made sure that he wasn't alone at night. So he had made sure he had his best friend with him, but that he had moved her into a space that didn't require everything from him.

He had his family, the ranch, and yet his finances were separate. His home was separate. He didn't put all his eggs in any one basket, because he didn't trust anything.

But he was still dying alone in the dark, and ever since Rue had left today, he had felt it. Keenly.

The rocks might not have crushed him, but he had been stuck in there ever since.

Rue was somewhere out there. On the other side

of this, and he couldn't get to her. That was what she didn't understand.

Because you won't let her understand.

Maybe that was true. Maybe the issue was him. What he refused to share. But the problem was he didn't know how to share it. He didn't know how to look his best friend in the eyes and tell her that he was just terrified. That he was a little boy who had never gotten out of the cave.

If he knew what he was afraid of. If he could just figure it out. If he just figured out what the hell was wrong with him, then maybe Rue wouldn't feel so messed up. Maybe he wouldn't feel so alone.

Alone.

He thought of Rue, wearing that necklace. Rue in the wedding gown. His great-great-great-great grandmother had worn that necklace out to Oregon, looking for a better life.

Rue was his better life. She always had been. The whole damned time.

She was everything.

That was what he was afraid of. She was *everything*.

And *everything* could be used against him. It had been done before.

And he knew what it was like to sit there in the darkness and feel like he had lost everything. To feel like no one was coming. He had never wanted to feel that alone again. Ever. And then there was her.

He had loved her from the moment he'd met her. Dammit, how he loved her.

She was everything. The most glorious, beautiful creature that he had ever known, and he found her all those years ago, but didn't know what to do with that.

Because he had never seen two people love each other in a real way. Had never seen a husband love his wife. Had never seen a father love his children.

Everything that the King children had scraped together had been out of desperation. And he had clung to Rue in the same fashion.

She was the one person who had the potential to be everything to him. Who had the potential to leave him alone in the dark, and now she had done it.

It was his fault.

He'd caused the cave-in. He had rejected her. He regretted it. But she had to teach him how to read. Was she going to have to teach him how to be a good boyfriend? Be a good husband?

That isn't the real problem. You're just scared. Stop trying to dress it up.

You're scared it'll be used to hurt you.

He took a breath and stood. Then he walked out of his house without thinking. He got into his pickup truck, and he drove to the watering hole where Rue had taken her polar plunge. When he saw the cave.

He wasn't a six-year-old boy anymore. He wasn't a fourteen-year-old whose father told him he just should have let him die. He was a grown-ass man, who had made decisions about how he was going to live his life. Who had made decisions about how to protect himself, and none of that had been about healing. It had been about protection.

He would rather face the cave than his father. Because at least the cave couldn't hurt him anymore. He took a step forward, and walked inside, letting himself be enveloped by the darkness. He didn't go in deep, but he stayed there, taking in the scent, the surroundings. He had been stuck here for three days. And those three days had defined the whole rest of his life. Because of everything that had happened afterward. Everything he had learned.

It had become a monster in his mind. This darkness. This place. But he realized now that it was just a place. And fear was just a feeling. What he wanted was her. Of course he was in love with her.

He grabbed his chest, afraid that his heart was going to burst right out the front of it. "Help me," he said. To what, he didn't know. To whom. He had cried out in the darkness before, and no one had come for him.

But Rue . . . He knew that she would never leave him. He knew that she would always care for him. That if they had an issue they would talk about it. She wasn't his father. So the idea that he was holding himself back because he couldn't trust her was just a lie. The real issue, when he drilled right down to it, was that love hurt. It had the power to devastate.

So he'd been very careful with how he loved in all the years since. She was right. She was right about him. He had been glad that there was another man that she would never love quite as much as she loved him. He had been glad that he had a stand-in so he could keep himself safe, and hold on to her. But this was another of those forks in the road. He couldn't leave Ruby Matthews half-loved. Not when she deserved everything.

Not when he *did* love her.

He did.

And he knew now why it hurt so much to think of them as kids. Because he'd fallen in love with her then. He had denied that little boy. He had denied himself. He had denied the man. Because of fear.

What bullshit that he'd told himself he was giving in to every indulgence. Every temptation.

Sex with strangers meant nothing. It was like eating and never being able to be satisfied.

Sex with Rue was something else. It was the substance of it all. The full expression of loving her. Accepting that was like taking a breath.

The first full breath he had taken in years.

Loving her was what he'd never let himself do. All this time. But it had been there all the same. Like all the wounds he never let himself deal with. So he had to tear every lock off every door, let them all fly free, because that was the only way. To get down to that love. To get down to the truth. And to let it all go. Finally.

He wasn't trapped in the cave anymore. And all there was left to do was walk out into the light.

So he did. Because Rue had shown him the way.

Bix, Arizona and Fia had done the hard work of packing everything up for her so that she could avoid him. And now her driveway was full of boxes and furniture that her friends were helping her unpack. Her friends. She had them still. At least there was that.

Bix had threatened to kill him, cheerfully, multiple times, while Fia and Arizona had been more measured.

They had talked a lot about old wounds, childhood scars and the damage that had kept them all from finding love for years.

"I don't have any patience for it," Bix said angrily. "I didn't have any patience for it when Daughtry had his big mantrum, and I don't have any patience for it now."

"You're consistent," Fia said, patting Bix on the shoulder. "I like that about you."

But then, they had gotten all the things moved, and everyone had left, and Rue was just there, alone with this big hole inside of herself that wouldn't ease up. Wouldn't heal. Because she wanted him. Regardless of whether or not he was being a dick. She wanted him.

She sniffed and wiped her eyes, trying to decide what she was going to do.

Because part of her really did think she had to take away the crutch of their relationship for him to ever get better. Part of her really did think she needed to demand the best for herself.

Part of her really did believe that staying away from him was the best course of action.

Another part of her felt like she had cut her own arm off and was just letting it bleed when she could easily reattach it.

And she hated the idea of abandoning him.

She kept imagining him alone. Alone and buried. With nobody looking for him. Nobody coming after him. Had she left him alone like everybody else?

This kind of thing was supposed to be so easy. The

decision to love herself enough to ask for what she wanted. Enough to demand she get what she deserved.

But it wasn't that simple. It never could be.

Because she loved him. Because she had loved him for most of her life. And losing her house, losing the wedding, all of that she'd been able to make a binder about, make new plans over. Deal with. But this... This wasn't the same. And she didn't know the right thing to do. She wanted to hold him. She wanted to go hide out in the barn with him. She wanted to talk to her best friend about her heartbreak, but he was the heartbreak.

She wanted him to come over and hold her and watch *13 Going on 30*. She wanted him. And she didn't know how that was ever going to be okay. They had been foolish. Because the stakes for this were far too high. And neither of them had been equipped to handle it. She had put it all on the line for love, and he'd held his ground of friendship. And they were left standing on two different sides of a line she didn't know if they could cross.

What did you do with something like that? What were you supposed to do?

She sucked in a sharp breath, right in time with the knock on her door.

She stopped, and went to answer it. The door pushed open, and there he was. Standing there in the suit he had gotten for the wedding she didn't have. Reminding her of that day he had come over for the fitting, and she'd been so damned proud of how beautiful her best friend was.

"What are you doing here?"

"I had to come get you," he said.

"Did you come to get me . . . to be your friend or . . . ?"

"Everything. Rue. Absolutely everything."

On a sob, she threw herself into his arms.

"I love you," she said.

"I love you too."

"I didn't know what to do," she said. "I didn't know if I should come back to you and tell you that we could be friends or if I should try and hold some kind of line. Because the thing is, I love you. Whether you're giving me exactly what I ask for or not. I love you. I hated being without you. I hated it so much."

"Me too," he said. "But I'm grateful. Because you taught me something. You taught me that I had to deal with myself. I was scared of being without you. Of being alone, and I never wanted you to be my everything because then if I lost you my world would end. I would be trapped in the cave all over again. I couldn't face it." He took a deep breath. "I didn't trust you, but it's because I didn't trust myself either. I don't trust my feelings, because they've been twisted and used before. But you've been there for me, Rue. You deserve my trust. You don't deserve . . . You didn't deserve what I did."

"Justice," she said. "It's okay that you didn't know what to do in a situation neither of us have been in before. You didn't need to be perfect. I know it seems like I was asking you to . . ."

"No. You were asking me to stand on my own two feet, and not use you to hold me up while I denied you what we both needed. You had to leave for me to realize it was too late." He took his grandmother's necklace out of his pocket and held it out to her. "I want you to keep this."

"Then it's not borrowed anymore," she said.

"No. You'll have to borrow something else for our wedding. But this is for you to keep. I want you to wear it. On your way to our better life. I have loved you from the beginning. But I didn't know what love was. And if I would've paid fucking attention, Rue, I would've realized that you were showing me."

"It wasn't just you. I was afraid of it too. I was afraid of giving all of myself to someone. I could feel myself wanting it from you. And I didn't ever want that to turn me into my parents. But that isn't us. It never could be."

He shook his head. "No. You were right. You never did anything to deserve my lack of trust. It wasn't you I was afraid of. I was just afraid in general. But our friendship was love without risk. I guess that was what was left. For us to take a risk. Do the zip lining, the polar plunge."

"Was I practicing for the two of us to get together the whole time?" Rue asked.

"Maybe. Maybe."

"I love you," she said.

"I love you too. I always have. It just took me this whole time to figure out how much I was willing to risk for that."

"It turns out we were both willing to risk everything." Then she laughed. Because it was true. They were just everything. That was all.

"Everything."

"I've always thought you were the most beautiful man in the world. But I didn't think you could ever really belong to anyone," she said.

"Don't you know, Ruby Matthews, I belong to you. Always."

She knew that it was true. Because she knew him.

Justice King was her best friend in the whole world. And he always would be.

"Remember how we talked about me giving you away at your wedding?"

"Yes," she said, laughing.

"What if I married you instead?"

"That sounds perfect."

Ruby Matthews had her life together. It just didn't look like she'd thought it would. She would be leaving this perfect little house, with a perfect little yard, for the place she loved most in the world, King's Crest.

All of her organization systems would have to change. They'd have to be shared. Because her life would be shared. She'd had plans before, but she had something better than plans now. She had life; she had love.

She'd be planning another wedding, and this one really would be perfect.

She'd always known Justice belonged right up at the front of the church with her, because he was her best friend in the whole wide world.

She just hadn't realized that he belonged there as her groom.

The love of her life. For always, forever.

Then he leaned in and kissed her, her Cowboy James Bond, in blue jeans or a tux.

"I love you," he said.
She sighed, then smiled.
Everything was perfect.
Everything was in its rightful place.
Finally.

* * * * *

Read on for an excerpt from Maisey Yates's next book from Canary Street Press, *Cowboy It's Cold Outside*.

CHAPTER ONE

DENVER KING KNEW that it was a lofty goal for a man like him to avoid hellfire altogether. Given his lineage, it was easy to see why many people assumed that in the afterlife he would be down south passing beers over righteous flame with some questionable characters for company. But in truth, he had done his part to try and balance his moral scales a little bit.

But for his sins, hellfire was currently headed his way.

He was standing out in the brand-new public area of King's Crest. Where they had just opened their new event venue, and several places that were equipped for overnight stay.

That was when she appeared.

Dark hair flowing behind her, the twining ink vines visible from her shoulder down to her wrist thanks to the rather brief tank top she had on.

And it was *freezing*. But sure. A tank top. That seemed about right for Sheena Patrick.

But it wasn't the tank top, the fierce look in her eye, her absolute smoke show of a body or the tattoos that caught his attention.

Tattoos he had often wondered about the intricacies of. The vine on her right arm disappeared beneath her tank top, and he felt it was human to wonder where it went from there.

But that wasn't it. It was the bright red chip she held in her hand.

Lord Almighty.

As she got closer, he could see she had a full face of makeup on at 8:00 a.m. He didn't know if it was because she was coming off the bar shift the night before and hadn't taken it off, or if she was ready for tonight. But the black liner made her green eyes glow, and the deep color on her lips was enough to make a saint consider what it might look like left behind on his skin.

And he was not a saint.

There was no denying that she was hot.

She was also a hundred percent completely off-limits.

And Denver King did not push limits.

He had no *interest* in hellfire. Whatever form it took.

That was the thing.

She stopped right in front of him, lifting one dark brow and holding the chip up just so it covered his view of her face. "I've come to cash in," she said.

Her voice was smoky. Like a late night and a shot of whiskey.

He looked at the chip. He didn't take it. "Have you?"

The truth was, he'd given out poker chips to any number of his father's victims.

In the years since, many of them had come asking for money. And that was the point of it. An acknowledgment that he owed them. That they had the right to come to him and cash in. Nobody had actually brought the chip.

Nobody else had waited this long.

Any chip that hadn't been cashed in so far belonged to dead men, who had continued on in the rough life his father had been part of.

Sheena was the last holdout.

But then, he had been sending money to Sheena and her family ever since that botched job that had cost her dad his life all those years ago.

He held his father, Elias King, personally responsible for that. And it was up to him to make restitution for it. He had always seen it that way. It didn't matter whether or not he had done it himself.

The sins of the father would be visited on the son. And God knew he meant to try and wipe that slate clean. He surely did.

"And what is it exactly that you want to collect?"

She lowered the chip. "I have a proposition for you."

"Name a dollar amount."

She shook her head. "I'm not after a dollar amount, King. It's not that simple."

He frowned. "Go on."

"I have a business proposition." There was something sharp and clear in her eyes, and he had a feeling this was going to be a long talk.

"All right. It's awfully cold. You want to go inside?"

She snorted. "Do I look like I'm shivering?"

No. She didn't. But he had always thought that Sheena might be powered by a hidden fire in her belly. God knew she'd been fighting a hell of a lot harder than most for a hell of a lot longer. He respected her. That was the thing. When her dad had died, she'd been left with three younger siblings to raise. And she had done a hell of a job.

She hadn't allowed his family to fully take her in. But that didn't surprise him. Not that he and Sheena knew each other. They didn't. In fact, other than him ordering a beer from her on the occasional night out at Smokey's, he didn't have anything to do with her. Not directly.

He would go up, lay eyes on the place, make sure nothing had burned to the ground. Put an envelope of cash in the mailbox and go on.

They saw each other from a distance, if that.

This was the longest conversation they'd had in thirteen years.

"All right, then. Tell me."

"It doesn't sit right with me," she said. "Being in your debt. But I have an idea that's going to help us both."

"You're *not* in my debt. Your father is dead because of mine. There's no amount of money on earth that can make up for that."

She snorted. "Your opinion, King, not mine. My dad was a worthless son of a bitch. Yeah. It was hard, being left without somebody bringing in money, but my dad himself wasn't worth the carcass of a moth-eaten buzzard. I'm not sorry he's gone. He did nothing but bring bullshit down on us. So no. It isn't like you robbed us of our loving patriarch. And hell, you didn't even have anything to do with it. Not directly."

"Close enough," he said.

He'd been drawn in by his dad. By his proclamations about how what he did, he did for the family. The truth was, he didn't care about his family. His wife had left him, and he'd painted it as a betrayal to their clan. He'd said he had to work even harder to make things right for the kids.

Denver had bought into it. But then their father's facade had started to crumble. The treatment of his sister after her accident was a red flag he couldn't ignore. And after that . . . the last job. The one where he'd really seen his dad. The violent man he could be.

And one thing Denver had learned that day for sure: violence begot violence.

"All right," she said. "That's your opinion. But I'm not putting that on you. I want to pay you back. To that end, I want in on the expansion here at King's Crest."

He owed Sheena, that much was true. But the control freak inside him balked immediately at the thought of allowing anyone *in*.

"Is that so?"

"Yes. I have a business plan. You know I work over at Smokey's."

She knew full well he knew it. He had a feeling she'd said that to highlight the total separation in their lives. They knew each other. They kept it brusque and bare minimum like they didn't.

"Yes," he confirmed.

"And before that I was tending bar down in Mapleton. People need more to do. More nightlife. Smokey's is fine, but it's a very particular thing."

"A meat market," he commented.

She shrugged. "Sure. Everybody loves a little beef."

He couldn't tell if she was smirking or smiling. Or some combination of the two.

"All right. Go on."

"Axe throwing."

"Excuse me?"

"Axe-throwing bars have begun to be a big deal. I hear you're making beer down here. Add a little bit of food, and you've got Pyrite Falls' newest hot spot."

"Axe throwing."

"Yeah. It's fun. You let off steam, you hang out with friends. You fling deadly weapons around."

"Sounds like a liability."

"I didn't take you for a bitch, King."

"I didn't think you took me for anything."

"Nothing but an envelope in a mailbox. And this chip," she said, brandishing it again. "Anyway. The point is, people do this all the time. It's perfectly safe. I had the opportunity to go check one out when I went down to Medford recently. It's a good time, and more importantly it's packed. I've got a lot of data about it as a growing pastime. Also, I'm great at it. You know, not so much in bars, but I do it for fun at home."

"It sounds like hipster bullshit."

"Do I look like hipster bullshit to you?" She put her hands on her hips, her dark hair sliding over her shoulder, shiny even in the overcast light.

"A little bit," he said, looking over the tattoos. Really, it was like one continuous tattoo. Vines and flowers that twined up her arm, down into the tank top, so where else it went, he didn't know. He wondered, though.

"That just goes to show that you don't know me."

It was deliberate. The not knowing her. He had wanted to help her while leaving her as untouched by all of this as possible. It was different with Penny.

Penny had been alone in the world. No one was coming to save her or take care of her. Sheena had her sisters.

She squared up with him, the determination on her face something no sane man would dismiss.

"I have a whole business plan," she said. "This isn't coming from nothing. Believe me when I tell you my survival instinct is strong. I'm not a dreamer. I'm a planner. I think this is really something."

"All right. Explain it to me."

"That's what I've *been* doing."

She reached into a bag she had slung over her shoulder and pulled out a binder. It was black and plain, with no adornment. His sister-in-law Rue was fond of binders. But hers were always floral. With decorative stickers for whimsy. The only thing ornate about Sheena was the tattoo.

"This is quite a bit," he said, opening up the binder and finding inside photos of different axe-throwing facilities. A proposed menu, projected expenses.

"I thought it best to be thorough. You told me that you owed me. That was why you gave me the poker chip. You said that all I had to do was cash in. That's what I aim to do. But further to that, I think it can be something that benefits both of us."

"Why don't you show me what you've got."

"Excuse me?"

"I'll tell you what. Let's go throw some hatchets. And I'll see what I think."

*

Sheena hadn't expected this to be *easy*. Denver King set himself up as being some kind of savior, but she had never seen it in that way. To her mind, letting Denver King near her property was a lot like letting a wolf offer protection.

They *could* protect you. But they could also decide to turn around and eat you. She wasn't a fool. She didn't buy into this whole idea that the Kings were so reformed. That Denver was entirely different from his dad. He earned his money gambling. She knew that. It was a fairly covert thing, but she kept her ear to the ground. Paid attention.

He had made big bucks in the professional poker circuit.

He might not have a bunch of illegal gambling happening on the property, but it was still an indicator that he was part of that world.

And she knew that she was playing it a little bit dangerous wanting to join up with him to do business. But her options were limited. There were very few people out there who felt that they owed her. But he was one of them. And that meant she was going to take advantage of it as and when she could.

She was a thirty-one-year-old empty nester—for all intents and purposes—with her youngest sister off at college and moving on with her life. Sheena was still tending bar, and she was beginning to feel . . .

Left behind. Which was dumb, and she didn't like it. So she'd taken a good look at that poker chip, and she'd decided asking for Denver's help was better than languishing in dumb, useless feelings.

She wasn't asking for a handout—the only money she'd ever taken from him was for her sisters' benefit, not hers—but using him to get a real business up and running? She'd made a bargain in her soul so she could handle that.

She was tough. Happy to use people as they used her. That was life, and she'd accepted it.

As long as she went in eyes wide open with Denver, she could do it with him, too.

She could admit she'd expected him to just agree. Which was strange because she'd say she didn't trust Denver or anyone to do what they said, but he'd always indicated that he felt responsible for what had happened to her father.

She also didn't want to owe him. But needed him to feel he owed her.

She also didn't want to rely on him or anyone, but had to.

She could appreciate the tightrope walk she was engaged in.

The red poker chip burned into her palm, and she squeezed her hand around it, before putting it into her pocket.

"All right. You've got yourself a deal. What do I have to do? Outthrow you?"

"No. I think I just need to see the appeal. I'm the kind of man who needs to see something to really get a feel for it. To visualize it. I want to understand what it is you're offering to people."

"Well. That's kind of lame. I was hoping this was some kind of Paul Bunyan thing. As long as I could out-hatchet your man-made machine, you would let me and my big blue ox have our way with the place."

"Do you have a big blue ox?"

"The big blue ox is metaphorical. Do you have a place where we can throw an axe?"

"Sure."

He moved in front of her, and she did her best not to pay too close attention to the fine, masculine figure that he cut. He was tall. Very tall. And she noticed because she was a pretty tall woman. A lot of men made her feel large and unfeminine, though she didn't really mind that, actually. But Denver King made her feel dainty, which was as disorienting as it was unique.

He was at least six inches taller than her. His shoulders were broad, his chest well muscled, his arms massive. Men like that always thought they would be great at axe throwing. In her experience, they tended to overdo it. Throw it so hard it bounced right out of the target. And it made them angry. She always enjoyed watching that.

He led her out to a space behind the shed, where a large axe was stuck into a round of wood. "I'll take you over to where we shoot," he said. "There's a couple of targets that are still set up."

"All right. Sounds good."

She did her best to not notice the way that his forearm shifted as he picked up the large axe and slung it over his shoulder.

He was a fine specimen of a man, that much was true. But she didn't have any use for men like him.

Sheena was in charge of her own life. In charge of her own destiny. *And that's why you're here asking him for a favor?*

Well. That little internal voice could shut its trap.

When it came to relationships, she didn't do them. When it came to sex, she liked to be in charge.

She got what she wanted, the guy got what he wanted. No harm, no foul.

She preferred men who didn't have ties to the area. Tending bar in Mapleton had been more convenient from that standpoint.

It made scratching an itch feel a little bit less risky.

Denver King might as well have been wrapped in caution tape.

The first time she'd noticed he was hot, the cops had just loaded her father's body into a coroner's van.

To say noticing Denver King's physical attributes was problematic was putting it lightly.

But also, it meant she was used to it.

He opened up the passenger door of an old blue truck, and she stared at it, and him.

"Get in," he said.

"I was unaware this was a whole field trip."

"We don't shoot near the buildings."

"Responsible," she said.

She waited until he moved away from the door, and climbed up inside the truck.

Then he rounded to the driver's side and got in.

He started up the engine, and she looked out the window. All the better to not look at him.

"How are the girls?"

Abigail, Whitney and Sarah were all off on their own now. Far away from this place. And good thing.

And if Sheena ached with loneliness sometimes, she dismissed it.

She could leave. She could start over somewhere else. When Whitney had moved out six months ago, she'd fully had that realization. But the problem was, nobody else owed her a favor. And then there was a tangle of the fact that she also owed Denver. And that didn't sit right with her. He might not feel like she needed to pay them back. But she wanted her personal ledger to be balanced up. It was important to her.

Because if she couldn't ultimately be free of that past, then nothing she had done since then mattered. And yes, she was aware that made it somewhat ironic that she was looking to actually get into business with Denver.

But she had a plan. Eventually, she wouldn't be here running the bar. She would open a second location elsewhere. Eventually, she would make her own way. Maybe somewhere closer to her sisters.

But after she got started. If there was one thing she was an expert at, it was surviving. But she wanted to be an expert at more than just that. She wanted to figure out how to thrive. They didn't speak while he drove them up to wherever that shooting range was. Somewhere out at the top of the ridge. It was beautiful.

This whole place was beautiful. But she knew that even with all of the magnificent surroundings, it was all only as serene as the life that you were growing up in.

The Kings had this place. She didn't deny it was possible that it might be a nice place that was shit to live in, given what she knew about their dad.

But she knew without a doubt her own growing-up years were worse.

The house had been small and ramshackle. Instead of kitchen cabinets and counters, they'd had tables lining a room, with a freestanding sink that leaked. She'd done her best to make that place a home after her dad's death.

Hung fabric from the tables to sort of mimic a cabinet and counter look. Something to make it seem normal. With sisters ranging in age from four to fourteen, it had been a struggle. And she'd only been eighteen herself. But they'd managed. For thirteen years, they'd managed.

And now it was her turn. To try and do something more than manage. To start the steps that she needed to build a life . . . somewhere else. A life that she had chosen. A life that was more than this.

It wasn't that it was a bad life. She liked to think that she had taken something really awful and turned it into something pretty decent for the sake of her sisters. But it had left her . . . hard. She didn't know another way to be. She was thankful for the resilience. She couldn't resent it. It had kept her safe. But she wanted to find a way to live where she didn't have to be this all the time.

An axe-throwing bar was admittedly a little bit of a funny way to go about that. But she knew bar work. This had a slightly different focus. It wasn't about getting drunk. It was about having a drink with friends, having a good time. A little bit of friendly competition.

She had been working the rough dive bars for years. She was ready for a change of scenery.

She had been waitressing early on, when the girls had been really little. But the money was just much better in bartending. So when she felt all right to leave them at night—tucked up into bed with the oldest well aware of how to use a shotgun if she needed it, and their trusty guard dog, Hank, on hand to create a ruckus if anyone should approach—she had started taking that night work. Down in Mapleton, the amount of work she had been able to get, the size of the tips thanks to the size of her . . . Well.

Her mama hadn't given her much of anything except her figure to hear tell of it. She was happy to make use of it. Consider it a gift from the woman who hadn't stuck around to raise her. It was the only one she'd gotten.

There were two ways to handle men. She could put them under her spell using her looks, and she could scare the hell out of them using her strength. She was familiar with how to do both.

She would like it if she didn't need to do it quite so often.

And being a business owner would be different than being a server.

Denver stopped the truck at the end of the dirt road. There was a view, spectacular, just behind a raised ridge of gravel with targets affixed to the front of it.

"Safety first," he said.

"Sure," she said. "Though I don't want to be flinging the axe over the top of the target and losing it down below in the draw."

"I thought you were an expert."

"I am. I actually meant I don't want *you* to lose your axe."

"I'm good," he said.

"All right. I'm going to demonstrate. And then I'll

let you have a couple of practice throws. We can do best out of five after that."

He looked at her, and she could tell that she had greatly offended his delicate masculine pride by suggesting that he needed to warm up. Or instruction of any kind.

"I think I can handle it."

"Just . . . based on your feelings?"

"Yeah."

"Your feelings aren't facts, Chief. No matter how much you might want them to be."

"Based on feelings and what I know about myself, I think I'm good."

She affected a very innocent expression, grabbed hold of the axe and slipped out of the truck.

Then she went to stand in front of the target. She squared up and decided to go with a classic, two-handed overhead throw. She lifted the axe over her head and drew it back.

"Don't do anything foolish like hopping in front of me," she said.

"Yeah, I think I can figure that one out, thank you."

Then without overthinking it, she let the axe fly. She did her best to gauge the distance between herself and the unfamiliar target, and it flew end over end, landing with a satisfying thunk at the upper left of the target.

"That's my favorite throw stance," she said. "And it's how I recommend you start."

"It wasn't a bull's-eye," he said.

She rolled her eyes and walked down the slight incline toward the target. She grabbed the axe and wrenched it out of the wood. "The next one will be."

She walked back up, lifted the axe over her head and let fly again. This time, she was able to correct and get it right at the center of the target.

She pumped her fist, unable to stop herself from celebrating.

"There you go," she said. She regarded the implement, then looked at him. "This is a pretty big axe. You might need a smaller one."

He lifted a brow. "I think I can figure out how to handle a big one."

She bit the inside of her cheek, uncertain whether the double entendre had been intentional. That was the problem. She really didn't know him.

"The size of the axe doesn't really matter, Denver."

"That sounds like something people with small axes say."

He took the axe from her easily and stood a couple of paces back from where she had been. Smart. He was going to naturally throw with a lot more strength, so he needed to put distance between himself and the target. She decided to focus on that rather than a comment on big axes.

He was a big man. She assumed he was . . . proportional. Though sometimes men could be a surprising disappointment. Sort of a theme in her life, she had found.

But that was why she didn't depend on them for anything.

He pulled the axe back over his head, and his shirtsleeves came up, revealing the definition of his bicep, and she couldn't help but look.

Instantly, for some reason, she took a moment to

imagine Denver King throwing axes shirtless. Okay. She was done with that.

There was really no point mooning after a specific nice-looking man. Because again, it was no guarantee they wouldn't be disappointing.

He let the axe fly, with way too much force. It bounced off the wooden target and landed in the gravel below, the head sinking deep into the ground. "Deep stroke," she said, her lips twitching.

He looked at her, his face completely void of expression. "I'm known for that."

She ignored the buzzy feeling between her legs.

"Go fetch your axe."

"Got any tips for me?" he asked as he walked over to where the axe was buried in the dirt.

He pulled it out one-handed, with ease.

"Well," she said dryly. "You don't have to go so hard. It's not a jackhammer."

"Noted."

Everything she said felt tainted by double entendres, and she had no idea what to do about it.

"You could also do it one-handed."

His lips went into a flat line. "Could I?"

"You could," she returned, not taking her gaze off his. "Of course, using two hands gives you a little bit more control. And you know, it's not the size of the axe, it's the . . ." She lifted a brow. "Motion of the ocean, so to speak."

"You're mixing your metaphors."

"Am I? Whoops."

She shouldn't be indulging in this. It made her blood feel a little bit fizzy. She was going to enter into a business partnership with him, and they didn't need to go teasing each other like this.

If he was teasing. She genuinely couldn't tell with him. He was inscrutable. Unknowable.

"Okay," he said. "I'll try again with your top tips in mind."

He stood back on the line, lifting the axe up over his head again. This time, he let it fly with a lot more control, and it hit the target with a satisfying thud. Her aim was still better. But he landed the shot.

"There you go. Now that you've found the sweet spot, you just have to keep throwing it at the same angle so that you can hit the same spot over and over again."

This time, she saw a glimmer in his dark eyes. "Is that how you do it?"

"For optimum satisfaction, yes. If you find a good spot, you keep going."

"I'll keep that in mind."

He went to the target and yanked the axe out again. Then she took it from him and went to stand in the ready position. "Best out of five, Denver King. And when we're done, you can tell me if you want to continue."

"Okay. In the meantime, though, tell me a little about yourself. Like a job interview."

"Well, that wasn't part of the deal."

"You aren't setting all the terms, are you?"

"Okay," she said, her teeth mildly set on edge. She drew the axe back and threw it, letting it fly true until it hit the edge of the target. She was distracted by him. Which was unacceptable.

"What is it you want to know?" she asked, turning to face him.

"I want to know where your sisters are."

"Sarah is in college. So is Whitney. Abigail graduated. She got a job in Fresno."

"Fresno. Wow. Sounds like hell."

She felt defensive of her sister's life choices, but he wasn't wrong. "Yeah. It does to me, too. But she's happy. And she isn't here."

"Right. But you want to start a business here?"

"Not my end goal."

She went and took the axe out of the wood, then reset her stance. She handed it to him and let him walk up to the line.

"Does this mean it's my turn to ask you a question?"

He let the axe fly, and it hit the outer edge of the target. Just barely in.

He didn't tell her not to ask the question. He didn't invite her to, but he didn't tell her not to either. So.

"What's your ultimate vision for King's Crest?"

"I want it to be a little bit of a destination. I want to bring more tourism into the area. I want to benefit myself and my family. But I also want to . . . to do something worthwhile. My dad did nothing but break shit, as you well know."

"I do."

"I want to do better than that. That's it. End of story."

"My turn, then?"

She put herself in the ready position and let the axe fly. It went true, right in the center.

"Go for it," she said.

"So you don't want to stay here."

"No. Not long-term. Wherever my sisters end up, I'd like to be a little bit closer to them. It's possible that they'll be far-flung. Maybe I won't quite be able to pull that off. But I'm going to try. I don't have a legacy here. Not one to fix. Not one to give even a single shit about. I lived here because this was where my dad decided to hunker down and get in bed with a criminal—that's your dad. We didn't have roots here."

"But you want to start your business on my land."

"I want to start a business, I want it to become profitable, I want to pay you back. And then I want to take some of what I made and open another location. I'll leave you the place when I leave. And keep collecting some of the profits."

"I see."

"I don't have happy memories here, Denver. I don't have a reason to stay. It was . . ."

It was tangled. Complicated.

For many years, Denver had been the reason she'd stayed.

Oh, not him personally. Because she didn't even know him personally. But that check he left in the mailbox.

And . . . in spite of herself, she had to admit that feeling that there was a wolf watching over them. Maybe even keeping them safe. Plus, things had been hard enough. Trying to figure out, as a teenager, how to put a house on the market, how to take her sisters and move them to a different school, all of it . . . It was just a little bit too much. Where she had lived, where she still lived, sat between Mapleton and Pyrite Falls. She split the difference between the two. Working in either one had always been about the same. And it might be kind of a pain sometimes, but it was familiar. And they could afford the cost of living.

In a city, that wouldn't be the case. And another small town would be just as difficult to navigate as this one.

So for years, it just hadn't made any sense.

He went and got the axe. His turn again.

"You want me to help you get a grip on that big axe of yours?"

He snorted, but when he threw the axe, it went wide.

That made her stomach twist a little bit.

Well. It was a good thing to know. That he wasn't immune.

He was just a dude, after all. Not really a wolf, or any of the other strange, fanciful things she had convinced herself he might be.

They didn't ask each other anymore questions, and she was the hands-down winner of the round.

"All right," he said, plunking the axe head down into the dirt with a thud, his large hand wrapped around the base of the handle. "You got yourself a business proposition, Sheena Patrick."

"Good. I look forward to doing business with you."

She reached into her pocket and took out the poker chip. Then she pressed it into his palm, ignoring the heat the transfer left behind on her fingertips. "Just let me know when you want to meet next."

"Depends. Are you going to quit your job down at the bar?"

"I have to put in my two weeks' notice."

"Fair. How about we talk after that."

"I guess we will."

"I guess we will."

CHAPTER TWO

"WHAT DO YOU know about axe-throwing bars?"

When they had their barbecue dinner set out on the table that night, Denver decided to pose the question to his brothers.

Technically, he didn't have to ask anybody's permission to do something like this. Yes, typically the money came out of the broader ranch pot for new endeavors, and they asked all four main families that made up Four Corners to vote. Meet with the whole collective at a town hall to make sure everyone was on board.

But in this case, he would be financing the whole thing from his own pocket. So he didn't figure it was up to him to consult anybody.

He realized, though, that his siblings might feel differently.

"Is this a trick question?" Landry asked, looking over at his wife and daughter, and then back to Denver. "Is someone in trouble?"

"I can't recall having done any raids on axe-throwing bars recently," Daughtry said, still wearing his uniform from his shift earlier in the day. "Or *any* raids, for that matter. Since our dad leaving town functionally removed most of the crime."

"Well, I warned all my friends at the axe-throwing bar that you were coming," Daughtry's wife, Bix, said. "Because I don't like cops."

"Which has made things very difficult for me," Daughtry said dryly as Bix grinned up at Daughtry.

Denver's siblings were disgustingly happy. He was thrilled for them. Honestly. It was all he had ever wanted for them. That was kind of the point of taking charge of everything. It was kind of the point of trying this to make a new life for them. A safer one. A happier one.

It was why he, who had never known anything about having a real family, who had never known anything about holidays or birthday parties or had one thrown for him, had decided that they all needed celebrations.

It was why they had crowded family dinners. It was why he had become a grill master. Not just because he liked beef. It was his life's work, after all. The gambling made a lot of money, because he was great at it. Because he was . . . He couldn't help it if his brain worked a certain way and he could count cards easily. At least, it wasn't his fault as far as he was concerned. He knew that other people, his competitors, might feel differently. He couldn't help them with that.

But the ranch, that was his passion. Doing honest work. He didn't gamble anymore. He'd made all he needed to. Between that and judicious investments, he'd netted himself quite a fortune. Enough to blot out some of the debt his father had left behind, enough to make sure that his family was taken care of.

Enough to support the ranch even when things weren't going well.

"I've been to one," his sister-in-law Rue said, down from her end of the table. "Back when I was with . . ." She slid a look over to Justice.

"I'm not threatened by Asher."

Justice and Rue had been best friends for years and years, and she had very nearly married another man a few months back. But fate had righted itself, and the two of them were together now.

"It was fun," Rue finished.

"Yeah. Well. We're going to open one up on the ranch."

"That's desperately random," Arizona said.

"Why is it random, Arizona?"

"It's random," Arizona's stepson said, chewing around a big mouthful of food.

"He says it's random. Therefore, it's random."

Denver looked to his brother-in-law, who simply shrugged. "I don't argue with either of them."

"Well, an opportunity came up. For me to go into business with Sheena Patrick."

"The bartender?" Justice asked, his brows lifting.

It was Rue's turn to shoot him a surreptitious side-eye. "The *hot* bartender?"

"I'm not blind," said Justice, who clearly felt convicted by his wife's characterization of Sheena.

"Yes," Rue said, sniffy. "But you've voiced your opinions on her very boldly in the past."

"In the past you were my friend, not my wife," Justice said.

"Yeah," Denver said. "The hot bartender."

"She's Dan Patrick's daughter," Daughtry pointed out.

As if Denver didn't know that.

Though, Daughtry was more connected to the fallout of that day than anyone other than Denver. They had both been enmeshed in their father's empire to a degree they were ashamed of. It was just that their hair shirts had taken different forms. Daughtry's was a badge and a uniform. Denver's was . . . the land, he supposed. The burden of trying to pay it all back. Ensuring that his family really was cared for this time. That it wasn't all a lie coming from a narcissist who was hell-bent on altering reality to suit his narrative.

"Yes. She is," he acknowledged. "I owe her a favor."

"You don't owe dad's victims," Arizona said. "Outside this house or inside this house. His actions were his own."

"But what people think of us comes down to him. And I can't just rest on the knowledge that I didn't do anything. It's not good enough. Not for me."

"I get it," Daughtry said.

Because of course he did.

Copyright © 2025 by Maisey Yates